DEFENDING SOPHIE

GHOST BOOK TWO

PJ FIALA

I've had so many wonderful people come into my life and I want you all to know how much I appreciate it. From each and every reader who takes the time out of their days to read my stories and leave reviews, thank you.

My beautiful, smart and fun Road Queens, who play games with me, post fun memes, keep the conversation rolling and help me create these captivating characters, places, businesses and more. Thank you ladies for your ideas, support and love.

The following characters and places were created by:
Shaina Fiala named Sophie Turner and also helped me out with military information.

Melissa Hultz created Sophie's MOS (Communications Specialist.)

Amy Higgison and Emma Sim named Kate Ryan.
Emma Sim named and Tate Turner.
Gigi Boyd named the baker, Gigi.
Teresa Russ named Canyon Creek.
Kathy Sheehan Copeland named Pine Lake.
Terra Oenning named Reed Killian.
Kristi Hombs Kopydlowski named Thomas James Taylor.
Georgine Wood chose Thomas Taylor's profession as a boat maker.

Debra Packer named Gaige's Aunt Beverly Taylor.
Yvonne T. Cruz named Windsor Heights.

Jennie Lee Ersari named Gaige's parents Elaine and Robert Vickers.
Janeen Wagner Phillips named Candace Phillips the coroner.
Terri Merkel and Melissa Hultz named Casper and chose his real name, which may be divulged in a later book.
Kimberly Slorf Veihl named Gavin Andrews, GHOST's pilot.
April Shindlebower Brown named Carlee Brown.
Carol Stout named Gayle Stout.
Sarah Brogni helped me out with the drugs used in this book.
A special thank you to Marijane Diodati, my amazing editor!

Last but not least, my family for the love and sacrifices they have made and continue to make to help me achieve this dream, especially my husband and best friend, Gene. Words can never express how much you mean to me.
To our veterans and current serving members of our armed forces, police and fire departments, thank you ladies and gentlemen for your hard work and sacrifices; it's with gratitude and thankfulness that I mention you in this forward.

COPYRIGHT

Printed in the United States of America

First published 2019

Fiala, PJ

DEFENDING SOPHIE / PJ Fiala

p. cm.

1. Romance—Fiction. 2. Romance—Suspense. 3. Romance - Military

I. Title – DEFENDING SOPHIE

ISBN-13: 978-1-942618-74-4

DESCRIPTION

She's the prime murder suspect.

He's the man she could never have.

Together, on the run and with a murder to solve, sparks fly and passion burns.

Army sergeant Sophie Turner would do anything for anyone. And after her best friend is murdered, she's hell-bent on uncovering the truth. But when all evidence points to her, Sophie must call the only man she's ever truly wanted for help.

Special agent Gaige Vickers has loved Sophie for as long as he can remember. The second she needs his help, Gaige is there. As they embark upon the truth together, Gaige and Sophie grow closer. Two things are clear: their attraction is undeniable, and Sophie's story doesn't quite add up. Gaige is suddenly torn between his desire for her and his determination to reveal the murderer. But one thing is certain: come Hell or high water, he'll do anything to DEFEND SOPHIE.

***

Let's stay in contact, join my newsletter so I can let you know about new releases, sales, promotions and more. https://www.subscribepage.com/pjfialafm

1

Looking over her shoulder, Sophie exited the little gas station just outside of Riverton, California through the back of the store and opened the package that held a burner phone. Pulling Gaige Vicker's phone number from her front jean pocket, written on a crumpled piece of a discarded newspaper she'd dug out of the dumpster at her apartment complex, she quickly tapped the numbers into the phone. She regretted having to dismantle and toss her brand new cell phone, but she knew they'd be able to track her with it and she just couldn't take the chance.

Throwing Gaige's number into a nearby garbage can so no one would connect them should she be captured, she quickly made her way across the quiet street and ducked between a large boxwood hedge and a wooden fence. Pressing her back to the warm wood, her eyes ever vigilant to her surroundings, she remained wary. Her heart was still pounding hard from her run through the woods. That bastard who was chasing her told her not to talk to another person about what she knew, her time was up. Swallowing the bile that threatened to rise at the thought of how close she'd come to dying today, she inhaled slowly. By the third ring her heart began racing. "Come on, pick up," She mumbled into the phone.

"Vickers." Her hand flew to cover her mouth as a sob almost escaped. Ducking down further behind the hedge, she whispered, "Gaige? Oh, Gaige, it's Sophie. I'm in trouble and you're the only one who can help me."

Taking a deep breath to regain her composure, she held her breath as she waited for him to respond. "Sophie Turner?"

"Yes." She hated that she sounded so desperate, but she was. Glancing around to make sure no one was nearby, she swallowed before continuing. "Gaige, I'm in trouble. I need help. I'm all alone."

"What about your friend, Kate?" Closing her eyes to stay the tears that threatened to spill, she took another deep breath. "Kate's dead. I'm in trouble. Can you come?"

"Okay, Sophie, tell me what's going on."

"I can't, Gaige, I'm afraid they're following me and I have to make tracks. I'm scared to say too much on the phone. I'm just outside of Riverton. Call me on this burner phone number when you get here. 939-202-9786."

"Sophie, you need to tell me something. What are you up against? What kind of backup do I need?"

"I'm sorry." Fighting a sob, her voice cracked. "Can you come? Can you help me?"

She heard him exhale and knew she was asking a lot of him, but she had nowhere to turn. Whispering, "please," she heard his voice change.

"I'll be there as soon as I can."

"Thank you." She broke down sobbing, but ended the call, nervous that she'd stayed put too long. Looking all around, she stepped from between the hedge and the fence heading south toward Canyon Creek. She could walk for hours, her Army training had conditioned her for that. Bonus that she wasn't carrying a ruck sack, so she was traveling light. She'd make better time that way.

Attacked from behind, strong arms wrapped themselves around her, she felt herself falling to the ground, face first and tried to twist to land on her attacker. Not quite managing, her right shoulder took the brunt of the fall but not before her attacker managed to reach around and punch her in the jaw once, bringing stars to her eyes. She heard her phone clatter to the ground and her eyes fell on it just in time to see it slide under a nearby trashcan with wheels. Shit.

Fighting passing out, she began kicking back at her attacker and heard him grunt when she managed a good solid kick to his shin. Taking the opportunity, she threw her head back and connected with his nose. Hearing the nasty crunch, she rolled away as he howled, scrambled to her feet, and took off running. The pain slicing through her shoulder hampered her pace, but she was determined to keep going. No way she'd allow them to kill her like they killed Kate. No way in hell. The bastards.

Setting her mind to hear the music she played in her head during their long and arduous runs in the Army, she steadied her pace and refused to look back. Reaching the nearby woods, she ducked in, and carefully watched the terrain as she navigated the downed branches and stumps of trees long ago fallen. Listening for anything behind her, she finally ventured a glance and saw that she wasn't being followed. At least not closely.

Slowing her pace to a fast walk, she looked up through the trees to see where the sun was in the sky. At 2:00 p.m., in California, the sun was just beginning its decent, toward the west, so she adjusted her direction and headed due south. The sun would still shine brightly for another five hours or so. She could realistically travel ten to twelve miles in that time. She'd done it more than once. But, she'd never been more determined than now to make time and distance.

She'd find a place to rest tonight, then she'd find a way to go back in the morning and retrieve her phone. That was the only place she had Gaige's number and it was the only way Gaige had to reach her. Hopefully, her attacker didn't see the phone slide to its landing place. If the grunt she'd heard from him was any indicator, he was in a fair amount of pain right now. But she wasn't going back there to look in case he had help. That would be tomorrow's task.

Tapping the end call icon on his phone Gaige stared at it for a moment, trying to get his head around his vague conversation with Sophie. She was in trouble, but she couldn't tell him anything and would he fly over a thousand miles to come and help her? If it were anyone else he'd tell them to take a flying leap, but this was Sophie. The same Sophie he'd dreamed of on and off over the years. The same Sophie who was his best friend, Tate's sister. The same Sophie, who he'd longed for but who had never given him the time of day. So, he'd moved on. So had she. She'd married, then divorced. Now, here she was calling him.

Shaking the melancholy thoughts from his mind, he pulled up the messenger on his computer and typed in a quick message.

To: GHOST Operatives
    From: Gaige Vickers

I have a mission, short notice, and sadly no pay. It's personal. Anyone interested in a quick op, meet me in the conference room in thirty minutes.

Gaige

Closing the lid on his laptop, he stood, stretched and headed downstairs. The GHOST compound was enormous. It was also gorgeous. An old Southern mansion style home, completely renovated with their needs in mind. Any operative who wanted a room had one here, free of charge as long as they worked for GHOST. Some of them stayed here, and some of them, mainly the bounty hunters they'd hired on recently and Jax, their only female operative, lived off site. The other five of them lived here. Why not? It was convenient, they had meals prepared, their place was clean, they had their computer systems, gun range, garage space and so much more. They didn't even do their laundry, Mrs. James and her daughter, Kylie took care of all of their needs.

Waving his security badge in front of the elevator keypad, the doors opened with a swish. He stepped into the large space, pushed the button that said "Conf", and directed his thoughts to the limited information he had about this mission. What on earth could she be in so much trouble over? And who was after her? And why a burner phone? And how in the hell did Kate die? Kate had been Sophie's friend forever. Tate had a crush on Kate for as long as he could remember. He said he was waiting for her to grow up. How ironic they were both dead now. Tate in Afghanistan, and Kate? Well, that was a mystery he'd soon figure out.

Stepping off the elevator, and crossing the hallway, Gaige smiled when he walked into the conference room and there was his entire team.

Nodding, he stepped up to the head of the table, but he didn't sit. Nervous energy was beginning to flow the more he thought about this whole cryptic call.

"I can't tell you how proud I am that all of you would show up knowing this is completely pro bono."

Wyatt was the first to respond. "You said it was personal. You'd do the same for any of us."

He watched with pride as each of them nodded in agreement. Clearing his throat of the newly formed lump, he began.

"Sophie Turner is a friend. Actually, she's the sister of my best friend, Tate, who died ten years ago on a mission in Afghanistan. She just called me, scared and on the run, saying someone was trying to kill her but she couldn't tell me more, and that her best friend Kate is dead. I don't know if the two are related. She's in the Army and stationed at the military base in Riverton. She said she's just outside of town and that I should call her phone, which is a burner, when I get there. So, I can't tell you anything about this mission except that I'd like one of you to come with me, to keep our profile on the ground small. I'd like a couple of you to be here on alert to come out should we need you and to monitor the computers and phone system for jobs while I'm gone. Also, there may be the need to run some intel for me, so, Axel, if you could do that, I'd appreciate it.

Axel nodded, his long dark hair still wet from the shower. "You got it."

"Wyatt, will you work with Axel, take shifts monitoring the phones and email for GHOST. I'll check the emails as often as I can. Once we know what we're up against out there, we'll fill you in."

Wyatt nodded. "No problem."

"Hawk, I'd like you to come with me. I may need the muscle and you've had some time off recently. If you're up to it, that is."

Hawk had recently been shot on their last big mission, though he stated just this morning, that if he didn't get out in the field soon he was going to kill something he was so stir crazy. He was perfect for this job.

"I'm up." He was also a man of few words.

"Okay then. Thanks everyone. Hawk, wheels up in an hour. Wyatt, contact Gavin and tell him to get the plane ready." Not waiting for any further conversation, Gaige left the conference room, hurried to the elevator, and upstairs to pack his bag, grab his computer, and get his head on straight for this mission. Just hearing Sophie's voice caused such a riot in his mind and heart. She sounded scared. Genuinely scared and yet her voice also sounded so good. He remembered the little dark-haired beauty that had haunted many of his dreams over the past 24 plus years. Off and on, he'd remember her and wonder what could have been if he'd just had the guts to approach her. And, if he'd been sure he wouldn't piss off Tate. Their friendship had been the most important thing in the world to him. The only person he had, who he considered his brother. They'd done everything together since they met in Basic Training. They stationed together as much as they could. Gaige often found himself going home with Tate when they had leave. They had such a great relationship and so much fun when they were together. But, he also went back with Tate, hoping to see Sophie.

When Gaige left the Army to run GHOST with his father, Tate said he was staying in the military until there was room for him at GHOST, since they were just starting out. Trouble was, that never happened.

3

Tired, sore, and hungry, Sophie finally neared the suburb of Canyon Creek. Estimating that she'd made it around eleven miles and happy for the dusk that had fallen to cloak her, she stopped at the edge of the woods and looked around for signs of movement. Mostly, signs that someone was looking for her. All she had for money was the change from the fifty that she'd used at the gas station to pay for her phone which was around $32. Not enough for a hotel room and not enough to survive on for long. Seeing a little bakery standing alone at the end of the street on the edge of town, Sophie slowly made her way through the darkness to the bakery and ducked around the back.

Even though it was closed, the delectable aromas that filtered out of the older brick building made her stomach growl. Estimating the last food she'd eaten to be breakfast that morning, she decided to find some water and fill her stomach and hydrate her body before she collapsed. At the back of the bakery was a spigot but no hose. Checking all around, she silently walked to the spigot, and turned it on slowly, so the water came out at little more than a trickle. Cupping her hands under the water she filled them and drank her fill. Once her thirst had been quenched, she filled her hands again and splashed water on her face, wincing when she touched her swollen jaw and cheek from where her assailant had hit her.

Turning the water off, she scooted to an alcove next to the backdoor where there was a dry patch of the warm blacktop and pressed her back to the brick still heated from the sun. Leaning her head back, she closed her eyes for a moment.

Waking later, Sophie startled herself by leaning over to the point of almost falling to the ground, caught herself, and righted before looking around. This section of town was quiet and now that darkness had fallen completely, she felt safe for a while. Looking across the alcove, she saw two wooden crates with "flour from the world's best" but couldn't read more.

Standing, she winced as her shoulder jostled, walked to the flour crates and lifted them with her left hand. They were empty. Scooting, she placed them in front of the alcove, she tucked herself behind them, pulled them slowly toward her and decided to stay there for the night. Warm, protected and somewhat safe, it was the best she could do for herself for the night. Tomorrow, she'd go back to that hedge and retrieve her phone from under the trashcan. It was the only way she had to reach Gaige, and he, her.

$\sim$

"**W**hat have we here?"

She heard the woman's voice before her senses fully woke. The top crate moved and Sophie braced herself for a fight.

A kindly looking woman, around her mid-fifties, peered over the top of the crate at Sophie. "Oh dear, hon, what on earth happened to you?"

Trying to stand unsuccessfully and wincing when she exerted her shoulder, the woman touched her other shoulder lightly. "Don't reinjure yourself, hang tight."

Moving the crates away and putting them where Sophie had dragged them from, she then turned, hands clasped before her.

"I used to have a husband who thought I was his punching bag. He's now someone's bitch in prison, and I own my own business."

She held a hand out for Sophie and waited while indecision played over in Sophie's mind. You could never be too sure who they'd hire to lure her into feeling safe.

"My name is Gigi. I own this bakery and I won't hurt you. I've been the recipient of a man's fist far too many times." She smiled sweetly and Sophie thought she looked like an angel. Her blond hair glowed where the rising sun caressed it.

"My name's Kate." She couldn't use her own name and it was the first name that sprung to mind. Thinking maybe that was too close to her real situation, she quickly corrected herself. "Katherine actually."

Quickly assessing Gigi's size and deciding, if need be, she'd be able to defend herself easily should Gigi decide to pull anything, she took the woman's hand. She allowed Gigi to help her stand, then stepped to the side, closest to the parking area in case she needed to run. Seeing her movements, Gigi smiled, "I'll bet you could use a bite to eat and maybe a shower."

Her traitorous stomach responded by growling and Gigi giggled. It sounded good to hear happiness, it had been far too long. As long as a month which was when Kate had been killed. Actually, it had been longer than that. A month before Kate had been murdered, she'd been raped and though Sophie managed to get a smile or two from her best friend in the month that followed, Kate's laughter had died that night.

"Ah, yes, see, you're hungry." Gigi turned and pulled her keys from her jacket pocket, and unlocked the backdoor to the bakery. "Come on in when you're ready, I'll whip us up a breakfast while the ovens are heating up."

She disappeared through the door but didn't close it completely. Swallowing to moisten her throat, Sophie stepped to the backdoor, listened for anything out of place, pushed it slightly open, and listened to Gigi's movements. She wasn't calling anyone to come and get her, she was pulling things from a refrigerator and setting them on the counter.

"Do you like scrambled eggs? I have plenty of eggs."

Entering the kitchen, Sophie closed the door behind her and stepped into the brightly lit and welcoming room. The far back wall was old red brick. Pots and pans hung from a brass rack hanging over a large stainless table, which was now covered with a frying pan, a towel with four eggs laying on top, butter, a glass bowl with a whisk in it and a carton of milk.

Gigi moved around the kitchen with ease. She nodded to a sink in the corner. "You can wash your hands there.

Paper towels hanging above the sink. Soap on the right." But she never stopped moving.

Sophie slowly walked to the sink, wary with each step, hoping this wasn't a trap. Her heartbeat was far faster than normal, but she didn't sense anything untoward about Gigi. Just the opposite, she seemed to be happy to care for someone. The water was warm coming from the tap and the instant she put her hands under the running water, goosebumps formed on her arms. The soap smelled of spring freshness and clean. She watched as yesterday's dirt and grime washed down the drain. Today was a new day.

Gigi whisked the eggs and began humming a soft tune that Sophie didn't recognize, but instantly loved. Reaching for a paper towel, she dried her hands, tossed the used toweling in the wastebasket under the sink and turned, unsure of what to do.

Gigi nodded toward a stool at the end of the table, closest to the sink, and said, "You can sit there. No one can sneak up on you right there and you can see the backdoor from that position."

Raising her eyebrows, Sophie cocked her head. "I told you, I had an abusive husband. I've felt all the feelings of someone who doesn't feel safe. I still have bouts with it, really, but I'm determined to push through. That bastard won't ruin any more of my life than he already has."

Deciding that using the battered woman guise and tamping down the guilt she felt for lying by omission, she nodded. "Thank you." It came out as a whisper.

"I noticed your shoulder is sore, are you broken?"

"No." It was so soft. Clearing her throat she began again. "No. I fell on it, I think it's just bruised."

"Okay. A bruise will heal." Pouring the eggs into the

frying pan, which was now on the stove, butter melting inside, Gigi continued to work as she talked. "I have a room upstairs. It's small. An open space with a single bed, a shower stall, and a chair. But you're welcome to stay as long as you like. I could use help here washing dishes if you need a job. I can't pay much more than a few dollars per hour, but if it suits you until you decide what you need to do, I'm happy to oblige."

"Why would you help me; you don't know me at all?" Blinking furiously at the generosity of this stranger quickly turning to friend, Sophie took a deep breath.

"I know you. All I need to for right now. You've suffered through something at the hands of an asshole. I've helped countless other women over the years. They come to me when they are in trouble. Somehow word travels silently through a system only we battered women are privy to. I assume that's how you've come to find me."

Deciding not to add to her lie, Sophie only nodded once and left it at that. "Thank you." And she meant it. For all of the women who had come before her, even though her situation was much different than what many had gone through, she did need a meal, and some shelter until Gaige could get here. Now she just needed to formulate a plan to get her phone.

4

"This is so fucking cool." Hawk stretched his long legs out in front of him.

He was a large beast of a man at 6'8" and brawny. Usually transportation was cramped for him. But, with the payment from the Santarino take-down, GHOST was able to purchase a plane and hire a full-time pilot. There may come a day when Gaige would complete his pilot's lessons and fly the plane himself, but he didn't have a ton of time to focus on that.

"I have to agree with you, Hawk. I think this was the best decision I've ever made. Having our own plane solves so many problems with getting to missions on time."

The large man chuckled, reclined his seat, and closed his eyes as Gaige pulled his laptop from its carry case, and set it up on the table in front of him. First order of business was checking out Kate Ryan's death. His contact in the State Department had given him security clearances years ago, which made things such as this a breeze.

Typing Kate's name into the database, he waited as the little circle on his screen turned. Slowly, data populated his screen and he began reading the reports. Her death, which was a month ago, was ruled a suicide, asphyxiation according to the report. She'd been found in her neighbor's garage, her car running and the windows open. The autopsy had been brief, and no report of alcohol was found in her system but there were opioids present.

He scrolled down to see her military record. She had four Article 15s on file. Tardiness, failing to man her post at night, failing to report on time to a training class. It seemed that Kate was a mess and not the Kate he remembered from years ago. Though, life had a way of breaking a person. He remembered Tate telling him years ago that Kate wanted to make the Army her career and retire from it, making civilian life easier with a pension and the ability to then work in the field she loved rather than one she had to in order to support herself.

Closing the lid on his laptop, Gaige leaned back in his seat and flipped the footrest up. A quick glance at Hawk told him the man was at rest, but one word from him and Hawk would be awake and alert. He could catnap at a moment's notice and be ready for action just as quickly. Actually, his whole GHOST team was trained that way. You slept when you had the chance 'cause you didn't know when you'd have it again.

Before closing his own eyes, he pulled his phone off the table before him, and scrolled through his contacts. Finding Henry 'Blake's name, he hit "call" and listened as the phone rang on the other end.

"Gaige, what can I do for you?" He chuckled then and Gaige made a mental note to call his friends for social reasons a bit more.

"Hank, sorry to bother, but I guess you already know I need a bit of assistance."

Chuckling as he replied, "You've always been business first, social later."

"Hmm, so I'm predictable. Noted. A colleague and I are in town briefly on a mission and need a quiet, private place to stay. You have such a place at your disposal?"

"I do. I think I do, anyway. I have a friend who has a little cabin just outside of Riverton in the woods. It was his parents' house but they've both passed now and he just can't let it go. Thinks when he retires he'll live there one day. Let me check with him and see if it's available."

"Appreciate it, man. Let me know."

"You got it. Call you later."

The call ended and it was then Gaige allowed himself a few moments of shuteye before they hit the ground running.

"I get we sleep when and where we can, but if I have to sleep in some little pink frilly bed, you'll pay for that." Hawk said without opening his eyes.

He couldn't help laughing. The thought of the gentle giant laying in a pink frilly bed would be worth a lifetime of laughs if he could just see that.

Allowing his eyes to drift closed the images of Sophie the last time he'd seen her came to him. Her hair had always been long, though she pulled it back into a braid or ponytail, it usually fell over one of her delectable shoulders. His fingers usually twitched because he wanted to feel her hair. See if it felt as soft as it looked. Smell it.

Her skin was tanned from being outside. She was fit, strong and yet so small and delicate looking. She was an enigma for sure. When she laughed, the creases around her eyes deepened and her lips, gawd her lips were full and shiny and just begged him to kiss them. It had been at Tate's funeral the last time he saw her, close to ten years ago. She didn't laugh much that weekend. She was married at the time and her husband, a pretty boy named Scott or something, seemed detached and constantly on his phone. Self-important, that was the impression he made. Sophie tried remaining strong for her parents as they nearly broke from the news that their son had perished.

Gaige remembered how Tate and Sophie's mom, Georgianna, shook in his arms when he'd hugged them. They all seemed so broken and so was he. Tate was a fixture in his life since they met in Basic Training. He'd imagined Tate as his best man for his wedding, if and when he married. And he assumed Tate would be the godfather to his children. All those plans changed the day he got the news that an IED had killed his best friend. Once GHOST had grown and had a place for Tate, he needed to finish out his contract with the Army, so he was killed before that could happen. The guilt that GHOST wasn't ready for him sooner was heavy in his chest every time he managed to lay back and sleep. Even after all this time, the pain was there.

Ringing woke him from his half-sleep, and he realized it was his phone. Snagging it from the table in front of him, he responded, "Yeah."

Sitting upright, his eyes glanced at Hawk, who did the same, his eyes alert and ready for battle.

"It's Hank. I've got the keys to the cabin with me. Are you here now and when can I get them to you? I can't leave base until later tonight, we're working a special assignment."

Glancing at his watch, he noted they were within twenty minutes of landing. "I can come to base. I'm still in the air but should be landing shortly. How about I meet you at the commissary around 18:00 hours?"

"Roger that. 18:00 hours at the commissary."

The line went dead and Gaige laughed. He wasn't the only one who was business first.

"Mr. Vickers and Mr. Delany, please fasten your seatbelts for landing." Gavin's voice sounded over the intercom system.

Doing as directed, Gaige packed his laptop away and relayed their first destination to Hawk, who in return only nodded.

Pulling up Sophie's burner phone number, he pressed, "Call" and listened as the phone rang. After the seventh ring the phone went dead. Furrowing his brow, he looked at Hawk and shook his head. What the hell did that mean?

5

"You're fast at the dishes, even with a sore shoulder. How is that by the way?"

Looking up from the steaming water in the sink, Sophie met Gigi's gaze.

"It's okay, but I think it needs a bit of a rest." She'd taken Gigi up on her offer to shower earlier. Luckily, Army life had taught her how to shower quickly. She was still waiting for someone to storm the bakery and attack her.

"Katherine, there's nothing wrong with taking a break. Those dishes will still be there later. I'll be closing the bakery in an hour. On Monday through Friday, I only stay open until 3:00 p.m. I work back here preparing for the following day and then I go home. This weekend, I have a wedding to bake a cake for, so that's what I'll be doing this afternoon. I bake them on Thursdays, let them cool and begin the decorating on Friday, then finish up the decorating at the venue on Saturday so nothing happens to them in transit."

"Thank you. I guess sleeping in the alcove outside

didn't offer me enough rest to actually begin the healing process."

"Go on upstairs and take a nap, Katherine."

Taking a deep breath and a huge leap of faith, she said, "Actually, I need to get to Riverton to find my phone. I lost it yesterday and I've called a friend to come and help me and that's the only way he has of making contact with me."

"He?" Gigi looked at her shoes for a moment, her face showed disappointment or sadness. Then met Sophie's gaze. "You don't have to go back to him, Katherine."

"No, it's not him." She hastily explained. "He's a true friend and one who lives over a thousand miles away. He's coming to help me."

Nodding, Gigi hesitated only briefly, then said, "I can take you."

"No." She raised her voice. At Gigi's flinch, she realized she'd overreacted. "I don't want you to go to any trouble, you've already done so much, I just need to go."

Gigi slowly approached Sophie, her arms crossed over her chest, "It appears as though your options are to walk, which I assume is how you got here, take a cab or car service, or let me drive you. Since it's only a bit over ten miles, it's really no imposition."

Pulling her bottom lip between her teeth and watching this lovely woman before her, give her understanding, encouragement, and support for someone she doesn't know anything about gave Sophie a pinch of courage to accept.

"Thank you. I appreciate it."

"Good, it's settled. In an hour I'll close the shop, take you to get your phone and when we return, I'll set out getting ready for tomorrow."

Without waiting for an answer, she turned and left the room to help a customer who had entered the bakery. Simple as that.

Deciding that she wouldn't tell Gigi where she'd lost her phone, she sat on the same stool where she'd eaten breakfast and the most delicious piece of chocolate cake she'd ever had as a snack after her shower, and slowly rotated her shoulder. It was certainly swollen, but she could move it, though not without pain. And she'd learned earlier this morning when reaching for a pot to wash, that she couldn't reach out in front of her quickly without a burning sensation running up her neck and down her right arm. Likely due to a pinched nerve which was hopefully only from the swelling.

Looking across this bright happy kitchen, she wished Kate were here and could see this place and meet Gigi. Kate would have loved her. And she wished Kate could have had a piece of that chocolate cake, she would have been in heaven. Which ironically is where she is now. Tilting her head back and looking up at the tin ceiling, stamped with rosettes and delicate vines, she closed her eyes and silently asked her friend to be with her now and help her get out of this situation.

Whispering to no one, "Kate, if you can hear me, I sure could use your help."

The bell above the front door rang and as she'd done all morning, Sophie held her breath, pressed her back to the wall, and listened to make sure it wasn't someone coming to get her. Hearing the female customer order six croissants, she let herself breathe again and stepped to the sink to finish washing the dishes soaking inside before the water cooled.

Rinsing the sink of last remnants of bubbles and food

scraps, Sophie jumped when Gigi entered the kitchen and said, "Ready?"

Drying her hands on a towel wrapped around her waist to keep her jeans dry from water sloshing around, she could feel her cheeks tint pink. "Sorry."

"Don't be sorry, dear. I've told you, I completely understand."

Removing her towel, she laid it over the edge of the stainless sink and followed Gigi to the backdoor. Gigi stepped out but Sophie froze. Glancing out the door and watching Gigi walk to her car, which was parked in clear view of the backdoor, she took a deep breath and stepped out.

"Lock it, please." Her new friend called over her shoulder.

Opening the door, and reaching around to twist the lock, she again stepped out and pulled the door closed once she felt that she wouldn't have to run back inside. Making a dash for Gigi's car, she jumped in, and locked the doors with the touch of the button on the right armrest.

Gigi started her car and put it in gear. "Buckle up." Was all she said as she pulled away from the sweet little brick bakery.

The ride was quiet and Sophie couldn't help but glance at her driver. Blond hair, fine lines around her eyes and lips. The skin under her chin sagged slightly, but no more than any mature woman's did. She was beautiful. Petite framed, her hands were work roughened but not like a construction worker, rather as if she did dishes a lot and worked with implements for her job. Her body was slightly rounded, but Sophie mused not as round as she'd be if she ate those delicious baked goods every day. Gigi could bake.

They drove along, and the closer they got to Riverton, the more Sophie twisted her fingers in her lap. By the time she saw the sign, "You are now entering the town of Riverton" her heart raced and her muscles tightened to the point of pain.

"Where to now?"

"Uh, if you could drop me at the Swanky Town Pub, I can find my way from there."

"Katherine, honey, I can help you."

She met Gigi's eyes and the worried blue ones that looked back at her made her sad, but she just couldn't put Gigi in danger if there was someone out there. "Please, Gigi, I need to do this my way."

Gigi swallowed hard and Sophie felt terrible for all this lovely woman had done and was doing for her, and yet, she'd been dishonest from the start. Not saying another word, Gigi pulled into the parking lot of the Swanky Town and put her car into park.

"Shall I wait here for you?"

"No. I don't want you to get any more involved than you already are. And, thank you so much for all you've done, Gigi. I'll never forget you."

Tears sprang to Gigi's eyes, but she nodded once and dug into her purse. "At least let me pay you for today's work."

"No. I used your shower, you fed me, and drove me here. Let's call it even. Please."

"Then, at least take my card. My phone number is on it, and I'd appreciate it if you'd call me and let me know you're doing okay." She pulled a card from an inside pocket of her purse and handed it to Sophie. As she gently took the card from Gigi's fingers, Gigi added, "or, if you need me to come and get you. You call me. Deal?"

"Deal." Leaning forward, she hugged Gigi with her left arm as much as she could in the confines of the car and with a seatbelt on.

Unlatching her seatbelt, she opened the car door without looking at Gigi again. Her eyes darted around the parking area making sure no one was around before she ducked behind the building and made her way across the back lot. Briskly making her way to the neighboring street behind the pub, which held houses and children playing. Just one more street down and to the east and she'd be on the street across from the gas station and that much closer to her phone. She had this.

The streets were busy, as it was now around 3:30 and school buses were busy dropping children at their various stops. Perfect time for her to blend in. She wasn't much taller than many children and actually much shorter than many of the high schoolers at only 5'2" feet tall.

Looking across the street to the gas station, she surveyed the parking lot for signs of anyone sitting in their cars or driving around looking for her. Quickly making her way to the wooden fence where she'd hidden, she tucked Gigi's card into her back pocket and swallowed the dryness away in her throat. Walking close to the fence and boxwood hedge she saw the trash can right where it had been yesterday and jogged to it. Dropping easily down to her knees and careful not to jostle her arm she glanced under the trash can only to see that it had been moved and her phone lay crushed under one of the wheels.

The tears that instantly sprang to her eyes blinded her vision. Immediate defeat washed over her and she let the tears flow. Scooting back against the fence, she pulled her knees to her chest and dropped her head to her knees.

"There you are." A deep male voice said. She couldn't jump up and run before he'd reached down and grabbed her.

6

G etting out of their rental, a sleek black Chevy Tahoe, Gaige and Hawk walked into the commissary on base. They all looked the same somehow, commissaries and bases. It was probably the utilitarian feel of the base and all the uniformed people walking to and fro, but that feeling of Deja Vu fell over Gaige every time he entered a military base or building.

The fast-food restaurants lined the outside of the actual shopping area, cell phone stores, computer stores, you name it they all had mini versions of themselves positioned inside the commissary all vying for those military dollars.

He saw Hank enter the front doors and look around. His black hair and tall physique were easy to spot, even among all of these other military personnel. Hank was a SEAL and SEALs held themselves differently. Taller, prouder, they carried that badass vibe with them everywhere they went. It was ground into them getting through BUDS.

Hank looked up and saw Gaige walking toward him

and laughed. When they met they embraced and slapped each other on the back a few times.

"Damn, it's good to see you, Gaige. How the fuck are you?"

"I'm good, Hank, how about you?"

"Same shit, different mission."

"That's for certain." Gaige and Hank had met years prior during a mission when GHOST was only a couple of years old and the SEALs had been called in. They weren't necessarily working together, but they had a common goal and he'd remained friends with Hank since that time.

Looking over at Hawk, he motioned him forward. "You remember, Hawk?"

"Of course. How the fuck are you, Hawk? I heard you got shot not long ago."

Gaige watched the two men hug and step back, Hawk towered over damned near everyone. Even Hank.

"I'm good. All healed and ready for action."

"Glad to hear, man."

Hank motioned them to a side of the commissary and pulled the keys from his front pocket. Handing them over, he also pulled his phone from his pocket, tapped a few times on his screen and Gaige's phone vibrated signaling a text.

"I just texted you the address. He said to make yourself at home, though you'll need some food. No one has been there in a couple of months."

Taking the keys, Gaige pocketed them before shaking hands with his friend. "We'll need to catch up one of these days. Sorry to grab and run, but I've got to find someone and I'm not sure how much trouble she's in. I'll call you to get the keys back to you."

Hank smiled. "I'll hold you to that. I've got an exercise I

have to return to across the way, but stay in touch. And keep your head down. Maybe once you find your person, we can get some drinks, it's been a while since we've all had the chance to knock a few back."

Hank turned to shake Hawk's hand, repeated the sentiment, and waved as he headed out the door. As Gaige watched his old friend walk out, a familiar face walked in. Fucking Reed Killian walked through the doors. Gaige remembered him from years ago during AIT and again when they were stationed at Fort Jackson. Reed was a major suckass who would stab anyone in the back if he thought the higher-ups would give him props. He ratted out any person in the unit, no matter how small the infraction just to get in good with the upper brass. Last time he'd seen this asshole he was a Second Lieutenant, though he'd heard he'd been promoted since then.

Their eyes met and Reed's face showed everything. First surprise at seeing Gaige here, then the mask came on and his military face with it. Walking straight toward him, Gaige stiffened and readied himself to be pissed off.

"Vickers, what are you doing all the way out here?" He looked the same. That same sickening smile that was more false than a stripper's tits. His white-blond hair slicked back made him appear bald from a distance. His light blue eyes always assessing and looking for a flaw.

"Just visiting. You stationed here?"

He wore civies so his rank wasn't apparent by his dress.

"Yes. I'm Captain now."

"Well, I think we all knew you'd climb the ranks no matter who you had to step on to do it." Even his chuckle was disgusting. "Same old Gaige Vickers, cynical and untrusting. What are you doing these days, bagging groceries I assume."

"Something like that." It wasn't worth correcting him, that's what he wanted. Besides, GHOST was under the radar and elite. "Gotta run."

Gaige moved toward the door, Hawk followed him, and they walked to the SUV. He jumped into the driver's seat, started the truck, pulled his seatbelt around him, and as he looked up, Killian stood just outside the door watching him. That same creepy feeling he always got around Killian crawled its way up his spine.

"Fucker."

"Yeah. Gotta story there I assume."

"You assume correctly. Look for a grocery store with my GPS, please. Address is in Hank's text. I don't want to shop here."

Hawk pulled his phone from his front pocket and began tapping. The GPS located a grocery store five miles away and on the way to the cabin, so Gaige pointed the SUV in that direction and took off. Pulling his own phone out, he tried calling Sophie again and still got no answer.

"My gut says somethings wrong. It could just be running into Killian, but something still feels off."

"I agree. Time to have Wyatt trace her phone." Hawk responded.

Gaige tapped a couple of icons on his phone, to call GHOST headquarters. Wyatt answered on the second ring. "Lawson."

"Wyatt, I need you to trace Sophie's burner. I also need you to trace her regular cell phone, too. I'll text you the numbers." He forwarded the numbers to Wyatt and waited until he had a response.

"Got it. I'll ring you as soon as I have something."

Stopping in the parking lot of the grocery store, they went in, grabbed some food, and left with little fuss. They didn't know what facilities they'd have at the cabin, but assumed the basics. Grabbing frozen meals that could be baked or microwaved, fresh fruit, instant oatmeal, coffee, and juices they left a few minutes later, each carrying two bags.

Setting the GPS for the cabin, they proceeded to find their home away from home, but each mile that passed, Gaige's gut tightened. Where was she?

Finding the cabin, they entered and dropped their groceries on the table. Hawk tossed the frozen goods into the freezer and Gaige wandered through the house. It was dated, that was apparent, but other than being dusty, it had been someone's full-time home at one point. It appeared everything they'd need was available. Two bedrooms, nothing frilly and pink, which Gaige admitted to himself was a bit disappointing as he'd love a picture of Hawk laying in a girly room.

His phone rang and he didn't let it ring a second time. "Vickers."

"I got a ping on her phone, though it's weak. It appears she's across from a gas station on the edge of Riverton. I'll send you the location on your phone. You're only eight miles away."

7

"I've been looking for you. Are you alright?"

Fighting to get out of his iron grip Sophie tried twisting and pushing away. She yelled out as the white hot pain slid down her arm and up her neck from her shoulder. She instinctively cradled her right arm in her left and the solid hands that had held her before, gentled and his arms wrapped around and pulled her into a hard chiseled body. The voice suddenly took on concern.

"Hey. It's me, Gaige. I'm here. I'm not going to hurt you."

Her watery eyes looked up the chest in front of her and into the face of the man she'd crushed on over and over through the years.

A sob broke out as all of the horrors of the past few days rushed through her. Gaige picked her up and carried her to a black SUV. Climbing in the back with her, a monster of a man climbed behind the wheel and began driving them. Somewhere.

"Hey. Why didn't you answer your phone?"

Clearing her throat, she sat up and his arms braced her and moved her to the seat behind the driver. He twisted to look at her and she knew the second his eyes landed on her face. More specifically, the bruise on her cheek and jaw. His tensed and his face grew hard and unreadable.

"Tell me what happened to you. I can see this." His fingers gently caressed the bruise on her face. "And it appears you have an arm or shoulder injury as well."

His fingers took hold of the collar on her button up shirt and gently pulled the collar back. She flinched away and his eyes, those gorgeous green eyes she'd been so mesmerized by years ago, landed on hers. "I'm a medic, remember?"

She hesitated, mostly because she wanted to stare at him for hours. Also because she'd now have to tell him what had happened. She hoped like hell he'd believe her and not think she was crazy.

Swallowing the lump in her throat, she nodded as her left hand swiped at the tears that trickled down her face. He gently moved her shirt from her shoulder and though it was barely perceptible, he grimaced. Ducking his head to capture her gaze, he said softly, "I need to make sure it isn't dislocated. It may hurt just a bit."

He held her eyes until she swallowed then nodded. Bracing herself for the pain, she had to admit, he was as gentle as he could be. His fingers kneaded the tissue around her shoulder joint to make sure it wasn't dislocated. She knew it wasn't but a masochistic part of her wanted him to touch her. She felt safer being with him already. For the first time in a while, she wasn't alone. Having no one to turn to when things got tough, sucked.

He touched a sore spot on her shoulder and she flinched. "Sorry, Soph, I'll be careful."

She nodded, still not sure she should trust her voice. Emotions were high and she didn't want to cry again and look weak to him. Not to him.

"Okay, rotate it as much as you can for me."

She moved her shoulder and winced when it pained her, but she still continued to move it. This was nothing compared to what she'd been through.

"Can you reach out in front of you?"

She did as he asked but sucked in air as the pain shot through her.

"Okay, we'll be at the cabin soon enough. There I can take a closer look, but I don't think it's dislocated, so that's good. But I do think you'll need to rest it to help it heal. We'll ice it and figure it out."

"Okay. Thank you." She watched his Adam's apple as it bobbed up and down. He swallowed multiple times and for some reason, it was sexy. Her eyes traveled up his throat to his jaw, then up until their eyes locked. "What cabin?"

He smiled for the first time and it was as if the sun shined right inside the vehicle. "I have a friend who has a friend with a cabin. It keeps us away from the general public and allows us the time and privacy to figure out what's going on with you."

"Okay." His fingers gently brushed her jaw again, but she didn't wince this time. "Who did this to you?"

"I don't know. He jumped me from behind. I dropped my burner phone and it slid under the trashcan with wheels. I came back this morning to get it because it was my only line to you. But, it had been broken when they emptied the garbage today. That's where you found me, crying and trying to figure out what I'd do next."

"Where's your phone? Your real phone?"

"I dismantled it, and then threw it away so they couldn't track me."

"Who is they?"

"I'm not a hundred percent sure. I only told one person that Kate hadn't killed herself and that was Chet Forest. He had to have told someone else. He wouldn't do this to me."

"Okay. It seems we have a lot to talk about. I did some research on Kate. She had quite the record and she was on opioids."

"No, she wasn't."

"They were in her system, Sophie. It's in the autopsy."

"She didn't take them. Whoever killed her must have put them in her system. Injected her or forced her to take them. She wasn't on them. She maybe should have been, but she wasn't."

"Why should she have been?"

His brows were bunched together, concern on his face. But his eyes never looked away from her.

"After she was raped she was...different. Despondent. Heartbroken. Maybe just broken. But, I stayed with her to make sure she would be okay; I cooked, cleaned, and helped her get through every day. She went back to work, right away even though she would have rather been anywhere else. She didn't take any pills. Nothing."

"Okay. So, how about this, we go back to the cabin and grab a bite to eat. We can talk while I make sure your shoulder is good and immobilize it. Then, we'll get some rest. You look like you could fall over from exhaustion. Did you sleep last night?"

She shook her head, "I tucked myself into an alcove at a bakery to get some rest. I walked about 11 miles yesterday to get away from here after I was attacked."

"Shit." She watched a silent message pass between Gaige and the man upfront by way of the rearview mirror. Gaige looked back at her, then said, "I'm sorry, I should have introduced you. Sophie, this is Hawk. Hawk, Sophie."

"Hi, Hawk." She hated sounding so weak. She needed to get her mojo back.

"Hey, Sophie. We're here now and we've got this, okay?"

Dammit. Tears sprang to her eyes. It was such a relief to have people she could trust help her. She simply nodded.

Hawk turned into the driveway of a little house tucked into the woods on the edge of town. It didn't look lived in, the lawn needed care, the windows were dirty, and the area around looked unkempt. Weeds had taken over the landscaping a long time ago. But it also looked to her like a place no one would come looking for them, so there was that.

"Honey, we're home." Hawk called out and she couldn't help it, a chuckle escaped her.

"Okay, let's get inside."

She and Gaige exited the truck, then Hawk pulled the SUV forward and around the back. The sound of a garage door opening reached her ears, but Gaige was ushering her into the cabin.

The inside looked like a place her grandparents would have loved if they were still alive. Frilly yellow curtains still hung in the kitchen window and the light pine cabinets and green counter tops practically yelled "retro".

Gaige began pulling food out of the freezer, and

opening boxed items to toss into the microwave. Despite the great breakfast and cake she'd had, her stomach growled.

"Do you still like oranges?"

Her eyes held his, her brows high on her forehead. He remembered.

"Yes. Do you still prefer apples?"

He pulled a gorgeous shiny red apple from the bowl on the counter and held it up for her to see. The smile on his face was mesmerizing and comforting.

Meals in the microwave, Gaige began peeling the orange for her. "Do you miss him?"

She didn't have to ask who, he was their link to the past. Her brother, Tate. "Yes. Everyday. How about you?"

"Damn, Soph. I miss him so fucking much. Anytime something good happens in my life I want to pick up the phone and call him. Then I remember that I'll never be able to do that again."

"Yeah. This past couple of months I needed him so bad. I talked to him and Kate and asked them both to be with me. To help me."

They were silent for a few moments, then Gaige chuckled, but it wasn't happy, sadder more, than anything. "Isn't it ironic that Tate and Kate are finally together?"

"Sad, too. They couldn't seem to get together in life, only in death. She really had a thing for him."

Surprise colored his face. "She did? Did she know he pined away for her, too?"

Huffing out a breath. "No. She thought he wasn't inter-ested so she loved him from afar. I knew though. I used to catch him staring at her. I'd catch her staring at him, but they were both too stupid to make the move. Or, I don't know, afraid maybe?"

"Hmm." Gaige said no more.

The backdoor opened and Hawk filled the room with his body. "Wyatt said he's found Sophie's other phone. It's on base in the Medical Examiner's Office and Morgue complex."

"It's not. I tossed it in the dumpster at my apartment building."

"It's not there now."

8

Gaige stood and tossed their microwave food containers in the garbage and tossed the three forks into the dishwasher.

"Okay, we need to talk about what's going on, Soph. Tell me what kind of trouble you're in."

He watched her throat constrict as she swallowed and the expression on her face changed to one of fear. "You already know that Kate is dead." Her fingers played with a crumb on the table and her shoulders slumped forward. "I told Chet that she didn't kill herself. I said I had proof that it was a set up to make it look like she did."

"Okay. Who is Chet?"

"He works in the Medical Examiner's Office on base. I went to him because I've known him for a few months and he always seemed like a straight up guy. I wanted a copy of the autopsy report to see if I could tell that it had been doctored and why."

"Did he give you a copy?"

"No. I saw the report Kate's parents received. It said

just as you mentioned that she had opioids in her system and that she eventually died from respiratory arrest."

"And, why don't you believe that?"

"She didn't have a car, Gaige. She had one three years ago, but it kept getting broken into on base. She got sick of fixing broken windows and trunk lids. So, she sold it and we either used my car or Uber when we needed to go somewhere. Plus, she wasn't on drugs. Any drugs."

Gaige stood from the table and grabbed his laptop from the duffle he'd set on the chair in the living room. Coming back to the table he lifted the lid and began typing.

Hawk leaned back in his chair and crossed his arms over his massive chest, but Sophie continued to look at the table. Defeated was the word he'd use to describe her. She looked defeated.

"The title was in her name."

"It wasn't hers, Gaige. That title was forged. I'm telling you she didn't have a car."

Shifting his chair to scoot closer to her he lowered his voice. "Sophie, so far we have a dead woman with opioids in her system and a death by asphyxiation in a car not hers but no proof. What proof do you have that you mentioned to Chet?"

Dropping her hand to her lap, she took a deep breath. Finally looking into his eyes she whispered, "I don't have any. I was hoping if I could figure out that the autopsy report was manipulated I'd be able to find the proof. I didn't count on Chet telling anyone what I said."

"Okay. So, let's get some sleep and talk about this in the morning. We're all running on lack of sleep, and we need clear heads to work through this. First, let me take a look at your shoulder and make sure you don't need more medical assistance than what I can supply you."

He walked back to his duffle and pulled out the medical kit he always had with him. Bringing it back to the table, he opened it up then turned to Sophie.

"I'm going to need to see your shoulder, Soph."

He saw the pink color her cheeks and his heart went out to her. She seemed like a scared little girl. But, her story had more holes in it than Swiss cheese, and he still wasn't sure what they were up against.

Hawk stood then, "I'm getting some shuteye. See you two in the morning."

"Take the back bedroom Hawk, Sophie can have the first bedroom. We can secure that one to make her feel safe easier."

Hawk looked between them. "Where are you going to sleep?"

"I'll take the sofa. I've got some work to do and that way I won't keep anyone awake."

Sophie said, "That doesn't seem fair, Gaige. I can sleep on the sofa."

"Nope. First of all, for safety reasons, it's better if you're in the interior bedroom. There's only one window and we can close the blinds and curtains to make sure no one can see in. That's the paranoid me wanting to make sure we're secure. Further we can block the window from opening with a board. Second, I really do need to get a bit of work done before I can sleep and out here I won't keep anyone awake."

Hawk nodded and left the room. Listening to his footsteps which were surprisingly quiet for a man his size, Gaige waited until the bedroom door closed.

Turning to Sophie he nodded and she slowly began

unbuttoning the top button of her shirt. His heart sped up and he closed his eyes for a moment and tried to remember, people could change and Sophie may not be the Sophie he remembered. Also, he still didn't know how much shit she was in. But still, he owed Tate to keep his sister safe and he'd do just that, if for no other reason than his dead best friend.

When he opened his eyes, Sophie had opened her shirt and struggled to pull her arm free from the sleeve. Seeing she had a tank top on underneath, he took a deep breath and knelt down before her to help tug the sleeve down her arm. He watched her face and noticed a wince, but nothing more. Not sure if that was toughness, lack of pain or both, he decided to proceed carefully. When he saw her swollen shoulder and the angry bruise around the swelling he had to tighten his jaw to stem the anger he felt at what she'd endured. It was bad enough seeing the bluing welt on her cheek and slender jaw. He'd watched her eat during supper and he knew it was tender to move, but she never whined, just ate the small amount she could and remained stoic. It was one of the things he'd always admired about her all these years. Any time he'd seen her, she managed a calm stoicism about her. Like the little soldier she was.

Repeating his ministrations from earlier he kneaded the area gently and had her move her shoulder. She did what he asked without complaint. In the end, he determined that she had a severe contusion on the bone of her shoulder. "I have some pain meds with me. They won't knock you out but will help ease the pain so you can sleep."

"I don't want them."

"You need to rest, Soph."

"I don't want them. I don't want to be drugged. I can't. Not now."

Nodding, he understood. "Alright. But if you change your mind, you just need to ask. Okay?"

"Yeah." Her voice was so soft. He wanted to pull her into his arms and hold her and tell her everything would be okay. He couldn't though, he didn't know if he could make that promise.

"Okay, hon. Why don't you go to bed? We'll have a conversation in the morning."

He stepped away from her and walked to his duffle. Pulling a white t-shirt from it, he brought it to her. "You can sleep in this, it'll be more comfortable. Bathroom is between the two bedrooms down the hall. While you're in the bathroom, I'll secure the window in your room."

"Thank you." She took the t-shirt from him and hesitated. Then she wrapped her left arm around his waist and hugged him. "Thank you for coming to help me."

Heart hammering, his skin grew clammy as his arms gently circled her petite body against his. He kissed the top of her head. "You're welcome. We'll work hard to get this straightened out."

She turned and headed to the bathroom and Gaige headed to the garage to look for a board to secure the window. This would probably be the toughest job he'd ever been on, one way or another.

esitating for all of thirty seconds, Sophie decided to jump in the shower. She didn't think either Hawk or Gaige would barge in, but taking your clothes off left you in the most vulnerable position. Still the call of feeling clean again won out. The shower she'd taken this morning was so incredibly brief that while it did a bit to clean off the surface dirt, she hadn't felt totally clean at all.

She lay Gaige's t-shirt on the counter, and turned the water on to warm while she looked around. Noticing that the house hadn't been cleaned in a long time, a layer of dust covered everything but she hoped there was some shampoo stashed away somewhere. Opening the tall cabinet next to the shower, she saw the towels and took one from the middle of the pile. Checking the bottom cabinet, she sighed when she found an older bottle of shampoo and a bottle of conditioner. Hallelujah. She didn't even care what brand. Setting them on the ledge of the tub, she began shrugging her blouse from her good shoulder and let the material fall from her injured arm.

Unsnapping her jeans and pushing them down her legs was a bit challenging but nothing she couldn't handle.

Finishing her undressing the hardest thing was removing her bra, but she managed. Pulling the shower curtain back to step in, she thought again, grabbed her clothes and brought them into the shower with her, she was at the end of day two with them and she'd sweated a fair amount yesterday.

Showering, shampooing, and running shampoo and water over her clothes she enjoyed a little longer shower, and for the first time in a while allowed a genuine smile to appear on her face. Feeling clean and safe again, or at least safer, she agreed with Gaige that a good night's sleep would help them all devise a plan in the morning.

Stepping from the shower she dried herself and her hair the best she could with her shoulder pain, then pulled another towel from the cabinet and opened it up on the long counter. Laying her wet clothes on top, she rolled them up in the towel and lay it on the floor. Stepping on it to sop most of the water from her clothes, she then grabbed her clothes in her wet towel and set it on the counter while she donned Gaige's t-shirt.

Sliding it over her head she closed her eyes as his scent surrounded her. Oh, all the times she'd remembered the way he smelled. Subconsciously she'd sought out men who smelled like him, or similar to his scent. It was the first thing she'd noticed about her ex-husband, Brad. When she asked him what cologne he used, he replied, "Cattleman." A shiver had run all the way through her body.

Taking a deep breath and grateful his t-shirt covered her body almost to her knees, she twisted the knob on the bathroom door and quickly ducked into her room.

Opening the closet, she was relieved to see hangers. Hanging her wet clothes on the hangers, including her bra and panties, she lay the towel under them to catch any dripping water.

Walking to the window, she gently pulled back the curtains and blinds to see that Gaige had wedged a section of 2 x 4 between the bottom window and the top sill to keep it from opening. She smiled that he worked so quickly and thought she'd need this to feel safe. Though in his line of work, no doubt he'd dealt with hundreds of women in need. Her stomach tightened and coiled with jealousy, though she had no right. Now she was just a job to him as well. She'd have to figure out a way to repay him. Though he'd probably say no, she'd still figure out a way.

She left the light on, darkness was too scary right now. Laying in the bed and pulling the covers up to her chin, she looked around the room, memorizing every crack and corner.

Not sure when she fell asleep, Sophie looked around the room. What had woken her up? She sat up, listened, then heard a door close. Her heart began racing, she jumped from the bed, grabbed her panties, they'd dried but not completely, but they'd have to do. Checking her bra, it was still wet, as were her jeans and shirt.

She walked to the door and listened but didn't hear anything. Turning toward the window, she walked over, pulled the piece of 2 x 4 from it, and walked back to the door. At least she'd have something if she needed it. She was still pissed at herself for not grabbing her gun when those asshats broke into her apartment and tried grabbing her. She was caught so off guard that her only thought had been to run.

Quietly turning the door knob, she pulled the door open and listened. Tapping sounded and she instantly recognized the sound of keys on a computer and realized Gaige was still working.

Making her way quietly down the hall, her ears hyper-aware, she neared the entrance to the living room. There sat Gaige on the sofa, his long legs propped up on the coffee table in front of him, crossed at the ankle, his naked feet in full view. Even his feet were sexy.

His head turned when he saw her, his smile beautiful, his green eyes bright despite the dark circles under them.

"Hey, what are you doing up? Are you in pain?"

She shook her head, "I heard a door close."

He patted the sofa next to him, "Come sit. Unless you're planning on bludgeoning me to death."

Her brows furrowed briefly until she remembered the 2 x 4 in her hand, and she felt her cheeks heat. "Sorry, I didn't know if someone was breaking in."

He chuckled. "No, sorry, it was me. I ran out to the garage to grab my phone cord from the vehicle."

Sitting next to him, she looked over at his computer screen and her heart hammered, her throat constricted and her hands began shaking.

"Why are you researching Captain Killian?"

10

L istening to the water running in the bathroom and the thought of Sophie slathering soap on her naked, wet body, almost became too much. Better to get some work done than torture himself with images that drove him crazy. Taking his laptop into the living room, he pulled off his boots and socks and lay them on the floor next to the sofa. Mrs. James would have a field day in this place. The dust alone would have her salivating for a good cleaning.

Placing his bare feet on the coffee table, he set his laptop on his legs and opened the top. First order of business was to check up on Reed Killian. The issue with him now was if he was a Captain, he'd have access to records, including his own. Manipulating them, while it could be tracked and get him in a shitload of trouble, there was little doubt the bastard would do it. He wanted to rise to the top so fucking bad, there was no doubt he'd do anything to get there.

Mentally noting when the shower shut off and closing his eyes for a moment as thoughts of naked

Sophie fresh from the shower, her long dark hair touching and pressing against that luscious smooth body of hers. Damn, he probably should have had someone else come on this mission and he should have stayed home. The bathroom door opened and he saw a flash of sexy leg and long dark hair scoot from the bathroom to the first bedroom. Within seconds the fresh scent of shampoo and woman wafted down the hall to his nostrils and he thought again that he should have stayed home.

Typing in Reed Killian's name into the internet search bar, he figured he'd start there and move into the military records. He liked starting with public searches first because you just never knew what you'd find. The search was fruitless. No big news, no pictures to speak of and no social media, which wasn't unusual for high ranking military personnel. It was unusual for Killian though 'cause that man loved blowing his own horn. He found every opportunity to talk and brag about himself to anyone who had the stomach to listen.

The next search moved to court records to see if he'd gotten himself into any predicaments outside of the military. When three searches popped up, Gaige sat up a bit straighter, now we were getting somewhere. It didn't take long for disappointment to set in. Two of those hits were divorces and one was a minor domestic dispute in which his ex-wife wanted him out of the house and he refused to leave. A fight ensued and she called police and then filed a restraining order against him. That would be something he'd look into further, since it may lead him somewhere.

His phone chirped that the battery was running low and he set his laptop on the sofa next to him and stood. Stretching he noted from his computer that he'd been on for well over two hours. Sometimes these searches could go on and on.

He grabbed a bottle of water from the refrigerator and popped the cap, took a long drink and recapped the bottle, setting it on the coffee table, he turned to head out to the vehicle to grab his phone cord. Making as little noise as possible, he noted a few things about being in California. The evening was still warm even though it was now around ten pm. He fought the urge to step outside of the garage 'cause he didn't want to attract any attention. He also didn't know if he could drag himself back in. Back home in Indiana, it was much cooler right now and not nearly barefoot weather. Thinking again that maybe he'd made a mistake in making Indiana the home for GHOST due to weather, he then reminded himself that the Midwest was the central hub to everything, which was the reason Indiana had been his final choice. There was never a one size fits all scenario.

Entering the house, he closed the door behind him and grimaced when it squeaked. Damned old houses. Nestling back into his little spot on the sofa, he picked up his laptop and pulled up his access panel for GHOST to enter into the military records the GHOST military contact, Casper, had given to him.

Sophie's bedroom door opened and he saw her from his peripheral vision slowly coming toward him with the piece of 2 x 4 he'd wedged in her window. At first he thought she was joking, then he turned and saw the frightened look on her face and his heart went out to her. The fears of the past few weeks had weighed so heavy on her. He could see it in her face. The fine lines around her eyes had deepened since he'd last seen her, but also the fine lines around her mouth had settled in. Though neither of those things had done anything to change how beautiful she was, she'd always been gorgeous to him, always would be. The first time he'd seen her she was sixteen and going out on a date. She'd come down the stairs at her family home and he and Tate were in the living room watching some football game on TV. They'd just graduated Basic Training, so he came home with Tate. He turned his head when Tate whistled and she told him to shut up.

His mouth went dry and his heart beat so fast he thought he'd pass out. She wore an electric blue short fitted dress and matching shoes. Her long dark hair hung in waves down her back and over her left shoulder and her brown eyes sparkled. He remembered with clarity the way she'd looked at him when she turned to see him sitting on the chair at a right angle to Tate. He saw her swallow and her fingers fidgeted with the edge of her dress.

"Sophie, this is my friend Gaige Vickers. Gaige, my little sister, Sophie."

He froze for a solid moment, then remembered his manners and decided to shake her hand to see what her skin felt like. He stood and walked the five or so steps over to her and held his shaking hand out and he saw her bottom lip quiver just before she sucked it in between her teeth. Fuck, that was sexy.

Her small hand grasped his and he remembered the feeling to this day. Soft and warm and her fingers tightened around his hand like she needed him to pull her to safety.

Finding his voice, he softly replied, "Nice to meet you, Sophie."

Her eyes, so beguiling without any pretense, looked

into his and the dark brown of her irises to this day is still his favorite color. Her thick black lashes were the perfect frame for her almond shaped eyes and he wanted to drown in them. Then, Georgianna, their mom, came into the room.

"Oh, I'm glad you were able to meet. Gaige and Tate met during Basic Training. They're stationed together at Fort Benning."

"Oh. That's great that Tate will have a friend with him." She swallowed. "Nice to meet you."

Tate walked forward then and hugged Sophie. "You call if any asshole decides to get too frisky with you. Gaige and I will wrap that shit up in two seconds."

Georgianna scoffed. "Tate. Language."

Sophie pushed on Tate's chest and chuckled. "I can take care of myself. No one touches me unless I say so."

What he would have given for her to say so right then.

Looking at her now, his heart ached for the time spent apart.

"Hey, what are you doing up? Are you in pain?"

She shook her head, "I heard a door close."

He patted the sofa next to him, "Come sit. Unless you're planning on bludgeoning me to death."

She sat next to him and his senses were assaulted on all levels. She smelled fantastic. He could feel her warmth the instant she sat down, even though they weren't touching. She wasn't wearing anything to cover her legs, which were amazing. Her voice still held that soft but strong quality he had played over and over in his mind and then she hit him with the final blow.

"Why are you researching Captain Killian?"

11

J ust seeing Killian's picture on the computer screen almost made her vomit. Her stomach twisted and turned and she wrapped her good arm around both her right arm which hurt to move much and her stomach to quell the roiling.

"Do you know him?"

Gaige's jaw tightened and she studied his profile. The almost imperceptible grimace that pursed his lips and wrinkled his nose hardened into a stony expression she'd never seen on him.

"Yeah, I know him. He and I were in AIT together."

"You went in to be a medic like Tate, right?"

"Yeah. After one deployment to Bosnia, my dad wanted me to come home and help him with GHOST. It was up and running and he wanted me to know the ins and outs of it."

"What did Killian go to AIT for?"

"I think he was a respiratory specialist."

She swallowed not sure what she should divulge.

"How do you know him?"

His green eyes locked on hers and she wanted so badly to tell him everything. But, she'd trusted too easily before and it nearly got her killed. She just had to be careful.

"I think he's the one who has framed Kate's death as suicide and is after me because he thinks I have proof that he has."

Gaige set his laptop on the coffee table as he pulled his feet off, then twisted on the sofa so he was facing her. His left leg folded on the sofa in front of him while is right leg rested on the floor. "Tell me."

"He had an obsession with Kate. Made passes at her, which she ignored. She noticed that he'd show up where she was. The store, the movie theater once when she was on a date. Then on base, he'd show up at her office, where he had no business being. Bogus excuses to be there and she was getting creeped out by him. After she was raped, he stopped coming around, but I noticed that his initials were on all documents surrounding Kate's disciplinary Article 15s. I don't have great evidence, I thought I'd have time to find it, but then Chet must have said something to him and my time ran out."

He never looked away and she felt better. Then, his left hand rested on the back of the sofa, and his fingers reached over and caressed her shoulder. It was light, almost imperceptible, but she felt it. Her heartbeat increased as she stared at him. Softly he asked, "Why don't you think he came around after Kate was raped?"

"My feeling is that she was tainted goods."

The frown that marred his handsome face was gone just as fast as it appeared. If she hadn't been watching him for expressions, she wouldn't have noticed it at all.

"Who raped Kate?"

Pinching her lips together she didn't want to risk lying.

Not completely anyway, so she slowly shook her head. It was a lie, but not a verbal lie. She'd deal with that bit of news later. It was too much to lay out right now.

"Okay, can you tell me any concrete reason why you think Killian is the one after you?"

Biting the inside of her cheek, she took a breath, "One of my attackers at my apartment said to the other one, "The Captain will be..." Then the other one told him to shut up. Killian is the only Captain with any interest in Kate, or me or the truth about all of this. It has to be him."

Gaige's chest expanded and then fell as he took a deep breath and let it out. "We have to be very careful. Hawk and I saw Killian at the commissary yesterday when I met Hank to get the keys for this cabin. The look he gave me when I climbed into my vehicle was creepy. It's been bugging me since. Now I think I know why. He knows of course that Tate and I were friends. And, he knows you are Tate's sister. Now, I'm in town and you're missing and he'll easily put two and two together. He isn't stupid. He'll assume I'm here to help you. I have to make sure he doesn't have access to the SEALS."

Picking up his phone, she watched his long sexy fingers deftly swipe and tap on his phone until he found the number he wanted. Putting the phone to his right ear, he kept eye contact with her, but his fantastic smile was gone and worry now played on his face and her stomach once again twisted. If her protector, friend, companion was worried, how could she not be?

"Hank, do you know Captain Reed Killian?"

She couldn't hear what this man, Hank, was saying, but she saw Gaige sit straighter, as if on alert. "Really. When was this?" Only getting one side of the conversation probably made it worse, because the following questions bothered her more than she imagined they would.

"What did you tell him?"

"Thanks man, can we keep it that way?"

He hung up, then cleared his throat. "How do you want this to work, Sophie? Do you always want info straight up or not?"

"Yes." She swallowed. "No matter how bad, I'd rather know what I'm up against."

He nodded, leaned over to set his phone on the coffee table, then looked at her. "Killian sought Hank out and asked him how we knew each other and why I was in town."

Sucking in air, enough to fill her lungs, she commanded her body to exhale slowly. "Okay. What did Hank say?"

"He told Killian to fuck himself." Gaige took a deep breath.

"So, here's what we have to do. We have to head back to GHOST headquarters in the morning and research from there. The needed resources are there. He can't reach you there. And we'll have time to figure things out without looking over our shoulders all the time and we'll be secure in the compound. Once we're armed with the information we require, we can come back and do what we need to do. I don't know what Killian has records to, but if he starts investigating the SEALS, it won't be long before he puts together that one of Hank's buddies' owns a house just outside of Riverton. We don't need him finding us."

"So, there's no chance that I will be able to go back to my apartment and grab clothes and supplies?"

"I don't see that as an option at all, Soph. But the

women back at the compound will have clothes for you and can shop with you to get you stocked up."

For some reason that just hit her like a punch in the gut. The women at the compound. He had women there. Did that mean he had a woman? A special someone? A wife?

"I didn't even ask if you have..." He dropped his left hand from the back of the sofa to his lap and she picked his hand up in hers. "Are you married?" Assessing his ring finger, no indentation was visible and he didn't have a tan line, but not all men wore wedding rings.

"No."

"Never?"

"No."

"I thought I heard you were engaged."

"You did, I was. But, I couldn't bring myself to go through with it and called it off a couple months before the wedding."

Relief raced around her body and she almost felt light headed from it. "I'm divorced. Brad was someone my parents approved of, and I wanted to make them happy, but after Tate..." Swallowing the tears that threatened, she gave herself a moment and cleared her throat. "After Tate died I kept hearing myself say, "Life is too short to be unhappy." So, I filed for divorce. I've never been sorry."

He chuckled. "Me either."

The air changed. It almost crackled with electricity. Her chest felt heavy with the need to touch him. She wondered what it had been about her all those years ago that he wasn't interested in her. She wanted to ask, but hated to sound so needy, after all the man flew over a thousand miles to help her, so she hated to keep compounding all of the emotions. Standing she softly said, "I'll see if I can get some sleep now, since it seems we'll be leaving right away in the morning. I don't have a plane ticket though and I'm worried about going through the airport, which I'm sure Killian will be watching."

"Ah, well, I have a private plane now and I have it in a private hangar with a small airline company close to the airport but not on airport grounds. The plane is not listed as a GHOST plane, it's listed as a plane for a company I formed to own it, so by the time, if at all, Killian puts that all together, we'll be long gone."

"Oh, I'm impressed, Gaige, I had no idea your company had grown so much."

His gorgeous smile appeared again and the thought that she could look at it for hours flooded her brain. "Take your 2 x 4, Soph, and wedge it back into your window. I'll see you in the morning."

Walking back to her bedroom, she had to fight the urge to look back at him and see if he was watching her. She hoped he was. But she wasn't ready to find out if he wasn't, so she kept her head facing forward. Stepping into her bedroom, she closed the door quietly, wedged her board in the window, and slid in between the sheets. Still not ready to sleep in the dark, she kept the lights on. The last thought she had before falling asleep was how many women were at the compound and who were they to Gaige?

12

"So, I won't be gone long, and as soon as I get back, we'll head to the airport. Are you sure you'll be okay here without a vehicle?"

He watched Hawk practically inhale a hardboiled egg, taking half of it in one bite, chewing briefly, and taking the other half before responding. Apparently he was hungry this morning.

"We'll be fine. I'll let her sleep and I'll keep lookout. When she wakes, I'll tell her you'll be back in a bit. And, we'll have the groceries packed up and be ready to roll."

"Okay. I have a comm unit here." He pointed to a unit he'd set on the table. "If you need it for any reason, don't hesitate to grab it."

Hawk sat back in the kitchen chair, which looked like it was far too small for a man his size. "I've done this before you know."

"Yeah. It's just personal this time"

He only nodded in response. Picked up another egg and began peeling it. "She the one who got away?"

Not sure how to respond to that question he stared at

Hawk's giant fingers trying to peel his egg without ripping it apart. He chuckled then. "Your silence says everything."

Their eyes met and Hawk's lips tilted up into a crooked smile. "Sad sack."

Shaking his head, he walked to the garage door. "Shut the fuck up. I'll be back within an hour."

Leaving the driveway, he kept his eyes alert to see anything that might seem out of place. It was doubtful that Killian would already know where they were staying, but he was a sneaky bastard and there was no telling how many men he had at his disposal.

But the other side of his life was his family, which was incredibly important to him, and he couldn't come all this way and not visit his maternal uncle and aunt. Besides, Uncle Jeff was a full bird Colonel, and while he'd never asked for a favor, he just may need to if things went wrong here. So, it was necessary to stop in, say hi, and ask for the stand-by just in case.

Taking the highway around Riverton, he turned off and maneuvered the coastal road until the sign for Windsor Heights appeared. The first time he'd visited this house he was highly impressed. Elite neighborhood with fantastic views of the ocean. The homes were all strategically nestled among the rocky terrain as if they'd grown from the mountains on their own. But, the first time his aunt and uncle had come to visit him at the GHOST compound, he'd felt like he made it given the praise by Uncle Jeff. He'd felt their relationship change during that visit. He was no longer "Little Gaige" Robert and Elaine's son; he was Gaige Vickers, Commander of an elite civilian special forces team of highly specialized men and women, and his Uncle Jeff, especially, beamed at him. Too bad his mother didn't feel the same way about GHOST. She hated it and refused to acknowledge anything about GHOST. She viewed it as the reason her husband, and Gaige's father, was dead. She wasn't totally wrong about that; he'd been working himself to the bone and had a heart attack at his desk at the original GHOST headquarters a few hundred miles from the current location. But, he spent all that time at his desk because he loved it. He fucking loved GHOST and what he'd built and what it meant. He was cleaning the scum from the earth by doing things that no ordinary person could do. The government and the police's hands were tied, GHOST was autonomous with all the cool access and equipment. It was perfect. Still is.

The entry gates to the back section of the neighborhood were open and Gaige maneuvered the SUV along the curvy, narrow street and up the drive of the Taylor home. It still looked the same. Even the foliage looked as if time had left this place alone.

Removing the keys from the vehicle, his phone rang just as his hand gripped the door handle to exit. He pulled his phone from the holder on the dash, turned off the GPS, and answered the call.

"Hawk, is everything alright?"

"Not sure. Sophie just had a fit when I told her that you were going to visit Thomas Taylor. I told her your connection and she freaked out. She said Thomas was dating Kate when she was raped. Sophie said he's the one who raped Kate. Date rape. Then she took off running saying something like she shouldn't have trusted you. I'm leaving to go look for her."

"Shit." His stomach dropped to his feet. First of all, Tommy was a bit full of himself, but rape? Never. Now, Sophie didn't trust him? She was out there alone again, and Killian was looking for her. Today sucked balls.

"Okay, I'll make this quick. Now I have to talk to Tommy and find out what the fuck is going on. Keep me posted and good luck. I'll be back soon."

He ended the call at the same time he exited the truck and made quick tracks to the front door. Ringing the bell, he checked the time on his phone. 6:30 a.m. He knew they'd be up early, Uncle Jeff went to the base by 7:30 every morning.

The locks twisted and the door jerked open. "Gaige." His uncle's booming voice exclaimed, and he was pulled into a bear hug before his mind could catch up with today's events.

"Uncle Jeff." He returned the hug, then stepped back. "I hope it's alright that I dropped in, but I'm on a mission and have no time."

"Come in, come in. At least you must have time for a coffee."

"Always." His uncle walked into the house and called up the stairs, "Tommy, Bev, Gaige is here."

"Tommy's here?"

"Yes. He's been staying for a short time."

Uncle Jeff's arm wrapped around his shoulders and pulled him toward the kitchen before any movement sounded upstairs.

"I'm so happy to see you, Gaige. How are you doing? How's GHOST? And, lastly, I spoke to your mother yesterday, and she's still as stubborn as ever about GHOST, but she's doing well."

"I'm happy to see you as well, Uncle Jeff, but I do hope I can speak to you before Aunt Bev and Tommy come down."

"Of course." He watched his Uncle turn to the side and pull coffee cups from a cupboard and set them on the counter. Easily navigating the kitchen, he pulled the creamer and sugar out and set them in front of Gaige.

"I drink my coffee as black as I can get it, but you may want to sweeten it up. Now tell me what's on your mind."

"Reed Killian."

His uncle scoffed and locked eyes with his. "Smarmy bastard is always trying to climb up my ass. But, he's useful when I need something done 'cause he's always vying for a promotion. Why are you asking about him?"

"How much access does he have to personnel records?"

"He has quite a bit of access, but not complete access. Why?"

"Uncle Jeff, I need a favor and it involves Army personnel."

"Gaige, I'm so happy to see you." His Aunt Bev breezed into the kitchen, looking shower fresh and ready to tackle the day. Her long blond hair flowed around her shoulders, and her blue eyes landed on his before she pulled him and hugged him. Turning, she walked around the counter and poured her own cup of coffee.

"I'm happy to see you, too. You look gorgeous as ever."

Aunt Bev giggled and it sounded as if she was a teenager. She'd always been youthful looking and her pleasant personality added to that youth and vitality. Living in California, she'd mentioned before, demanded that a woman take care of herself. Being married to a full bird Colonel, further added to that pressure. So, her job was to keep up her appearance, exercise, stay fit and trim and volunteer at the base. But, she loved it.

His eyes slid to his Uncle Jeff's and locked when he saw his uncle staring at him. He didn't seem angry, but he was trying to figure this out. And, suddenly, Gaige began to think this was not the right move to make.

Angry at himself for blindly trusting that this was the right move given what Sophie told Hawk about Tommy, he turned his attention to his Aunt Bev as she chatted about her day and all she had to do. She didn't even seem to notice that no one was paying attention.

His phone chirped that he had a text and he quickly pulled it from his shirt pocket, glanced at the text, and let the phone drop into his pocket.

"I've gotta run, I'm sorry. But, I'm on a mission and things aren't turning out like they should."

He leaned forward and shook his Uncle Jeff's hand, then began walking to the front door as his Aunt Bev walked around the counter and hugged him briefly. Hugging her back, he kissed the top of her head. "I'm sorry I couldn't stay, I actually thought I'd have more time."

Aunt Bev squeezed then replied, "Next time let us know you're coming and I'll have a meal planned and we'll visit properly."

"That sounds great, Aunt Bev." He opened the front door, turned to wave to his uncle who stood a few feet behind them, but simply nodded at him.

Quickly walking to his SUV, his gut told him to get the hell out of town. His text told him they'd have a bit of trouble finding Sophie. Hawk said he'd lost sight of her, but was still following a trail.

He needed to make time.

13

F ighting the urge to break down and cry or slam her fist into a tree, Sophie kept her head low. She knew Hawk and Gaige were good at their jobs. Over the years before Tate died, he bragged endlessly about GHOST and how good all of the guys were. He was so proud of Gaige. She needed to use every bit of her survival training and keep herself hidden. From GHOST and from Killian and from the Army. Today was turning into a bigger pile of shit than the days before Gaige got here.

To find out he was related to that fucking piece of crap, Tommy Taylor, well that just figured. She was more pissed than ever that she'd trusted him and mad at herself for not telling him that Tommy was Kate's rapist. She would have known last night that they were related and could have snuck out of the house and been gone by now.

Finding a primitive shelter in the woods that someone had built a while ago, she hesitated then knew it was a bad idea to hide inside. They'd come looking for her soon enough and she couldn't be idle right now. Thing was, she couldn't go back to Riverton. She needed to find a phone and call Gigi, but that was the tricky part, finding a phone. She would have taken Hawk's, if she thought she could've gotten away with it, but they would've just tracked it anyway. Luckily, she did grab a go bag from Gaige's duffle, which would offer her some minor comforts, but there'd be no phone in there.

Ducking behind a small hill, she pulled the go bag from her left shoulder and unzipped it. Inside were some small bottles of the basics, soap, shampoo, coffee packs, which were kind of neat, little baggies with a k-cup, filter, and a creamer packet inside. Then there was clean underwear, which wouldn't help her much, a clean t-shirt, socks and gym type shorts. Another baggie held a disposable razor, and a mini bottle of shave cream. Finally there were about five meal bars, that would get her through a couple of days. But nothing else that could really help her.

As she began putting the items back into the bag, she noticed a tab on the inside. Pulling it up, she saw material folded inside. A label lay tucked alongside and she looked closer at it. This damned bag turned into a small tent. Eureka, she'd have a bit of shelter at least and some food. She could survive overnight and figure this shit out.

She leaned against the tree, careful not to be seen, and tried to get her head around all she knew so far. Gaige was a cousin of Tommy Taylor. Which meant that Colonel Taylor was his uncle. Which likely meant they knew Killian. She couldn't recall if Killian reported directly to Colonel Taylor, she'd need the Brigade website to see that chain of command. What a fucking mess this was all turning out to be. Her heart felt heavy, as if it was weighted down by a boulder. She'd felt almost like a teenager sitting with Gaige early this morning. They still had so much to figure out, but she was hopeful and he promised to keep her safe and she believed him. And, a part of her hoped that maybe things could be different for them this time around. Whatever had kept him from noticing her before had maybe changed and he'd notice her now as a woman.

Taking a deep breath, she solidified her plan in her mind. She needed to get back to Gigi, even if it meant another eleven-mile hike today. She stood and peeked over the hill, feeling a bit lighter that she at least had a plan now.

Footsteps in the dead leaves on the forest floor made her drop to the ground on her belly. Her heart hammered in her chest and her mouth grew dry. She listened for movement, her ears tuning into anything of note. The light rustling she heard was definitely not an animal. The crackling slowed and she turned her head slightly to ascertain the direction the footsteps were coming from. Nothing. They seemed to stop. She paused for a long moment, in case whoever it was intended to wait her out. Slowly raising herself with only the strength of her left arm, she pushed herself back on her haunches, and waited to ensure she was undetected. Silence ensued, so she slowly raised herself into a crouch, then gently lifted herself up to peer over the hill. That's when she saw him.

Twisting to run in the opposite direction, she leaped over a dead branch laying between two trees and maneuvered herself between the trees that came next. The spaces in between the trees narrowed and she turned to keep herself in the smaller passages between the smaller trees. It was unlikely he'd be able to follow her through trees this close together.

Leaping once again, a massive arm encircled her waist

and pulled her back against a solid wall of chest. The quick breathing of her captor huffed in her ear.

"Not so fast, Sophie. We have to talk."

She squirmed but her right shoulder thumped into his muscle-hardened chest and she cried out as the pain shot down her arm.

"Easy." His voice was calm as he easily carried her deeper into the woods and through a small copse of trees which helped to shield them from anyone else lurking about.

Setting her feet on the ground, he didn't release her but whispered close to her ear, "At least give me a few minutes to explain."

What choice did she have? Reluctantly she replied, "Okay."

Feeling defeated for about the tenth time in a couple of days, she slowly turned to face Hawk and wrinkled her nose when she noticed he wasn't allowing her to step away from him.

"How did you find me so quickly?"

"Soph, you took Gaige's go bag. We have tracking on everything, just in case." He pulled his phone up and showed her the map location with the red dot right where they were standing.

Nodding her head once, she made a mental note not to steal GHOST stuff.

He continued. "Why did you take off?"

"Why do you think? He's working with Kate's rapist."

"No, he isn't. He didn't know anything about Tommy and Kate until you told me and I called him when you bolted."

"How can I believe that? Even you have to see how

convoluted this is and how coincidental all of this seems to be."

"It's just that, coincidence. He thought his Uncle Jeff might be able to help us out."

"But don't you see? His son is a rapist. And, it's all coming together for me now. I'd bet Killian helped Colonel Taylor get rid of Kate because she wouldn't shut up about Tommy raping her."

"If that's true, and I'm not saying it isn't, you don't know Gaige at all. Even if his cousin is a rapist..."

She opened her mouth to tell him Tommy was a rapist, but he held his forefinger up to stay her. "Even if Tommy is Kate's rapist, one, Gaige did not know and two, he wouldn't help a rapist get away with it. That's not who Gaige Vickers is. The very principals that GHOST was founded on are just the opposite of what you're saying and I've known Gaige for more than ten years now, and never once...Not once, did he ever waiver on responsibility or integrity."

"But, it's too coincidental that he'd come here and then go to see Colonel Taylor."

"I'll give you that. But not because he wants any harm to come to you. He has feelings for you and he'd never put you in a position to be harmed."

"You mean he has feelings for me because he loved my brother."

"If that's what you believe, you're sadly mistaken." He looked around at the sound of a snapping branch. "We have to go, Sophie."

He gripped her left arm, and began leading her through the woods, deftly navigating the terrain, which she had to admit was impressive for a man his size.

Nearing the cabin, Hawk slowed them down, then

watched with interest as a black car slowed as it drove past the cabin. After the car moved past, he steered them in the direction of the backdoor, then opened the door, letting her enter before him.

As soon as the door closed, Gaige came around the corner from the bathroom. "We have to go. I think they're on to us." Running into the living room he nabbed his duffle, which she noticed had been packed up. "We'll get into the SUV while you grab your gear, Hawk, we need to roll."

Quick as lightening, Hawk disappeared into his room and Gaige locked gazes with her. "We'll talk in a bit, Soph, but know this, I'd never hurt you and we've got to make tracks."

Nodding because she didn't trust herself to talk right now, she moved toward him as he held his arm out to the garage door exit. He waited for her to proceed him, then held the backdoor on the driver's side open for her and settled her inside, stowing his bag in the back. Hawk appeared soon after, tossed his bag into the back and hustled around to the driver's side. Gaige tapped the garage door opener on the wall and jumped into the passenger seat as Hawk started the vehicle.

Slowly exiting the garage, Gaige said, "I was followed by two black sedans once I neared the outskirts of town. I don't know if Uncle Jeff put them on to me or not, but he saw what kind of vehicle I was driving and it's too coincidental that they'd be on to us this fast. It makes me sick to think he and Tommy are involved in something like this. I've always admired him."

Hawk turned briefly to Gaige and said, "We don't know for sure."

"No, we don't but at this point we have to assume. I

asked him if Killian had access to personnel records before I clearly realized I shouldn't say anything based on what Soph told you. Head to the hangar, I'll call Gavin. It's the only way to stay safe."

Turning left onto the road that took them away from Riverton and toward the major highway that sent traffic around the town, Gaige pulled out his phone and tapped a couple of times before speaking.

"Have the plane ready to take off in thirty minutes to the compound. Don't tell anyone who isn't necessary when we're taking off or where we're going."

Gaige twisted and looked at her. "It'll be okay, Soph. We'll talk more on the plane."

Before she could respond Hawk said, "We have a tail."

14

What a mess this all was turning out to be. He was so good at his job but he'd let a few things blind him this time. His feelings for Sophie and the love of his family. He needed to set aside some of these feelings and start using his head.

Turning to see the car trailing them, he recognized a sedan that had followed him earlier from Windsor Heights.

"I only see one. Is there anywhere we can get off this highway and dodge them?"

From the backseat Sophie responded, "Take the next exit, number 13A. That will take us through the south end of town and it's riddled with narrow winding streets and paths where we can hide if need be."

Hawk switched lanes in front of a dump truck at the last minute, which not only pissed off the dump truck driver but threw the sedan off enough that it couldn't change lanes.

"No doubt he's in contact with the other guy and they're headed our way now. We need to ditch this car."

Pulling his phone from his shirt pocket he began looking for another rental car company. Last case scenario, he'd call Hank and see if he'd help out once more. He was going to owe Hank big time for all of this.

"Gaige?" Her soft voice belied her strength. He admired her more each day for her grit and determination.

Turning in his seat he locked eyes with this brown-eyed beauty. Looking forward to a time when he'd be able to sit with her and actually take in all that was Sophie Turner.

"Yeah, Soph."

"I have an idea." Her hands were laying in her lap, her fingers were twisted together and he realized how scared she must be. They'd had no time to talk, she likely thought he was working against her, which he'd never do. He nodded. "The night before last, I stayed in Canyon Creek at a bakery. The owner, Gigi, mistook me for a battered wife and took pity on me. She'd help us. If we head through town, and maneuver down Fourth Avenue, which is where you found me, we can hike through the woods. I made it in a few hours last time, but we could call Gigi and ask her to meet us closer to the edge of Riverton. She'd help me, I know for certain."

Watching her face, the blue-yellow bruise beginning to fade from her attack, but the firm set of her jaw, he nodded. He handed her his phone, "You have her number?"

She nodded, then pulled a business card from her left back pocket and began dialing her number. Her fingers rotated the business card as she waited for Gigi, or whomever, to answer the phone. "Hi Gigi, it's me, Katherine." Her eyes flicked up to his, then out the window, and he realized what she'd done to stay safe. "I'm in need of your assistance. Again."

He faced forward to give her the sense of privacy and watched in the passenger side mirror for anyone who looked as if they were tailing them.

Sophie cleared her throat from the backseat and he twisted to see her handing him his phone. "She said to meet her halfway out of town in the township of Glenco. She said to pull off the road at the Bakery Supply Store, which is usually never that busy, but far enough off the highway that it takes a few moments to get to. Across the street from the store is a used car lot. She said to park our vehicle in the back behind the office. We can call the rental place to have them pick it up."

Hawk swung around in the road, using the opening of a driveway for the room he needed to do so. Gaige wished they had the Beast with them right now; she was fully equipped with all the bells and whistles and they'd have better communication to the compound, too. As soon as they got to wherever Gigi was taking them, he'd call and check in. He needed Wyatt to run some information for him and that just might mean bringing in Jared Timm, who was a computer hacker of epic skills, to do some computer magic and find out some details for him.

As Hawk guided the vehicle down the on-ramp to the highway, Gaige twisted his head to and fro, looking for any vehicle that looked suspicious. The drivers tailing them might even switch out the black sedans for something else and they needed to be vigilant. Fuck his Uncle Jeff. Never in his life did he ever think his family was capable of shit like this. Rape? Covering it up? Possibly murder? He hadn't even had the time to sift through his mind on any of this, but it sure wasn't looking good.

Turning to look at Sophie, he was startled to see she was staring at the back of his head. He tilted his head to the side and her lips turned up at the corners in a soft smile.

"What can you tell me about Kate's death?" Her smile faded and a haunted look passed over her soft features. He hated asking, but he needed to know.

She turned her head to look out the window and he saw her swallow a few times. Her eyes blinked rapidly, then she cleared her throat quietly and turned to face him. Hawk maneuvered the SUV off the highway and he braced himself with his hand on the console between them to keep from falling over. Sophie held onto the armrest in the back to keep herself upright.

"The day she died, she was feeling better. I even got a bit of a laugh out of her in the morning at breakfast. Then she got a text from a friend of ours telling her that Killian slammed her with another Article 15 for being late the day before. She wasn't late. We went into PT together. I'm Sergeant First Class in our Company and Kate was my next in command. We walked in together, then went to our posts. We weren't late. Killian had been harassing her like that since the rape. She was pissed and later that day told Killian she'd be filing a complaint against him and she was going to the police to give them as much information as she could about Tommy. The Army's Criminal Investigation Command, CID, were doing nothing by way of investigation and that was the last straw.

Hawk parked the truck behind the used car dealership and turned to look at him.

"Now what?" He asked to no one in particular.

Sophie turned in her seat and saw the Bakery Supply Store across the road. "We need to meet Gigi over there."

She pointed out the window and the uncertainty that flashed across her face saddened him.

He jumped from the SUV, ran around to the driver's side, and opened her door. He saw her struggling a bit with the seatbelt. Since it latched on her right side and that was the side she'd injured, he reached across her and whispered, "Let me help you."

He could smell her. The fresh shower soap from last night still lingered and in the heat of the vehicle it intensified. He tried to focus on what he was doing but he was acutely aware that his body leaned over hers. He was bent across her breasts, and he fought the urge to touch his lips to hers. His heartbeat pounded through his ears as awareness of Sophie took over all of his senses.

The seatbelt unlatched and he stood back quickly, the heat on his face near burning. Hawk had walked to the back of the SUV and pulled their bags out, but he smirked when their eyes met.

Pulling his thoughts back to their safety, he took Sophie's left hand in his right and tugged her forward. "Let's make tracks and stay low."

15

———

She could have kissed him. Just once to see what it felt like. He had on his Cattlemen's aftershave and it gave her goosebumps, even in the heat of the vehicle. His face was even with hers and he had looked up at her once and she could have sworn he wanted to kiss her, too. Why did they have to be joined together because of her bullshit? Oh what she wouldn't give to spend a carefree day with him, not worried about being hunted or afraid.

Stepping from the vehicle her nipples pebbled when he took her hand in his. His was work roughened and masculine; and while her hands had never been soft and supple due to working with weapons and her work as a communications specialist out in the field, hers felt soft next to his. It gave her a bit of a thrill to feel feminine and be in the presence of a man. A real man. Her ex had been such a soft boy-man. No work roughened hands on him. He was more of a girl than she was in so many respects. He sat at a desk, looking over spreadsheets all day. When something needed to be done on their home, he'd call someone, but never attempt to do something himself. The day he announced that he was late coming home from work because he'd stopped for a pedicure was the last straw for her. Sadly, she knew right from the start that he wasn't 'the one'. But, her parents forced the issue. He was the son of their good friends and they wanted this match to happen. Now, having a new appreciation for arranged marriages, Sophie knew two things: one, she'd never again marry someone she didn't love, and two, if she ever had a little girl of her own, she'd never force her to marry someone she wasn't madly in love with.

They walked between the cars at the used car lot, and at one point a car drove past on the road. Gaige wrapped his arm around her shoulder and turned them so it looked as if they were car shopping. Feeling his body pressed firmly against hers did funny things to her body. It screwed with her mind, too. She continued to get off track.

"Okay, let's go." Gaige whispered in her ear and shivers ran down her body. He removed his arm from her shoulders and took her hand again. Hawk was watching them on the other side of a vehicle. Gaige nodded and Hawk took off first, walking brusquely. He was surprisingly agile, but, at first glance, you'd never guess it.

Hawk looked both ways, nodded that the coast was clear, and walked across the road. She and Gaige followed close behind. Her eyes scanned the parking lot for Gigi's car and she prayed Gigi wouldn't be mad at her for her little white lie. Actually, lie by omission, but she needed help and didn't know if Gigi would help her if she knew the truth. But, she also didn't tell her she had Gaige and Hawk in tow, and this might piss her off. Gawd, she wanted life to get back to normal.

Not seeing Gigi's little SUV she worried that she

wouldn't come, but something told her to walk around the back of the building. She pointed toward the back, and without saying a word Gaige headed in that direction. They stayed close to the building, all of them were hyper-aware of their surroundings and they continued to look for black sedans that might contain the enemy. Whoever that was, it seemed they had a few and they were multiplying.

Just as they turned the corner she saw Gigi's vehicle and her heart hammered in her chest and her tummy felt queasy. Gigi sat in the driver's seat and the look on her face said anger. She ran to Gigi's vehicle and as soon as Gigi saw her running toward her, she opened her door and stepped out.

"Gigi, thank you so much for coming. We need your help."

"We. Is this the man..."

"No, he's a friend. He flew out here from Indiana to help me, and now we're all in trouble. You're the only other person I feel like I can trust. Can you help us get away from Riverton?"

She felt Gaige stand next to her without looking. His presence calmed her in some way, even though they still had some talking to do. She realized at this moment that if he were helping his uncle, he would have driven her right to base and turned her in.

Gaige held out his hand to Gigi. "Gaige Vickers. This is my colleague, Hawk."

Gigi eyed them both up, suspicion clear on her face, but shook hands with each of them.

Inhaling deeply, relief flooded her body when Gigi finally said, "Get in. We need to move. But I want to hear all about what the hell is going on while we drive."

Gaige walked Sophie around to the passenger side of the vehicle and held the front door open for her. Climbing in behind her, Hawk climbed in behind Gigi.

Gigi's Ford Edge, was a nice vehicle, but Hawk made everything look ridiculously small. She stifled a giggle 'cause she didn't want to start something, but his knees were seriously high in the back of the SUV. She assumed Gaige looked similarly, he was only a couple inches shorter than Hawk.

"Let's hear it." Gigi maneuvered her Edge out of the parking lot and onto the road.

Sophie filled her in on the details as she drove them back to Canyon Creek. Surprisingly, Gigi listened without interrupting and seemed to understand the situation. At least as much as anyone could.

"I'm sorry I let you think I was a battered wife. That wasn't fair."

Gigi shrugged. "As far as I'm concerned you were, still are, a battered woman and that's enough for me. I help women when I can." She drove past the bakery and Sophie's brows furrowed. "This is the first time I've helped men though. But I guess there's a first time for everything."

Turning to the east and down a country road, which wove itself around the bottom of the rocky hills above it, she softly asked, "Are you AWOL?"

A frown instantly appeared and sadness fell over her. "I'm sure they've reported me AWOL. It would be a tactic Killian would use to get everyone out looking for me. I've been a stellar soldier and worked my ass off. This bastard is going to kill my career."

"As long as he doesn't kill you, Katherine, the other can be worked out."

For the first time Gaige spoke up. "I'll be able to fix this once we get everything sorted out. I've got some contacts I can rely on."

She twisted in her seat to look into his eyes. "What if your uncle gets to them first?"

"He doesn't know who they are. It's all good."

Pulling up to a neat ranch style home with a stone exterior, which made it look as though it was part of the terrain behind it, Gigi hit a button on her visor, then softly said, "We're here."

16

Gaige looked around the area. "I don't want to seem unappreciative, but where is here and do I assume this is your home?"

Gigi looked into the backseat at him. "Yes, this is my home outside of Canyon Creek."

"And, why are you bringing us here?" They had to be careful, and he didn't know Gigi. Apparently she helped battered women, but what did that mean for he and Hawk?

"Katherine said she needed help and I could tell yesterday that she indeed was afraid of someone. But, as is usual in cases like this, it takes a while for some women to open up or ask for help. When Katherine called me today, I felt that was a step forward."

Clearly Sophie had given Gigi Kate's name to hide her identity, that was a plus. He hadn't done that, but wasn't as worried about it as he wasn't wanted. Until maybe now. He nodded his head and locked eyes with Gigi. Hers were pale blue, clear and bright. She held herself with a confidence and strength that was impressive.

"Fair enough." He waited for her to turn and tap the garage door button on her visor and watched as the door slowly raised. The interior of the garage was neat and clean, the walls were drywalled, plastered, and painted white. Nothing hung on the walls. The back wall held four flat doors, also painted white, and behind which he assumed were the gardening, yard tools, and other things normally stored in a garage. Slowly moving into the garage, she tapped the button to close the door behind her. He watched as she sat still and waited for the door to close before opening her door. Her eyes caught his in the rearview mirror.

"Old habits. In case you haven't figured it out, my ex used me as a punching bag for years. He'd jump out from behind doors to scare me. He loved it when I was frightened. Once I got rid of him, I still couldn't shake the feelings of not being secure. I never get out of my vehicle until I know someone can't run in and grab me. I've changed all of the doors in my house into sliding barn doors so no one is hiding behind one. All doors are opened wide and stay that way until I go to bed at night, in which case, I lock myself securely behind my bedroom door. It may seem weird to most, but I'll never live in fear again."

For the first time since they all got into the vehicle, Hawk responded. "No one should."

But sadly, she was living in fear, she just managed it in a way to make herself feel safe again.

They exited the vehicle and waited as Gigi walked them to a door on the driver's side of the vehicle. She unlocked it with her key then entered the room. The lights immediately turned on and the room flooded with light. The kitchen was neat and clean and brightly lit. The open concept meant the living room was visible from the kitchen, with no spaces available for a body to hide. Gigi meant what she said, no doors where someone could hide. Living like that for so many years played on a person's psyche. There was only a short hallway in the home. From the kitchen, an open sliding door lead to a bedroom, which was decorated in muted greens and ivory. Two open bedroom doors lead off from the east side of the living room. The living room didn't hold the usual large picture window, but two smaller windows with decorative grating in the glass. He'd bet she never opened those windows, keeping them closed and cooling the house with the air conditioner. Clearly, she'd thought all of this out.

"I've got two spare bedrooms." She held her hand out toward the living room. "Take your pick and partner up how you choose. There'll be no judgment here. My room is off the kitchen." She pointed to the room with the muted green decorating. "I have my own bathroom, but I'm afraid you'll all have to share the one between your bedrooms."

Not seeing a bathroom door, Gaige entered the first of the rooms and noticed a barn door to the left. Looking into that room he saw the Jack and Jill bathroom which was open to the other bedroom. Stepping back out he saw Sophie standing perfectly still, her thumbs tucked into her front jeans pockets. If he didn't know better he'd think she was looking casual, but her shoulders were stiff, her back rigid, and her jaw was tight.

"Soph...Katherine, why don't you take the room you like and Hawk and I will bunk up together in the other."

She stared at him for a few moments, her long dark

hair hung limply over her shoulders, her eyes held uncertainty and he saw her swallow. This was not the Sophie he knew from before. This woman before him had lost her spunk. He'd love to help her find it once again and he wondered if he should have Jax come out here and room with Sophie to help her get her sass back. No one had more sass than Jax.

"I'll take that one." She pointed to the farthest from the kitchen and he nodded.

Gigi then said, "I'll have something whipped up for supper in about an hour. You all make yourselves comfortable. I have a Murphy desk against the far wall." Pointing to a wooden cabinet, she continued. "Wi-Fi password is taped to the desktop and if there is anything you need, just ask."

Gigi went into her bedroom and closed her door. The lock clicked from the inside and his heart felt heavy for her. A woman who had been abused and scared to a point that she'd probably never feel totally safe again. People could really suck.

He walked into the bedroom he'd share with Hawk, set his duffle on the bed and dragged his laptop, cord and mouse from inside.

Hawk entered behind him and quietly said, "You think she's been reported AWOL?"

"I'm going to check that first. Then I'm going to email Casper and find out what he's knows about this and if he's heard anything regarding my presence here." Casper was GHOST's military contact who reported to their main contact in the State Department and his code name was the only name Gaige knew. His real name was top secret to everyone for safety purposes.

Walking out of the bedroom and to the Murphy desk he gripped the handle on the wooden door and gave it a tug. The desk slowly pulled down, and a panel which served as it's legs, moved out to support it. Ingenious way to hide a desk. Inside the cabinet, were cubbies and slots where Gigi had billing and paperwork organized. She was neat in all things.

Bending he plugged his laptop into the wall receptacle to the right, set it on the desk, and opened the lid. Entering his password, he looked to his left and saw a chair on wheels in the corner of the room. Pulling it up to the desk, he sat, his hands folded in front of him, his chin resting on his knuckles and he took a deep breath and let it out slowly. Today certainly didn't go as planned. Remembering Gavin, he tugged his phone from his pants pocket and called him up.

"Sorry, we ran into trouble. We won't be flying out tonight, stand by for morning."

"Yes, sir."

The line went dead and he silently offered a thank you to the Lord above for giving them Gavin, not only was he a great pilot, he was discreet and professional.

As soon as his computer finished loading, he tapped the icon for GHOST's military access software and entered his user name and password.

A few clicks and he was on the screen to access military personnel files. He typed in Sophie's name and watched as the information slowly populated the screen. He read the information on her and his heart beat with pride at the soldier she was. Top of her class in AIT, top 95% in shooting, perfect attendance, communications specialist and a good one at that. She had five special accommodations added to her credit for outstanding work. Damn it, Tate would be so fucking proud of her. Gaige was proud just reading it all now. Then, his blood ran cold.

She was not only listed AWOL, she was wanted for murder.

17

A soft knocking sounded at her bedroom door and Sophie jumped. She'd been sitting on the end of the bed, not sure what to do next. She thought about taking a nice long shower, in a clean bathroom with fragrant soap. But, she didn't have clean clothes and nothing to wear while her clothes dried. She could ask Gaige for his shirt again, but she was undecided if she should even do that.

She stood and walked to the door, slid it open and smiled when she saw Gigi. "Hi, come in."

"I brought you a few things to wear. I hope you don't mind, but I noticed that you are wearing the same clothes you had on yesterday and you don't have a bag with you, so...."

Her words hung in the air. "Thank you, Gigi, I really appreciate it. I haven't had the chance to get anything and Gaige said I can't go to my apartment because we don't know how secure it is."

"Well, these are just hand-me-downs, nothing fancy, but over time women have left things, or donated things as they've gotten back on their feet, and I hand them out when there's a need. You'll also find basics in the bathroom. Deodorant, shampoo and conditioner, lotion, shower soap, toothbrush, toothpaste, etc. Make yourself at home."

Clearing the lump from her throat, she replied, "Thank you, Gigi, you're very generous."

"Nope, no worries. I've got supper to make, why don't you take a nice hot shower and put some clean clothes on. I can show you the washer and dryer when you're ready."

"Do you need help? I can do...something." She smiled, not knowing what she could do. She could cook but when she did, it certainly wasn't in front of a professional, so embarrassing herself would be certain if she tried. On top of that, she was still a bit jumpy from all this upheaval.

Gigi turned to exit the room, "Nope, I've got this."

Just like that she was gone. Looking out the door and across the room she studied Gaige sitting at the desk. His fingers flew over the keys of his laptop, the fine hairs on his arms sparkled in the sunlight that shown through the windows on him. Almost as if he was being blessed by the bright light.

Suddenly his hands froze over the keys. He read something on his screen and she saw him swallow. Then, slowly, his head turned to her and their eyes locked. "What have you done, Soph?"

Her heart hammered in her chest and her mouth grew dry. She could feel her pulse pounding in her ears and the look on his face was absolutely devastating. What did he think she'd done? "What are you talking about?"

He turned his laptop toward her and she forced her feet to move to him. He never looked away from her and that made her nerves tingle. Reaching the desk, she looked at his computer screen and saw her name at the top. Glancing through the document without reading every word, her eyes landed on the most hated word of all. Murder.

Blinking to clear her vision she stared at that awful text hoping it would go away. Shaking her head, she finally glanced at Gaige. "That's not me. I didn't... I wouldn't ki... No, I didn't kill anyone."

Her knees shook, her bottom lip quivered, and the fact that she was about to have a meltdown scared her more than anything. Now more than ever, she needed to be strong. Present. Aware. She couldn't be weak. Not now. Not ever, apparently.

He stood abruptly and gently wrapped his hand around her upper arm, guiding her to his newly vacated chair. Kneeling down in front of her, he collected the clothing still wrapped in her arms, set them on the desk, and then took her hands in his. "We have to talk. About everything. I need to know what we're really up against."

From her peripheral vision she saw Hawk enter the room from the bedroom, but her brain didn't seem to want to cooperate. Gaige turned to his friend. "Hawk, can you get Sophie some water?"

"Yeah." He paused for a moment, taking in this weird scene then headed to the kitchen. Within a minute or two he was back in front of her holding out a bottle of water. Gaige gently took it from his friend, twisted the cap on the bottle, and handed it to her.

Numbly she reached for the bottle and sipped the cool water while she heard Gaige ask Hawk to take a seat, they had to work this all out. Her hands continued to shake as she set the bottle on the desk. Stupid thoughts ran through her head like, 'Don't spill water on Gaige's computer' and 'She should have jumped in the shower right away'. Why was she worried about those mundane things when she'd just read that she was wanted for murder?

"Come on over here, Sophie." Gaige urged her to stand and she felt as if she'd fall flat on her face, her legs didn't want to move. He picked her up without a grunt or a huff of air, as if she weighed nothing and easily set her on the sofa, taking a seat next to her. Hawk sat in the armchair at a forty-five-degree angle to her and watched silently as Gaige cleared his throat.

"Sophie's wanted for the murder of Chet Forest, Hawk."

She gasped. "Chet?" She looked deeply into Gaige's eyes to see if he was lying. "Chet's dead?"

"Yeah, Soph, he's dead. Didn't you tell me that was the guy who worked in the Medical Examiner's Office and you asked him for the autopsy report? You thought he was the one who told Killian about your evidence."

Swallowing what felt like a gigantic cotton ball, she nodded.

"When was the last time you saw him?"

She licked her dry lips before responding, trying to recall the last time she saw Chet. "About four days ago I think. I went to see him at his office in the Medical Examiner's Office. I asked him if he could get me Kate's autopsy report. I told him that she didn't kill herself. I said I had proof that it was a set up to make it look like she did. He told me he'd see what he could do, but then two men tried to grab me at my apartment complex and I had to run. I knew then he must have said something to Killian, but I still wasn't able to confirm it."

Hawk leaned forward, his forearms on his knees. "When was Chet murdered?"

"Three days ago."

"That was the day I called you." She whispered.

Gaige nodded, his lips formed a straight line and her heart began pounding again.

"I didn't do it, Gaige. I'd never do...that." Nervously she tucked her hair behind her ears and wracked her brain. "How? How was Chet murdered?"

"The report doesn't say. I'm going to see what I can find out. But, for now, we need to have that long awaited conversation."

18

He saw her spine straighten and her hands balled in her lap. She swallowed then looked him in the eye.

"Okay."

"First, and foremost, I'd never betray you, Sophie. If I would have known Tommy was accused of raping Kate, I would have gone to Uncle Jeff's and I'd have handled this differently. I still have to find out what has gone on in their house since that day."

"I realize that now, I just got freaked out when I heard where you'd gone." She lightly cleared her throat. "My trust levels are at an all-time low I guess."

He kept his eyes trained on hers, it was the best way he knew to convey honesty. "With good reason. But, Sophie, we're here to help you. We came here for you. No one else."

She blinked rapidly and he saw her eyes glisten, but she composed herself and shyly said, "Thank you." Turning to Hawk she repeated her thanks.

Hawk leaned forward again, his forearms on his knees,

his eyes locked on Sophie and said, "You're welcome, Sophie. You mean a lot to Gaige and therefore you mean a lot to all of GHOST. Our whole team volunteered to come here and help out. The rest are standing by at the compound, waiting for instructions on how they can help. That's the honest to goodness truth."

Her eyes widened and she relaxed her back just a bit, then she looked into his eyes once again. "I don't know how I'll be able to repay you, Gaige, but I will."

"We didn't come here for payment. When I asked the team if anyone wanted to join me, as Hawk said, the whole team volunteered. When I told them it was pro bono, not one person backed out."

"Wow. I don't know what to say."

"Let's start with the basics. How is your shoulder today?"

"It's sore, but it's healing, I think. It isn't worse than yesterday, so that's a good sign."

"It is. Now, tell me what you know about Kate's rape."

She squirmed a bit on the sofa, and inhaled a deep breath, held it a moment, then released it slowly.

"Kate and Tommy were dating. At least, they'd gone on about three dates. She told me they hadn't had sex yet, neither of them rushing it. She really liked Tommy."

She closed her eyes for a moment, then continued. "They went out that night, I think it was a Wednesday, and there was a place he said where he liked to eat, just out of town off the highway, called Kickers. It's a bar and restaurant and they're known for their ribs and home cooking. She was excited to go 'cause he was sharing things about himself. She thought that was a good sign that they were progressing as a couple."

Her cute little nose wrinkled and she bit her bottom

lip. "She dressed in jeans and a bright yellow button up blouse. She looked beautiful, but she always did. Her blond hair had been recently cut into an adorable bob and her blue eyes sparkled when she talked about Tommy. She was smitten."

Wriggling on the sofa to push herself back into the cushions a bit, he watched her face. This was difficult for her to share. He'd bet she hadn't told anyone, except CID.

"Go on, Soph." He gently pushed her to continue. It was too important to know everything that happened up till now so they could figure out which direction to take from here.

"Tommy came to Kate's apartment, I was still there, so I took off. They seemed excited to be together, happy and nothing seemed off. Not until around 7:30 the next morning when Kate called me. She was crying and asked me to come over. I just lived across the parking lot from her, so I ran over right away."

Tucking her hair behind her ears, he watched her fingers, though they were slender, he knew from the work she did they were strong and he knew from holding them they were soft.

She looked into his eyes, her deep brown irises glinted in the waning sunlight streaming in through the window. Her lush lashes framed her eyes perfectly. Even with the fine lines around her eyes and mouth, she was the most beautiful woman he'd ever laid eyes on. He'd thought so from the moment they met.

She took a deep breath. "She was crying, her hair was disheveled, and she was wearing her robe. She cried, "He raped me." But couldn't say much more. She pointed to the bedroom floor where her cute yellow blouse lay with a large rip down the front, and three of the buttons missing.

She had bruises on her wrists where his hands held hers together and she had a bruise on her jaw."

She absently rubbed the yellowish mark on her own jaw with her fingertips before returning her hands to her lap. He glanced at Hawk who sat staring straight ahead, as if imagining what the scene must have looked like, though his jaw was clamped together tightly and his fists were balled.

"Was Tommy still there?"

Shaking her head, she replied, "No, she said she'd just screamed at him till he left. He kept saying he didn't do it, he didn't remember anything and she was enraged. She was raped and he denied having anything to do with it, despite the fact he was the only one there with her."

"Did she say how Tommy looked? Were his clothes ripped? Did she scratch him anywhere?"

"No, she didn't remember it at all. She said she didn't even remember leaving the bar that night. And she remembered feeling weird about that because she only had one drink."

Hawk leaned forward again. "Sophie, did you take Kate in for tests? Did they do a toxicology report on her?"

"I took her to the hospital and they did a rape kit. They took blood but we never got the results. About a week after that was when things started happening to Kate. She was continually harassed in our unit, the men calling her a liar and a cock-tease. She couldn't believe the guys would do this. She said she felt raped all over again. When she went to our superiors they said they'd look into it, but nothing changed. After the third week she got mad. She told me she wasn't going down without a fight. She had a stellar career in the military and she wasn't going to let one asshole ruin it. There were so many things that just didn't add up."

She rubbed her forehead with her fingers, her brows drew together, and he could tell she was puzzling everything out in her mind.

"The harassment seemed off base. Other than Colonel Taylor being Tommy's father, why would our unit get involved? We tried getting information on the investigation from CID, but they just kept blocking our attempts telling us it was an open investigation or they were still waiting on lab results which seemed ridiculous to us after all that time. She then went to the local police and told them what had happened and that CID wasn't investigating or, at least, didn't seem to be and she was being harassed. They told her it was a military issue. Her next step was going to be to see an attorney who could help her out. She told CID afterward that she had seen the local police. Two days later, she was dead and a month later I'm on the run."

19

This was hard. She'd only told CID this information so far. Everyone else seemed too risky to say anything to. After all, look what happened to Chet. Her stomach twisted and she wrestled with whether she was hungry or nervous. Probably a little of both.

Gaige watched her and she wondered why he was here for her at all. Tate was gone, and though he probably felt like he owed it to Tate to help her, he didn't.

When he spoke to her, his deep sexy voice felt like a warm blanket wrapping around her shoulders on a chilly day. Her nipples puckered when he looked into her eyes and spoke. It was a heady combination. If only...

His voice softened. "What about Tommy? Did CID interview him?"

"I don't know. They'd never give us that information. They just kept saying when their investigation was complete they'd be in touch. It was so damned frustrating."

His eyes darted to Hawk's and she swallowed to moisten her parched throat.

"Look, Gaige, Hawk, here's what I do know. Kate wasn't on drugs. Any drugs. Her parents came after she died and I helped them clean out her apartment. We didn't find anything more than a bottle of aspirin and over the counter meds for cramps when she got her period. There was nothing anywhere. And, the garage that Kate was found in wasn't hers. It belonged to some guy in our apartment complex. It wasn't her car. The garage had been pried open, and the car backed in. And, my hunch is that the autopsy report will show there wasn't any carbon monoxide in her lungs or blood. That's why I went to Chet."

Gaige's phone rang and he reached over to the desk where it lay next to his computer. Glancing at the screen he looked her directly in the eyes. "I have to take this, it's Tommy. I need to find out what's going on with him."

Swallowing the gigantic lump that instantly formed in her throat, she wrapped her arms around her middle and nodded once. Gaige moved to sit at the chair in front of the desk, but he turned the chair to face in her direction.

"Tommy, what's up? Sorry I wasn't able to stay and see you this morning."

She watched his face, his handsome face. His eyes were the color of the grass late in the summer when the color deepened to a dark green. Fine lines had grown at the corners of his eyes since she'd seen him last, which was so many years ago. She assumed GHOST and its missions kept him up until all hours and the worry of keeping his team working, safe, and happy probably weighed on him, too. And he was doing it all alone. No one to help him bear the burden. No one to share that burden with, discuss it with, and make plans with. So much like her it was pitiful. Neither of them had found someone to spend their life with. Neither of them had really lived a full life. At least not in the sense that they had jobs they loved, and a family to come home to. Not everyone wanted or needed that, but for most people that was the definition of living a full life.

"Where can I meet you?"

Her ears began picking up the conversation again. He was going to meet Tommy? "No, I'm not really staying anywhere right now, so you'll need to come up with a place."

He turned to his computer, tucked his phone against his shoulder and his ear and began typing. "I see it, I can be there in a half hour."

Tapping the screen on his phone he looked at Hawk. "Call the compound, check in, and have someone rent us a new vehicle and tell the rental agency where to pick up our other one."

"You're not going to see Tommy alone are you?" Hawk asked, concern in his voice.

"No, I'll need you to come with me." He turned to her. "Sophie, I need to ask you to stay here with Gigi until we return."

"Gaige, I'm not a helpless..."

"I know." His hand raised to ward off her anger. "I need to deal with Tommy and find out, first of all, if this is a set up. If it is, I don't want you to get caught in the middle. If it isn't, he claims he's in trouble and needs my help, I may be able to get information from him that can help us out."

He waited for her and it melted her heart a bit. He wanted her permission.

He quickly moved from the desk chair to sit next to

her on the sofa. "Take a nice long shower. Dress in clean clothes. Have a nice woman to woman chat with Gigi and we'll be back as soon as we can."

Oh, she could stare into his eyes forever. His strong jaw and short dark blond hair made the rest of the package appear rugged and so damned alpha, but she could almost see his soul in his eyes. He was honest and true.

"Okay." She agreed. Though, the thought of a shower gave her goosebumps.

Hawk stood up and left the room as he pulled his cell phone from his back pocket. She could hear his voice from the bedroom he'd be sharing with Gaige. It was deep and smooth as he checked in, but she didn't listen to the actual words.

Gently taking her hands in his, Gaige hesitated before saying words she'd always wanted to hear from him. "Sophie, I'm here for you and I won't let anything happen to you. We're a team, the three of us. We're on the same side."

Her heartbeat sped up and she could still smell his scent. Musky and masculine, all the running they'd done today hadn't washed away the aroma of him. His body felt warm pressed against her arm, his knee against her leg. She watched his lips, the full bottom lip spread into a soft smile and butterflies took flight in her tummy. Then he licked his lips quickly and chuckled, but his words were serious.

"You need to be careful looking at me like that, Sophie. You'll never know how many times I've dreamed about you looking at me just like you are right now."

What? Was he kidding? What the hell... She leaned in

and softly touched her lips to his. She'd thought about kissing him for twenty-ish damned years.

His lips were soft and instantly molded to hers. His head tilted slightly and their mouths fit together like long lost puzzle pieces, locked into place. Moving her lips slightly against his she felt a little sigh escape her throat and he swallowed. Almost as if it was too much.

Pulling away slightly she watched his face to see what he was feeling. He looked bewildered. Surprised even. When he spoke, his voice was raspy. "I don't know why you did that, but I've dreamed of that kiss for a long damned time."

"Really?" She sat straighter and pulled away a bit. "I didn't think you were interested."

His brows raised high. "I didn't think you were."

Hawk cleared his throat from the bedroom door and Gaige turned to look at his friend. Hawk approached and handed her a phone. "It's a GHOST burner. I programed my number, Gaige's number, and the compound number in it in case you need to get in touch with us."

Reluctantly she looked away from Gaige and took the phone from Hawk. "Thank you for thinking of this."

Hawk nodded to Gaige. "Thank this guy right here. It's his money that buys us all these cool things we have."

She turned to him again but before she could say anything he said, "We'll be back soon."

20

She didn't think he was interested? They'd been stupid for years, each thinking the other wasn't interested. A simple word, a phone call, anything would have ended all this longing. It was fucking frustrating.

Walking into the kitchen his stomach growled as delicious aromas reached his nose. Gigi giggled, "Hungry?"

"Yes. Very. But, we have to go. We won't be gone long, but I need another favor."

"Keys are on the desk over there, and the gas tank is full."

He blinked as her words caught up to his ears. Hawk reached over and grabbed the keys, then walked to the counter where Gigi had a vegetable arrangement waiting for dinner. He plucked a couple carrots off the plate and shoved them in his mouth. Grabbing a celery stalk, he headed to the backdoor without a word. He saw Gigi smile but she kept working and never said a word.

"If anything happens and you need us, Sophie has our numbers."

Gigi stopped cutting up potatoes and looked him in the eye. "We're safe here, I've got a security system to beat all security systems. I told you, I'll never be caught off guard again. Now go so you can get back here in time to eat with us."

Gaige followed Hawk out the door and climbed into the passenger seat as Hawk jumped in the driver's seat. Taking his phone out of his pocket, he pulled up the location where Tommy asked to meet; it was a bar just off the highway on the opposite side of Riverton, which meant they had a few miles to trek, but it made him feel better that they were a good distance from Gigi's place.

After pulling from the garage, he tapped the button on the visor to close the door and waited until it closed before backing from the drive. Hawk didn't say much, but he always paid attention. Once they were on the road, he asked, "Which direction?"

"Head north on Hwy. 2."

His mind floated to Sophie and his lips tingled once again. He needed to keep his wits about him but dammit, she was making that difficult. His skin prickled to get back to her and get down to some things that had been left for far too long. But, first, they needed to have a different kind of conversation and this one would change everything for both of them.

"What do you think this is?" Hawk asked.

"I'm not sure and I hope to hell Tommy or Uncle Jeff isn't setting me up, but my gut tells me Tommy isn't. He said he'd gotten in trouble a month ago and he's been laying low because his dad wanted him to. But, when he heard I was there today, he realized he needed to talk to me to see if I could help him. He sounded sincere."

"Is he a good actor?"

"My first instinct is to say no, that's not something I ever thought about him. He's always been a stand-up guy. I haven't seen him in a few months, but the last time I did, he seemed happy and was doing well. His job was great, he's a boat builder and works for himself. But he had plenty of orders and he was excited about the future of his company.

Hawk nodded but stared at the road. The miles ticked away as his thoughts were all over the board, no matter how hard he tried to rein them in. Hawk broke the silence once again. "We'll be able to pick up an SUV on our way back to the house, Wyatt has it set to go and the company is picking up our other vehicle."

"Great. Thanks."

Hawk nodded, "How's this going down?"

"We'll go in separately. It's a bar, and hopefully, there aren't many people inside. You come in and sit close, keep your eyes peeled for signs of anything off. I'll try to get Tommy to talk. If I feel like I can trust him, I'll introduce you. Right now, they're not looking for you. I'd like to keep it that way."

"Killian saw me with you."

"Right, but Uncle Jeff didn't. I'm not sure who our enemy is this time around."

Hawk cleared his throat. "You've got a lot at stake on this one, Gaige. Sophie clearly is important to you and I can see you wrestling with your feelings for her. Now your uncle and cousin may be involved in a bad way. You gonna be okay on this? We can always call in some of the others to free you up a bit."

He looked over to see Hawk's face. But as he usually was, Hawk was a closed book. "I'm good. I need to see this through. If Tommy raped Kate, he needs to be punished. I have no idea how Kate ended up dead, but something tells me Killian is involved. Uncle Jeff said he came in handy even though he's a smarmy bastard. My best guess is Killian wants a promotion and he felt he'd get it by taking care of Tommy's alleged issue so Uncle Jeff would owe him. Plus, no doubt he's collecting evidence along the way for protection to use as blackmail if he needs to."

Dropping his head back against the headrest, he let out a long breath. "I want to figure this all out for my family and for Sophie. Now her career is in jeopardy because of all of this. Not to mention, the murder rap."

Hawk nodded and Gaige grabbed his phone from his shirt pocket. Tapping a couple of times on the screen he raised it to his ear and listened to the phone ring on the other end.

"Gaige, what's up out there?"

"Josh, I need you to do something for me. I need intel on how Chet Forest died. If you can hack in or have Jared Timm hack in, do it. Get everything you can get. He's a Medical Examiner's Office employee. Army. Died a couple of days ago."

"Got it." Josh was a longtime member of GHOST, his father and brother, Jake, were former members of GHOST, both deceased now. His sister Jax and future brother-in-law, Dodge were GHOST members as well. It truly was a family affair.

"I also need Kate Ryan's autopsy report. Rape kit, blood work, any lab results, too, most of it except the rape kit should be in the ME's report. Check the hospital, too. CID reports if you can get them. Everything either of you can find."

"Okay, we're on it. Everything else okay out there? Hawk said you were up against a bunch of shit."

"Yeah, you could say that. My cousin is accused of rape. The girl he is accused of raping is dead. Sophie is wanted for the murder of Chet Forest and she's being hunted and reported AWOL. It's a regular shit show out here."

"Fuck. We're ready to come out and take care of shit."

Gaige chuckled. "Thanks, but coming in guns a blazing right now isn't going to help. We've got to lay low and play this smart. Get all the intel we can and expose whoever is behind all of this shit. My gut tells me the person who killed Kate, also killed Chet. They were both in the way."

He saw Hawk nod from his peripheral vision, and it made him feel good about bringing Hawk along. He was smart. He'd already puzzled this out as well.

Pulling into the parking lot, Gaige watched his cousin Tommy walk across the blacktop to a side door of the bar. He looked guilty as hell of something. Gazing around as if he was afraid he was followed and shifty as well.

"I'll go in first before he runs out the backdoor. He looks like he's scared of his own shadow at the moment. Give me three then come in."

21

S he turned and watched them pull out of the driveway and heaved out a long breath. She'd kissed him and not only did he reciprocate, he said he'd thought about kissing her for a long time. Both of them had thought of the other for so damned long and neither of them did a thing about it. Of course it didn't help that she was only sixteen when she first met Gaige. Then, he'd finished AIT with Tate, then been deployed. Then she got married. Tate died. Then she divorced. Then he was engaged. Time. It never seemed to be on their side, but now? Maybe now would be their time. If she wasn't in jail or dead.

Frustration rolled over her like a steamroller and the full weight of all things lost. Lives lost and time long past threatened to suffocate her. She stood and walked into the kitchen. Gigi stood at the counter, crushing garlic while something totally delicious simmered on the stove. Gigi's blue eyes met hers and she smiled.

"I see the sparks flying, girl."

"Yeah." She sighed and leaned against the wall across

from the counter. Her shoulder was beginning to ache and her head throbbed.

"You don't sound very happy about that." She turned and scraped the garlic into the pan on the stove, stirred the ingredients together then came back to the counter and set the cutting board in its place.

"I kissed him."

"I saw."

"He told me he'd thought about kissing me for so long."

"Mmm Hmm."

"Well, I've thought about him for all that time, too. Since I was sixteen."

Gigi remained silent, going about the business of chopping up an onion.

When she realized she wasn't going to get anything more from Gigi, she continued. "We've been stupid." Tucking her hair behind her ear, she grimaced as her thoughts raced through her mind. "A phone call, an email, a message, anything could have changed both of our lives."

Gigi looked up from her cooking and took a deep breath. "But you didn't. There's no sense worrying over what could have been. It wasn't. What you have is here and now. You need to clean up your shit and then see if you two have something tangible."

She held the kind gaze Gigi bestowed upon her then nodded. "Go on Katherine, take a hot bath or shower, get dressed, and when the men come home, we'll eat."

"You sure you don't need any help?"

She giggled and it sounded nice. "No, I'm like a kid at Christmas right now. I seldom have this many people to cook for. I bake all day long, but this is fun. Go on and relax, get your head around your situation, and when they get back here, you all can put your heads together on how to fix this mess you're in."

"I owe you an apology, Gigi. I didn't let you know my situation when you first found me. And things are worse now."

"You don't owe me anything, Katherine. Once you've got this under control, maybe we can share a glass or two of wine and you can tell me all about it. Then, all I ask is for you to pay it forward. Simple as that."

"I'd like that." Swallowing she added, "My name isn't Katherine, it's Sophie."

"Mmm Hmm, got that too, hon. Doesn't matter to me what your name is, I'm not telling a soul."

Gigi turned to scrape the onion in the same pan as the garlic and Sophie turned and walked to the desk where the clothes she'd been given still sat. Picking them up, she smelled the shirt on top and the fresh laundry scent made her close her eyes. It reminded her of an easier time, her mom doing laundry while Sophie sat in the kitchen doing her homework. Her mom. Her parents didn't know any of this and she hoped she could keep it that way, but she'd need to call them soon or her parents would panic if they couldn't get in touch with her. The last thing she needed was for them to contact someone else and hear the worst of this situation without understanding Gaige was here to help her. She turned to her bedroom, slid the door closed and fought back the tears that once again tried leaking out. Gigi was right. Maybe a hot bath, a good cry, and clean clothes would clear away all the darkness and allow her to focus on a plan. And Gaige, she'd think about him, too.

22

The door closed behind him and the light from outside shutoff. The darkness of the bar took him a moment to allow his eyes to adjust. The dank odor of stale beer reached his nostrils, but he tried his best to ignore it. As his vision came back to him, he scanned the room. Dim lights hung in various places within the bar, all of them decorated with one brand of beer or another, all of them far too dull to do much in the way of illuminating the place. As he moved his feet and the sound of stickiness reached his ears, he figured the low light served more to hide the grime from the few patrons in this establishment than anything else. The one small window in the far wall angled a shaft of light across an empty table, but landed at the boot of a patron at another table. Looking past that man and to the dark corner, he saw Tommy's light head nod toward him.

Picking up his pace, he sauntered to his cousin and when he was three steps away, Tommy stood. The hollow look on his face wasn't the same Tommy he'd seen a few months ago. This man looked as if he hadn't eaten or slept in months. Dark circles framed his light blue eyes, and the skin on his cheeks sagged and were colored gray. Where once they were bright and vibrant, so much like his mother, now he could pose as a zombie.

Tommy reached forward and grabbed Gaige in a bear-hug. His face buried in Gaige's neck, but he heard Tommy say into his shirt, "I'm so glad to see you, Gaige. I'm so fucked right now and you're the only one who can help me."

Gaige tightened his hold on Tommy to sooth him, and himself. His stomach knotted up and the acid that built-up in his stomach soured anything he had by way of food in it. Pulling back, he placed his hands on either of Tommy's shoulders and looked him in the eye. "I'll do what I can, but you have to tell me everything."

Tommy nodded, swiped at his nose with the back of his hand, and then sat with his back to the wall. That left the chair next to his for Gaige to also be able to put his back to a wall. It would be funny if it weren't so fucked up.

"Tell me what's going on, Tommy."

"I didn't remember for a long time. But, I've been having like, visions or memories or something. I told dad and he told me to shut up about it. But, it's not right, Gaige."

"Okay. Start at the beginning."

Tommy swallowed then let out a shaky breath. "I was dating Kate. Kate Ryan. She was great. Blonde, blue eyes, smart, great sense of humor, she was a dream. After getting divorced a few years ago, I haven't found anyone that held my interest for more than five minutes, but Kate, she..." His voice cracked and he stopped to swallow.

"We'd gone on three dates. No sex, some great kissing,

and she was the best hugger. Gawd, she made me feel like I was the most important man in the world."

His hands lay on the table in front of him, his fingers shaking slightly, and the pads of his fingers followed some of the various imperfections and gouges in the wooden table top.

"Two months ago, we went on our third date. Damn it, Gaige she looked perfect. Bright yellow top, it made her blue eyes look bluer if that was possible. We went out to Kickers, to have bar-b-que."

He sniffed and his eyes shifted around the room to make sure no one was listening. The door opened and Hawk entered the bar, practically had to duck through the door, but he was used to being a big man in every room. Hawk's eyes perused the room, then he strode to a table two away from Tommy and him, and sat down. For the first time since he'd entered the bar a waitress came around and took Hawk's order first. She tried flirting, which went nowhere. She was older and not well kempt, she was sure barking up the wrong tree with this group. Then she turned and tried her best to sashay across to them. Gaige clinched his jaw at the interruption more than anything.

"What'll you boys have?"

"I'll have a dark soda, whatever you have. He'll have the same." He motioned to Tommy with his head, wanting this woman to move on sooner rather than later. She wrinkled her face before turning and heading back to the bar. Gaige reached into his wallet and pulled a $10 bill out, laying it on the table top.

"Go on, Tommy."

Clearing his throat, he softened his voice, "We walked in and took a table. The waitress came around and took our drink order. I ordered a beer and Kate ordered a Cosmo. Then we looked at the menu. I knew what I was going to have right away and she teased me about that. Then, she decided to have the same as me and we sat and talked. She was telling me about her day, they'd had an incident at work with one of the civilian employees on base showing up late and generally being an asshole to all of the military employees. I shared a story about a boat I was working on then we moved on to favorite movies. Our drink order came, the waitress took our food order and left. It was nice. Easy. I felt so good to have found her. She smiled all the time. She was like a ray of sunshine.

"The next thing I remember was Kate screaming at me. We were at her place, she was clutching a sheet around her breasts, she seemed as if she was naked under the sheet. She kept yelling, 'You raped me. Get out. You raped me. How could you do that to me?' It was horrible. I didn't remember getting back to her place. I didn't remember having sex with her. I'd never, ever..."

His voice cracked and his shaking fingers brushed along his temple. The waitress brought their drinks, picked up the ten and said, "I'll be back with your change."

"Keep it." He replied, he just wanted her to go away. Taking a drink of his cola to wet his dry throat he waited for Tommy to get himself together.

He leaned in and whispered, "I didn't rape her, Gaige. I'd never do that. I was willing to wait no matter how long it took. She was special. I felt like it was a relationship that would last."

His fingers wrapped around the glass in front of him, more to steady himself than anything.

"I got off the end of the bed where I was laying and pulled my shirt closed. It was a button up. I stood up and zipped my jeans. My head was pounding and all I could hear was Kate yelling. Her cute yellow blouse lay on the floor, ripped. Her jeans were on the floor, her panties and bra..."

A sob escaped his throat and he put a hand over his mouth. Gaige's gut wrenched for his cousin. This wasn't a man who was trying to get out of a rape charge. He was devastated.

"It's okay, Tommy. Take a sip of your cola and take a minute."

"I can't." His voice cracked again. He swallowed and continued, "I think we were drugged. I can't drink something that I haven't opened, I'm so afraid it'll happen again."

23

G lancing over at Hawk he saw the slight nod his friend gave him. A signal he was listening. Watching.

"Tell me what happened when you got home."

"I didn't go home. I was freaked out. I couldn't get my head around what was happening and I felt dull and like my brain was working in slow motion. I walked out of her apartment and looked around for my car. I found it at the end of the lot, but I don't remember parking it. I don't remember driving. It's fucking scary. I drove to mom and dad's and I've been there since. I didn't realize what happened right away. I called dad once I got to the house and he came home. I told him what had happened and he told me to go upstairs, take a shower and then a nap and he'd make a couple of phone calls. Unfortunately, I slept for about five hours. It must have been the drugs 'cause with all of this bullshit swirling around in my head, that would have been the last thing I'd do. Later that day dad came home and told me that I was never to tell anyone anything and that he had it worked out so I wouldn't be implicated. I asked what that meant and he told me to let him handle everything and put it out of my mind. He also said I was never to contact Kate again."

"Did you ever try to contact, Kate?"

His bottom lip quivered and he sniffed. "No," he softly said. Then he inhaled and held his breath a moment before letting it out. "I wanted to. So bad. I wanted to tell her I hadn't raped her; I'd never rape her or hurt her. Never. Dad didn't want to talk about it. I asked him what he did and he would just walk away. He told me to forget it."

He scraped a shaking hand through his sandy blond hair and sniffed again. On the verge of crying, his voice cracked when he finished with, "then I heard she...she was gone."

Pulling a napkin from the metal holder on the table next to theirs, Gaige handed it to Tommy. Blowing his nose, Gaige took the time to glance at Hawk. Hawk was on his phone, no doubt looking up drugs that would knock a person unconscious or something similar. He was a great teammate. Gaige had a couple ideas of his own to research.

Returning his gaze to Tommy he prompted him a bit more. "What have you started to remember, Tommy?"

He sat up straighter and rotated his shoulders. "It's not clear. More like I'm in a fog or a haze but I hear clothing ripping. I can hear Kate whimpering or crying softly. I see a man with white hair laying on her in bed. I'm at an angle at the end of the bed. I try to move to help her and he turns his head and stares at me. His face is evil; his eyes are so light they look evil. He kicks me in the face and I don't remember anything else."

"And you told Uncle Jeff this?"

"I tried to. About two weeks ago when I first remembered. He told me to shut up and never talk about it." His hands continued to shake and he folded them together on the top of the table. "He left the house after that and he didn't come home until late that night. He'd been drinking. He's been avoiding me since then. I've barely seen him."

Looking over at Hawk, his friend met his gaze, held up his phone with Killian's picture on it. White hair, light blue eyes almost giving him the appearance of an albino. He'd always given Gaige the creeps. Of course his personality didn't help that any.

Tommy scooted his chair back abruptly. "He's listening?"

Gaige reached over and lay his hand on Tommy's arm. "He's with me. He's GHOST. I wasn't sure if this was a set up or not so I asked him to hang back."

Hawk stood and all 6'8" of him slowly approached the table. Gaige was only a few inches shorter than Hawk, but the black hair and green eyes of Hawk, the plethora of tattoos on his arms gave him the immediate impression of badass. It was only one of many reasons he'd brought Hawk along. Even the meanest son-of-a-bitch thought twice before tangling with Hawk.

Leaning over the table, Hawk locked eyes with Tommy and held his hand out to shake. Tommy froze in place, swallowed, then his eyes slowly traveled up Hawk's body to his face. After what seemed like ten minutes, he finally reached over and shook hands with Hawk. Sitting at the table with them Hawk once again held up his phone. "This the man you saw?"

Tommy looked at the picture and his eyes welled with tears. He sniffed a few times and swallowed rapidly.

Finally nodding his head his voice came out in a whisper. "Yeah."

Gaige leaned in toward Tommy. "You sure, Tommy?"

"I know I was drugged and hazy, but that's him. I've seen his face in my nightmares since I first started to remember."

Hawk lay his phone on the table and crossed his arms over his chest. "Name Reed Killian mean anything to you?"

"Is that his name? Is that who that is?" Tommy seemed hopeful to find out who his nightmare was.

"I asked you first."

"Yeah. But only because I've overheard dad on the phone with him a couple of times. Once was right after..." Clearing his throat he finished, "Right after Kate was raped. They were arguing, but I couldn't hear exact words. I only knew that's who he was talking to because my mom made a comment. We were both in the kitchen and we could hear dad from his study on the phone. Mom said, "He can't stand Reed Killian, I don't know why he continues to take his calls."

Swiping his hand through his hair again, he continued, "The next time was after Kate...passed. They were talking on the phone, then dad left and said he'd be out a while."

Gaige asked, "You didn't think that was weird or out of character?"

Tommy looked him in the eye, his defeated look was so fucking sad. "Gaige, man, I hate to say this, but I've been living in my own fucking world since this all happened. I feel violated in some ways. I'm brokenhearted that Kate died thinking I had raped her. I'm brokenhearted that she's gone and that the life I was beginning to picture in my head will never be. I haven't thought for two seconds about dad's behavior. Mom's behavior. My own for that matter. I've been cooped up in my room at my parents' house hiding from life."

"Okay, I get it. So last question. Why were you looking around like you were being followed when you walked in here?"

"I'm so fucking paranoid about everything now, Gaige. Someone drugged me. Got me and my date out of a restaurant. Drove us to her place. Raped her. And left me there to take the fall. I don't know who did it. How he did it. Why he did it. But, as I've been thinking about it, he had to know Kate. Otherwise, how would he know where she lived?"

24

She felt like a new person. Almost. For the first time in days now, maybe even weeks, she felt clean, safe and as if she had help to sort out all of this mess for herself and Kate, too. The fragrant, steamy hot bath did wonders for making her feel clean. The tears cried while soaking did a lot to clear out the angst, sadness, and left over fear. Blow-drying her hair, touching it up a bit with the borrowed curling iron from Gigi and the cute jeans and sleeveless blouse made her feel sexy once again.

Leaving the bathroom and sliding the door closed, the delicious aromas from the kitchen filtered into her bedroom. Carrying her wet bath towel and dirty clothes into the living room which flowed into the kitchen, she saw Gigi look at the clock, turn a dial on stove, and then begin pulling dishes from a cabinet. Setting a stack of four plates on the counter, she pulled open the drawer just below and counted out four forks and knives.

Glancing over her shoulder, Gigi asked, "Do you feel better, Sophie?"

"I do, yes. Thank you so much. I guess I needed the time to myself to get my thoughts on track."

"There's nothing more healing than time. Even in small spurts." Walking around the center island with the plates and silverware she set them on the table. "Follow me and I'll show you where the laundry room is."

She followed Gigi down the short hallway to the back of the house, where the bright laundry room was located. No door on this room, but from the hall all you could see was a wooden bench with two yellow pillows on it for decoration. A mirror was hung above the bench, allowing her to see into the room from this vantage point. No surprises.

"Washer and dryer are here. Soap is between them on this roll out shelf unit." She pulled a built-in unit on gliders from between the front-load washer and dryer. Two shelves held laundry soap, fabric softener sheets, bleach, and a bottle of stain remover.

The room had the feel of an old farmhouse with the shiplap boards whitewashed in white. The decorations on the walls had splashes of the matching yellow from the pillows on the wooden bench. A backdoor opened to a gorgeous patio enclosed with a tall, wooden privacy fence. The plants and shrubs were healthy and colorful. Six brightly-colored chairs waited at the perimeter, in groups of two, for various conversations but not so far apart that all guests couldn't have a nice chat. Many colorful yard ornaments were disbursed throughout. It was comfortable and relaxing with a touch of whimsy.

"Wow, Gigi, this is beautiful."

She looked out the window onto her patio and smiled. "Thank you. When I first divorced, I spent loads of time out here growing these plants, tending to the garden, and painting the decorations. I did it for therapy. Getting my bearings as a person and who Gigi was. What did Gigi like to do? What was she good at? I'd lost all of that during a prolonged, difficult relationship. I wasn't allowed to do anything I wanted to do. I was suffocating and didn't even know it, till I landed in the hospital for the fifth time. With the help of my sister, I got my ex arrested, then jailed, and now he's sitting for a good long time for the things he's done to me and so many others. I needed to find out who I was before I could move forward."

She turned then and looked Sophie in the eye. "Then one day it was cold outside and raining so I decided to bake something. I took the cupcakes I made to my sister's house for her and my niece and nephew and they raved about them. I came home and baked more, I took those to therapy that day. One of the women in my group therapy asked if I could bake a cake for her daughter's birthday party. I did. I enjoyed it. I blossomed. Then the opportunity to buy the bakery came along, and I managed to make that purchase work. The rest, as they say, is history."

"Good for you, Gigi. It sounds like you've been through an awful lot, but it also sounds like you've come out on the good side of the storm."

The door to the garage opened and the deep voices of men floated down the hall. Without so much as a prompt, her cheeks flushed crimson and heated her face. Gaige was back. Gigi giggled and headed down the hall. Laying her wet towel filled with her dirty laundry on the floor in front of the washer she stepped down the hall to see if they had any good news. She'd also ask them if she could do their laundry. It wasn't much, but she'd feel helpful being able to do something for them.

Gaige and Hawk filled up the room in the most delicious way. Hawk began setting the plates and flatware around the table, but Gaige was watching her move toward him. Her heart hammered in her chest and her stomach felt as if it was filled with butterflies. He moved two steps to meet her and the instant she was within touching distance, his hand reached out and cupped the back of her head, pulling her into his body. His arms instantly circled around her. He was warm, and firm against her and he smelled heavenly. Spicy and musky. Laying her cheek against his chest she inhaled his scent, wanting to memorize it forever, in case things didn't work out for them. Again.

He kissed the top of her head, then said, "After dinner we need to talk."

She felt the words rumble through his body just as she heard them and her knees began shaking. Yes, they needed to talk about a lot of things. But, she also intended to make sure she told him how much he meant to her. How many times she'd thought about him? How badly she wanted to be with him. In every way.

That was going to happen tonight.

25

Gigi took charge of the room. "Sit down, everyone, I'll pull supper out of the oven. I've made roast beef, braised potatoes, and baby carrots stewed in the beef broth. I have a spice cake for dessert and there's plenty, so I hope you're hungry. And, before anyone asks, no I don't need help, let me enjoy having company and playing hostess."

"I'm starving," Hawk said as he promptly sat down.

Pulling away from Sophie, something he hated to do now, he looked into her gorgeous brown eyes. "You hungry, Kate?"

She smiled sweetly and nodded. Watching her swallow, his heart grew for her right then. She'd been stoic, strong, and smart through so much of this ordeal. "I told Gigi my real name."

He kissed the top of her head, his heart hammering away in his chest. Turning he held out a chair for her to sit on one side of the small square table. Gigi carried a glass roasting pan filled with delicious smelling food and his stomach growled. Gigi giggled and turned to the refrigerator. "What can I get you all to drink? I have a lovely red California wine, water, juice, or milk."

Sophie smiled. "I'd love a glass of wine, please."

"Gentlemen?"

"I'll just have water, Gigi, I need to stay alert, just in case,"he replied.

Hawk leaned forward, "Have a glass of wine with Sophie, Gaige. I'm on alert tonight."

Was Hawk playing matchmaker? Nodding, he replied to Gigi, "A glass of wine would be great, thank you." He glanced at Sophie and saw her cheeks turn pink. Some of her brightness was coming back.

Gigi poured two glasses of wine, placed them on the table, set two tall glasses of ice water on the table for Hawk and herself, and then sat across from Sophie. "Dig in while it's hot."

After a few quiet bites of food Sophie looked at him and asked, "I just have to know, Gaige, what did Tommy say?"

Swallowing the food in his mouth, which was beyond amazing, he set his fork on his plate and took a drink of wine.

"I don't think he raped Kate." He looked at Hawk who nodded. "He's been having memories or flashbacks. He remembers being at the restaurant with Kate and the next thing he remembers is her screaming at him that he'd raped her. But lately, he's been remembering other things. Someone on top of Kate, her whimpering or crying. He tried to help her and got kicked in the face."

"But she was so sure."

"Could it be because he was left there to be implicated in the rape?"

She thought about it a minute. He could see her

wrestling with his comments that Tommy hadn't raped Kate. When you'd believed something for so long and it was so personal, it was difficult to change your thoughts in an instant.

"I suppose. She said he left and never tried to contact her to explain."

"My Uncle Jeff told him not to contact her. Uncle Jeff said he'd take care of it and that he wasn't to talk about it ever again. He said he wanted to. Then he heard she'd died and he was just devastated."

"So was she."

Hawk set his fork on his plate. "Sophie, if you could have seen him, you'd have believed him, too. He's shattered. He looks horrible as if he hasn't eaten or slept in days. As a matter of fact, he wouldn't even take a drink of the soda Gaige bought him because he said he can't drink something he doesn't open. He doesn't know who drugged him and Kate or why and he's freaked out."

Sophie lay her fork down and moved both of her hands to her lap. Her head was bent and she stared for a long time at her plate. He glanced at Hawk, not sure what should be said or done.

"Soph, I'm not saying this answers all of our questions and I'm also not saying we shouldn't continue to investigate Tommy. There are things that can be done, such as a hair analysis. I asked him for a few pieces of hair so we can test for drugs. He readily agreed. That will help us with some answers. If Tommy was drugged, it's unlikely he raped Kate or even had the capacity to rape her. That will allow us to focus on other suspects."

"What other suspects?" She turned her head and locked eyes with him.

"Killian."

Immediately her spine stiffened and her mouth formed a straight line thinning her lips. "Why?"

"Why Killian? Tommy told us he remembers the person on top of Kate had white hair and light blue eyes. Hawk showed him a picture of Killian and he identified him as the man."

Her eyes, her gorgeous chocolate-colored eyes glistened as tears filled them. She swallowed a few times in rapid succession and inhaled a deep breath. He assumed to gather her control.

"He had not quite been stalking her but showing up at odd places where she was and he had no business being. Places on base like her office with feigned excuses to be there. He showed up at the bowling alley one weekend night when we were there with a group from our unit. He was at our apartment complex, which is on base, and, of course, he has access to, but he lives off base and had no business being there. But we'd gone to my apartment for lunch because we were planning a baby shower for a friend and we were using every spare moment to plan. When we left to go back to work, he was parked outside. But he was facing Kate's apartment. We thought it was plain weird. After she was raped, she didn't see him anymore and she thought it was because she was damaged goods then."

"How would he have known?"

"Word ran rampant through our unit. We were contacting CID all the time trying to get answers. Then Kate started getting verbally harassed, called a cock-tease and a liar. She went to our upper command but it continued. Then she saw an Article 15 accusing her of being late and others signed by Killian. That was just a couple of days before she died." Tucking her hair behind her ear, he noticed that her fingers shook slightly. "At least that's what we thought at the time because he had no other explanation. But, if he was there that night and he was the man who raped her, he'd have known and had time to set things up including the Article 15s that started cropping up to discredit her."

Her eyes flashed in anger then defeat in a matter of seconds. "I don't know how I'll ever be able to prove any of this."

"We. How we'll prove it. We have some ideas." He reached over and covered her hand with his and squeezed.

"We need to talk to the medical examiner. Find out if there were drugs in Kate's system when she died including the opioids. We need to have Tommy's hair analyzed for drugs so we know which drugs to look for and find the origin. We have to tie this all to Killian. Then, we need to find out how my Uncle Jeff is involved in any of the cover up and fix it. After that, Soph, between my Uncle Jeff, assuming he's not involved, and my contacts, we'll get your record and Kate's corrected."

"What about Chet?"

Hawk finished his plate of food. "I have Josh working on Chet's death to find out how he died. Once we know that, we'll figure out how to prove you weren't there and didn't murder him."

Gigi spoke for the first time in a long time. "Well now, you all have quite a bit of work to do, so you should go on and get cracking at it. Dig into your food, then I'll clean up and make myself scarce. The leftovers will be in the fridge, and if you get hungry, please help yourself."

26

They moved into the living room while Gigi cleaned up after dinner. She hummed as she cleaned and generally seemed happy to have people around. It was nice, hearing a happy person putter around her kitchen, reasonably carefree and it was nice to be cared for again.

Gaige opened his laptop, grabbed his duffle bag from the bedroom and brought it into the living room. He pulled a baggy from his duffle bag and then a gadget that looked like a handheld recorder. Pushing a button on the gadget, a vial popped out from the end. Opening the baggy and using a pair of tweezers taken from inside a zippered case, he pulled a hair from the plastic bag and dropped it into the vial. Tapping a few buttons, he set it on the desk next to his computer then began typing.

"Soph, I'll have test results in a few minutes on Tommy's hair. But, that's just for our use. I have more samples that GHOST's contact will send to an appropriate lab so we'll have the official test results needed to prove that Tommy didn't rape Kate and the chain of custody verified. I've collected the hairs properly and will get them to GHOST's contact."

"That little machine can give you drug analysis on hair?"

"Yeah, among other things."

"You have a lot of cool tools."

"We do."

She still stood, watching him, unsure what she should be doing. "I'd like to help, Gaige; I'm not used to sitting on the sidelines and doing nothing." It was driving her crazy. She was finally starting to feel like herself again and it felt good.

Gaige turned, his green eyes locked on hers and she felt the flush rush up from her toes. It came so fast and furious she caught a chill and shivered. Seriously, she could stare at him all day, this man about whom she'd lay awake at night thinking, wondering what it was about her he didn't find appealing. Just today he'd dispelled those thoughts admitting he'd been thinking about her, too. If their situation wasn't so serious, her clothes would already be off. Hopefully his would be, too. When he finally spoke to her, his voice was raspy, the deep tenor slid over her like a warm sweater fresh from the dryer.

"I'm glad to hear you're ready to help out, Soph. Based on what we have to do, tell me how your computer skills are."

She smiled then, almost laughed. "I'm an expert on the computer, Gaige. Tell me what you need me to do."

"I've logged into the military database. GHOST has high level clearance so we can't abuse it, promise me that."

She held her right hand up, "Scouts honor."

He laughed and it was the most fantastic sound. The fine lines next to his eyes crinkled and gave him that sexy mature man vibe. His full lips formed the perfect smile and his teeth were enviable, straight, and white. There wasn't anything she didn't enjoy looking at.

"I didn't know you were a scout."

Giggling, "I wasn't." She shrugged and his grin said so much.

"Okay, then you sit here." He stood next to the chair he'd just vacated. She sat down, the seat still warm and she got another whiff of him. He still smelled simply fantastic.

"Okay, from here you can access Kate's record. Pull it up and see if you can find her autopsy report. If it isn't uploaded yet, see if you can at least find the name of the medical examiner who did the autopsy."

The device sitting next to the computer beeped and Gaige lifted it from the desk. He looked at the readout, then pulled his phone from his pocket. Hawk walked out of the bedroom he was sharing with Gaige and waited for Gaige to tell them the analysis details.

"He was drugged approximately two months ago with a drug named Versed. It's a drug that's usually used for colonoscopies and other surgeries for pre-anesthesia sedation, but they also use it for some outpatient procedures. Usually given via IV it can be taken orally in some circumstances."

She stopped typing and searching and looked up at Gaige. Tommy didn't rape Kate, they were likely both drugged. His eyes dropped to hers and held.

"This is good news, Soph. Tommy didn't do it, which makes me so fucking happy. I've been a bit freaked out that he'd resort to doing something like this, and he'll feel so much better knowing he's innocent now, too. Our biggest hurdle will be figuring out how Killian had access to them at the restaurant and how he drugged them."

"It is good news. It just feels as if we're starting all over again." The news almost felt heavy and suffocating. Starting over again was the last thing she wanted to do. "Also, why is Tommy just now beginning to remember things?"

"I don't know for sure. But, my best guess is that either he was given more Versed than Kate, provided Kate was given Versed. Or, he metabolized it differently. He's also never been as mentally tough as Uncle Jeff. It's why he didn't go into the military. On top of that, he hasn't been eating well, or sleeping properly. Uncle Jeff won't let him talk about it, and he hasn't gotten proper medical help. All of this could hamper the progression of the drug leaving his system and his memory still being foggy."

He kneeled down beside her. "We're not starting over. We have a lead, we know who didn't do it and we have access to some pretty amazing tools, so we'll get this all sorted in no time."

Hawk broke his silence. "Josh just got back to me. Chet was found lying in the Medical Examiner's Office. It looked at first like he'd had a heart attack. But since he was only 28 years old, that seemed suspicious, so an autopsy found that he had Fentanyl in his system. His heart couldn't take it, which is what killed him."

She wrapped her arms around her waist, "Oh my God, that's so horrible."

Gaige stood next to her, his warm, strong hand pressing against her neck and nape. Supporting her. He squeezed a couple of times to let her know he was there, but said nothing.

After a few moments she stood and inhaled deeply. Then she looked at Hawk as a memory ran through her head. "Hawk, there are records of who enters and exits the Medical Examiner's Office and of the morgue itself where the bodies are stored until the autopsy is complete and any necessary examination of the bodies by the authorities are conducted. You have to sign in and out and there are security cameras everywhere. It would be impossible for someone to erase all of the footage."

He smiled at her and it struck her what a handsome man he was. So different than Gaige. Gaige was all, sandy blond hair, green eyes, and fair skin while Hawk was dark. Dark hair, green eyes, even his skin was olive toned. And, the presence he emitted when he walked into a room was impressive. All badass and gnarly.

"I'm on it." He disappeared into the bedroom and came back out in a minute, a laptop in his hand.

He sat in the armchair across from the desk and began typing away. She resumed her seat at the desk and began scouring Kate's record for the autopsy report, the medical examiner's name and anything else she could find. It made her sad digging through personal stuff about her friend, but it also made her happy that she'd avenge Kate's death because she had the power to do it with GHOST.

The next thing she knew, she was floating on air. She felt as though she was being carried on a cloud. The aroma of Gaige enveloped her and a heat warmed her body. It was delicious.

"Here you go, Soph, rest now."

Her eyes flew open and she realized she was in her

bedroom at Gigi's and Gaige had laid her on her bed. Her arms encircled his neck and she pulled him down, her lips capturing his. Her heart raced when he kissed her back, his hand sliding up her abdomen to find her breast and gently squeeze.

27

The kiss grew heated, his body enflamed. He tried pulling back and giving her some space, but also to make sure she was actually awake, as she'd just been sleeping. As soon as he pulled back, her arms pulled him forward with a strength that both surprised and impressed the hell out of him.

His tongue delved into her mouth, the warmth felt amazing. Her tongue slid along his and circled his mouth. Both soft and firm at the same time if that was possible; he wanted to be consumed by her. Or perhaps that was he who wanted to consume her. His cock throbbed and it thickened and he could feel the dampness on his skin as he fought the natural urges a man would feel in the arms of a beautiful woman. But, he didn't want this to be a mistake. Something they'd both regret tomorrow. That was the last thing he ever wanted to feel about Sophie. Regret.

"Soph." He managed to pull away just far enough to whisper her name.

Her eyes opened and glistened in the moonlight streaming in through the window. "What?"

"You know where this is leading don't you?"

He stared into her eyes, looking for any sign that she didn't understand what he meant. That maybe she'd been caught up in the moment and she would realize that she didn't want to be with him now.

She raised up onto her elbows, which God help him, thrust her breasts forward. He looked, he had to. The thin fabric of the t-shirt she wore did little to hide her nipples, which were erect and brilliantly calling to him. "Of course, I do. I've thought of being with you for what seems like forever."

His heart raced and he could feel the pulsing in his neck and lower in his cock as his mind grappled with what she'd just said.

"We can't take it back once it's done."

She tilted her head to the side, "I'm aware." Her brows furrowed and she bit her bottom lip. "Gaige, if you don't want to be with me, let's call this..."

"I didn't say that, Soph. I wanted to make sure you were awake and clearheaded."

"I'm as clearheaded as I've ever been. I've never been more certain of anything in my entire life."

He stood and in one swift motion he reached behind his neck and pulled the t-shirt he wore over his head. Turning quickly, he walked to the door and slid it closed, engaging the lock. Moving to the bathroom door which lead into his room with Hawk, he repeated the motions then turned to Sophie. His mouth instantly dried and his heart picked up its rhythm when he saw her topless and shimmying her jeans and panties down her sexy legs. The moonlight caressed her skin like a lover. The silvery glow it shone on her added a mysterious element to her enchanting features; and if he didn't know better he'd think she was a mythical creature here to lure him. Fine with him, at this moment, nothing would stop him from finally making her his.

He stalked toward her, unzipping his fly as he neared her. His cock damn near sighed as he freed it from inside. He tugged his pants and briefs down his legs and stepped out of them, his eyes roaming over her body, capturing her eyes then floating down her body once again. The flowery scent from the soap she'd used earlier wafted to him and it was like a siren song.

The instant his legs touched the bed, his hand reached out and roamed over the warm skin of hers. From thigh to ankle he marveled in her body. Then slid his hand back up the inside of her leg till he touched her pussy. A soft moan escaped her lips and the dampness and warmth he felt called to his fingers. Softly he parted her lips and slid his fingers up and down smearing her wetness and enjoying the textures his fingers met.

She spread her legs apart and it was honest to God, the most sensual experience he'd ever had. How sad was that? He could see the shimmer of wetness as he smeared it over her skin. Her breathing grew raspy and uneven. But, he couldn't look away from his fingers. Dipping his forefinger inside of her she moaned as he pulled out and pushed back in a few times. The feeling so unusual and yet so fucking erotic that he felt like he was living in a dream or watching a sexy show on television. Slowly pulling his finger out, he slid it up to her clit and circled it marveling at her quivering legs. When he rolled over her most sensitive spot he added a bit of pressure and focused on that area.

"Gaige," She whispered his name and he added a bit more pressure.

Her hips thrust up into his hand and he increased his speed and pressure, on and on watching her body fight for the orgasm he knew was coming soon. Her skin glistened as her body heated and the floral scent from before mingled with the musky scent of her own juices and his cock pulsed. He wrapped his free hand around his cock, as much to keep it in check as to offer himself a bit of pleasure. He glanced at her face and locked eyes with her. Her soft lips parted in a smile and he pressed firmly on her clit and watched her explode. Her lips now formed a perfect "o", her eyes closed, her hands fisted the comforter on the bed, and her legs quivered. Fucking perfect. He'd never forget this moment in time.

Slowly he climbed on the bed at her feet and kissed his way up her body, beginning at her pussy, offering a few kisses and a few laps with his tongue which had her gasping in pleasure. His lips dusted kisses up her abdomen, to her breasts where he then pulled a nipple into his mouth and suckled a few times before giving the other nipple the same treatment. Her hands framed his head as his kissed her neck, her jaw, and then her lips.

His cock lay at her opening and her legs wrapped around his waist and without letting their lips part, he slid his cock into her.

Fireworks exploded behind his eyelids as her heat enveloped him. Her tight channel wrapped itself around him and sucked him into her depths. Un-fucking believable.

His hips worked in time with hers, their breathing raspy and ragged, their bodies perspiring and working in time with the oldest dance in the world. When their lips parted, her soft moans filled his ears and sounded like the sweetest music. She whispered unintelligible words but they sounded like words he'd want to hear forever. Her hands roamed his back, then grabbed at his ass, then up his back again as if she wanted to touch him everywhere she could and it was like heaven.

"Gaige," Her hushed voice whispered in his ear. "Oh my God, Gaige," she whispered once more before her legs tightened and her body stiffened. She turned her face into the crook of his shoulder and moaned.

He increased his speed, needing to cum now more than ever. The quivering of her pussy damned near sent him over the edge alone. But the feel of her warm body under him, and her soft words in his ear. "Cum in me." Shot him right. Over. The. Cliff.

He stiffened as his balls drew up painfully tight and finally he released himself. The white hot pulsing of his cock as he emptied his load almost blinded him. He groaned loudly into her hair on the pillow and he heard her giggle softly and her hands held him against her.

He paused a few moments, letting his heart and his breathing mellow, enjoying the feel of her hands on his back, rubbing softly up and down.

Then she whispered. "We didn't use protection."

28

She didn't care. Not really. Though getting pregnant wasn't something she wanted or needed right now, with this man, she didn't care. She also didn't have the time to concentrate on what that would mean for her or them.

Gaige had never been a whore hound. Not according to Tate. That didn't mean he didn't have women at the snap of a finger, but he didn't do the ugly bar scene or the sluts that hung around looking for the military men they so loved to climb into bed with. He'd been focused on his career, and frankly, himself at an early age. Tate once said that Gaige was impressive in that he wasn't putting himself in a position to ever get a disease from one of the skanks that constantly made themselves available or get roped into a pregnancy that so many of their military brothers found themselves in. Something about his mannerisms now told her he was still that man.

Laying here with him now, his abdomen pressed firmly into her back as he spooned her in a warm cocoon, his scent mingled with hers, his deep even breathing in her ear, she couldn't imagine how she'd gotten through life without him in it.

A muffled phone rang and she opened her eyes. The window she faced reflected the pink sky from the sunrise just outside. Never having been a morning person, it took her brain a few moments to realize that they'd slept for a few hours, which was more than she'd slept in the past week combined. And that she was in love with Gaige Vickers. She'd been whispering her declaration of love as he'd made love to her last night, though he didn't hear her.

He kissed her temple and gently slid his arm from under her head. She felt the bed move as he got up so she turned to watch him. His fine naked ass was available for her admiration as he walked to his pants laying on the floor and fished into his pockets. Pulling his phone out, he answered, "Vickers." Then turned toward her and walked back to their bed.

Though his cock was not erect, it was still impressive, thick and perfectly shaped. A finger under her chin brought her eyes up to his and the smirk on his face caused her cheeks to burn. She'd been caught admiring him.

"Okay, that's fantastic, can we get her back here or do we have to go to her?"

He climbed back in bed with her, laying on his side facing her, his phone pressed to his other ear. She perused his magnificent body, first with her eyes, but her fingers decided to take a trip through the ridges and planes of his physique. His nipples puckered as her fingers circled them softly, enamored at the response of them to her touch. Scooting down a bit she licked his nipple and giggled when he flinched stopping his conversation mid-sentence for a fraction of a second before continuing.

Softly her fingers explored his abs, tracing the lines between his finely formed muscles watching in fascination as the goose flesh formed on his body.

Moving down lower she was slightly stalled at the full erection that presented itself to her, the slit in the head glistening with pre-cum. Using her forefinger, she swirled the sticky substance over the tip of his cock, amused when it jumped and moved under her fingers. Running her wet fingers along his shaft until the slipperiness halted, she looked up at him to see him watching her. Dipping her finger into his pre-cum once more she repeated her previous motions once again. Never looking away from the intense green gaze that captured her attention, she smiled softly, lifted her leg slightly and gathered moisture from between her legs, then slid it onto his cock. His nostrils flared and his pupils dilated at the same moment he said to his caller, "Gotta go. Call you in a bit."

Tapping his phone, he then tossed it on the pile of clothing on the floor and swiftly rolled her to her back, climbing between her legs.

"I only want to talk about this once, are you clean?"

She smiled, "Yes. Are you?"

"Yes. Are you on birth control?"

"No."

He hesitated a moment and saw the frustration float across her face. Wrapping her legs around his waist she lifted her hips, feeling the hardness against her clit and moaned at the glorious feeling it created. His body shook slightly. She opened her eyes and saw the indecision but she wanted him again. Badly. Raising her hips again she whispered, "You can pull out just before."

His hips arched as the tip of his cock seated itself and he slid inside of her, causing both of them to moan. He took his time this morning, rolling his hips slowly in and out of her, the soft sounds of their mating, heavy breathing and pleasure swirling around making the most beautiful music.

"Open your eyes and look at me."

She did as he commanded, and what she saw in his eyes was intense. Bewildering. "Your body fits mine perfectly, Sophie."

"I know." She arched her back then lifted her hips again driving him deeper into her. They both grunted. He reached back and lifted her left leg higher, wrapping her leg over his arm, as he drove into her deeper still. Her eyes closed at the beautiful intensity of having Gaige Vickers so deep inside of her she could cry.

"Open your eyes." The gruffness in his voice told her just how much he felt right now. The green that met her was consuming. "While I'm in you, making you mine, you look at me. I want you to remember this forever." His hips continued to pump into her, but he was taking his time. Thrusting in deep he held himself inside then swirled his hips, grinding against her clit. She moaned and almost closed her eyes, but she didn't want to lose one second of that look on his face. "Watching your face while I give you pleasure is a dream come true for me."

"Watching your face while I give you pleasure is better." She whispered.

His speed increased, his muscles bunched and flexed and his skin grew damp as he worked to drive them both to a point they couldn't control.

She reached down with her right hand, grabbed his ass and squeezed. Her left arm couldn't reach around because her leg was lifted so she lay her hand on his face, her thumb gently swiping his lips. He grunted as she touched him, he pushed his face into her hand, adding more pressure and her heart grew a hundred fold for the intensity in this moment. He wanted her as much as she wanted him.

He rolled his hips into her clit over and over until she exploded, the speed of it numbing her mind. He smiled at her as he watched her come, then his speed intensified and he managed to husk out, "My turn."

His face grew taught, his lips pressed firmly together as he spewed into her a low growl from deep in his chest the only sound he made. His eyes never left hers.

29

S tepping from the shower he wrapped a towel around his waist, brushed his teeth, then walked into the bedroom he was supposed to be sharing with Hawk.

Hawk lay on his bed, fully dressed, ear buds in his ears, scrolling on his laptop. He glanced up then pulled his earbuds out.

"I've got the information from Wyatt on the location of the medical examiner. She had been stationed here. Perhaps coincidentally, she was transferred after Kate's autopsy. Now, she's on base in Maryland. Gavin is ready to fly us out there to interview her. Wheels up in an hour."

"Thanks for taking care of that, Hawk. I'll be ready."

Hawk swung his legs off the bed and stood. "What about Sophie? Will you be bringing her with us?"

Wasn't that the million-dollar question? He wanted her around always, but they needed to make this a quick trip. But, he also worried about her staying safe here. Walking to his bed, and the duffle that lay on top of it, he pulled a clean t-shirt and khakis from inside as well as clean underwear and socks. He dropped his towel and began dressing, his mind rolling over all of his options.

Hawk interrupted his thoughts. "I can go alone and you can stay here and deal with the car Kate was found in, Tommy's hair analysis, and Killian."

Zipping his pants, he locked eyes with Hawk. "You gonna need backup?"

"I shouldn't. No one will know why I'm there."

Nodding Gaige grinned. "Thanks, Hawk. I'm a bit out of my element here. I promise I won't let this interfere with getting the job done, but this is...she is..." Holding his arms out, he shrugged.

Hawk raised a hand to stave off any further words. "I get it. Sort of. Don't stress over it, let's just get her cleared of all of this bullshit. Tommy, too, and go home."

"10-4." Tugging his t-shirt over his head he turned and walked out of the bedroom. The desk had been folded back into the wall and his laptop was not there. He turned to see Hawk grinning and pointing to the dresser across the room.

"I didn't think we should leave that out last night and when you didn't come back out of Sophie's room right away, I took care of it."

Not for the first time, or hundredth time, did he thank the Lord above that Hawk was on his team. The man was positively invaluable.

"Thanks again."

Chuckling he only shook his head, pulled his phone from his pants pocket and tapped a couple of times.

"Gavin, it's just me; I'll be there soon." Tapping his phone again, he tucked it back into his pocket.

"I hope you're all hungry. I have pancakes, sausages, fresh fruit, fresh squeezed orange juice, and bacon." Gigi called from the kitchen stove. The aromas mingled together to create the smells of his childhood.

"Smells great, Gigi, and thank you again." He walked to the kitchen as Gigi pointed to the coffee pot and the cups on the counter.

"Help yourself."

Next to the coffee pot on a tray were three coffee cups, each with funny sayings, a little container with creamer and one with sugar. He poured coffee into the three cups and handed the black cup with yellow writing, "Shut dah fah cup" to Hawk with a grin on his face. Hawk read the saying and chuckled.

"Perfect."

Adding creamer to his cup, he walked to Sophie's bedroom door and knocked. The door slid open and Sophie's shower fresh face greeted him with a smile. He leaned down and kissed her soft lips, earning himself a slight moan and her warm body pressed against him.

"Morning," She whispered. Her cheeks tinted a pretty pink. "Again."

He chuckled. "Morning. How do you like your coffee?"

"Aww, you're sweet. Just creamer, please." Her hair was still damp from the shower but it was beginning to lightly wave as it dried. The dark richness of her long thick hair had been one of the first things he'd noticed about her. She always kept it shiny, though lately she'd worn it in a ponytail or a braid more often than not. "I'll be right out. I just need to braid my hair."

"No. Please leave it down for a bit."

She cocked her head to the right and looked into his eyes. "Okay." Her lips turned up into the most beguiling smile and her dark eyes sparkled.

Stepping back for her to proceed him he only let her

get two steps in front of him before taking her hand and giving it a quick squeeze. The kitchen wasn't more than twelve steps away, and Hawk had a bullseye view from his seat at the table.

He pulled a chair out for Sophie to Hawk's right then went back to the coffee pot to put creamer in Sophie's coffee before bringing both cups to the table. Gigi joined them at the same time. The food had been set out and it looked simply amazing.

Sophie read her coffee cup and giggled. "'Make today your Bitch'. I'm going to do just that."

She leaned over to read his cup, "Coffee 'cause adulting is hard". Grinning she sipped her coffee but watched him over the rim of her cup. He could get used to waking up and looking at her smiling face after making love to her.

Gigi urged them on, "Dig in before it gets cold. I'll eat quickly then I have to get to the bakery. If one of you wants to drive me there, you can use my car."

He responded " Thanks, Gigi. We can all take you. Hawk has to get to the airport for a quick flight out and Sophie and I have some investigating to do today. So, if you don't mind, we can drop you at the bakery, then drop Hawk at the airport, then swing by and pick up our new rental and we'll drop your car back at the bakery by late morning."

She nodded. Sophie then asked, "You have a plan for us today?"

"I do. Hawk found the medical examiner who was transferred to Maryland. He's going to interview her and see if she remembers anything about Kate's autopsy that can help us determine what really happened to her. You and I are going to see what we can find out about the car Kate died in and the DMV records."

"I found Kate's autopsy report on file last night."

"We know. We have that. You fell asleep but we forwarded what you found to GHOST and Ford and Lincoln did some researching last night. That's how we found out the medical examiner had been transferred. If Killian's behind all of this, he's got a long reach."

Sophie took a deep breath. "Gaige, what if it isn't Killian?"

"I don't know, Sophie. My gut tells me it's him. But Tommy can't remember yet and I'm hoping the longer he's clean the more his memory will come back and he'll remember a more thorough description of the man he saw raping Kate."

Hawk then asked, "Sophie, was there anyone else that seemed to have a crush on Kate? Anyone who called her or asked her out or hung around a bit?"

"No, she was friends with some of the guys but no one that seemed truly interested in wanting to date her. We are all like brother and sister . We've known many of these guys for years. So, no one stands out."

Nodding, Hawk went back to his breakfast.

A thought popped into his head. "Sophie, when you're finished with breakfast, as we drive Gigi to work and Hawk to the airport, I'd like you to write down the names of all of the men in your unit. Maybe we can pull pictures of them from their records and see if Tommy recognizes any of them."

"Okay. I sure wish I had my phone back."

"That I can help you with. GHOST has someone who can obtain access to many things. Since he found your phone on base, I'll ask him to hack into your phone and pull down your contacts."

Her smile was brilliant. "Do you think he can pull my pictures down, too? Oh, I'd so love to get those back. My last photos of Kate were on there."

"I'll ask him to pull them down as well."

30

H aving done their taxi duties for the morning, they finally picked up the new rental. Sophie pulled Gigi's car into the lot at the back of the bakery and put it in park. Undoing her seatbelt, she looked around the car before opening the door. Gaige jumped out of the white Tahoe Wyatt had rented and came to the driver's door. Unlocking it and pulling the handle, he swung the door open and held his hand out to her. Her tummy flipped a bit at his traditional manners and she warned herself to keep her heart in check. Today and last night had been simply wonderful, but she needed to keep her head on straight. After this was all over, he'd go back to the GHOST compound and she still had some contract time on her service she had to finish up. No telling if the distance would kill them or not. And, she thought they shouldn't play with fire while having sex, so she'd asked Gaige to purchase some condoms. He agreed, though she thought he hesitated before responding.

He kissed her lips the instant she stood outside of the car and her heartbeat skipped. He was a fantastic kisser.

His lips molded to hers perfectly. Soft, warm and supple and he seemed to enjoy kissing her, too. Bonus. Her ex-husband didn't enjoy kissing. He told her he preferred to get to the good stuff. What an ass.

"Okay, let's be quick with this. We've got a ton of work to do."

"Okay." She locked Gigi's car and led Gaige to the back-door of the bakery. The back hallway was empty, which she expected, but so was the kitchen. She turned and spoke softly to Gaige, "Gigi must be out front with customers."

She located a pad of paper on the small wooden desk in the corner and wrote Gigi a note. Laying the keys on top of the note, she then walked out of the kitchen, Gaige closely behind her. A male voice filtered out to the hallway.

"Are you sure you haven't seen her? Her name is Sophie Turner. She's AWOL and wanted for murder. We're asking all of the business owners if they've seen her. Take another look, please."

Her heart raced in her chest, but Gaige turned her to look at him. His forefinger held in front of his lips to signal her to be quiet, he took her arm and quietly led her to the backdoor. Silently opening the door, he ushered her out first, then followed closely behind. Brusquely walking to the rental, he opened the passenger door for her then gently pushed the door closed and made his way around to the driver's side. Starting the vehicle, he eased the SUV out of the parking lot and down the back alley to the street behind the bakery.

"Okay, we knew they were looking for you, so this isn't a total surprise. But, we need to find you a cap to wear. And some sunglasses without looking obvious. Then figure out how to get into the impound yard to take a look at the car. I want the VIN off of it so we can run it through all the records." Turning onto a back street he handed her his phone. "See if you can pull up the impound yard on my phone, along the way we'll look for a store to stop at."

What was so damned impressive was that she was shaking and trying super hard to not freak out and he seemed perfectly calm and onto the next thing as if this was his daily life. Which she supposed it was.

"Hey, look at me."

She turned her head and looked into his eyes. "I'll keep you safe, Sophie. It's not unusual that someone would have grunts out looking for you to keep them busy and Canyon Creek is only ten miles from Riverton. Okay?"

Nodding she replied, "Yeah. I guess I wasn't expecting it, though I should have been. I just feel so safe with you that I forgot for a while that I'm still wanted."

He picked up her hand and tugged it to his lips. Kissing her fingers briefly he chuckled. "You're wanted for sure."

Her eyes began tearing up and she shook her head and closed her eyes reminding herself to stay strong. He let go of her hand and she inhaled, then began looking for the impound yard on his phone.

Forty minutes later they'd stopped at a dollar store and found a pink ball cap with a rhinestone heart on it and a pair of sunglasses. She'd braided her hair and tucked it under the cap. Glancing in the mirror on the back of the visor she giggled. "I don't look any different. Not really."

Gaige chuckled. "You're always beautiful, but at this point we can only hope they solely have grunts out looking for you and they won't be all that observant. Looking just for long dark hair and such. Unless you want to get radical and cut and dye your hair, this is what we've got to work with."

She scrunched her face and glanced out the window. Shrugging she finally replied, "I'll do whatever I need to do to prove my innocence and bring Kate's rapist and killer to justice."

Gaige turned into the driveway of the impound yard which actually looked like a junkyard. A tall chain-link fence surrounded the large area. Junk, dilapidated cars, and trucks were lined up, in some semblance of order, she supposed made sense to whoever owned or ran this place. They pulled up to the door of the office, which looked like a gas station from days gone by. The faded red stripe around the top of the building still shown through years of dust and sun bleaching. The glass doors were covered with fliers and signs taped to the inside in a haphazard manner.

"Okay, stay in the truck, doors locked. I'll be right back out." Gaige locked eyes with her and raised his brows when she didn't respond immediately.

"Okay."

"I'm just going in to inquire about a Pontiac Grand Prix that was stolen from me. Since this is the place where shady characters come first, I'd prefer you weren't seen. You never know if someone paid off our clerk in there to call them if they see you."

Nodding, 'cause he had a good point she pulled her lips between her teeth and said nothing. He leaned in and kissed her softly. "You have the phone Hawk gave you?"

"Yeah."

"Okay, if you need help call me, text or whatever, but I won't be in there long. If someone pulls into the lot, duck down or look like you're sleeping. Capeesh?"

Smiling she replied. " Capeesh."

He exited the vehicle and strode to the glass door. Tall and broad, he was an easy man to admire. He'd managed to stay in shape over the years, though in his line of work, it was most likely a necessity than anything else. In her case, she had regular PT exams she had to pass, so it was also a necessity for her.

He turned briefly and winked at her before disappearing behind the dirty front door. Damn, she hoped this worked.

31

"Hi, I'm looking for a black Pontiac Grand Prix. It was stolen from me a couple of months ago and I've been checking places like yours out here and there to see if I can find it."

The clerk behind a grimy counter stacked with dirty papers and miscellaneous pens, paperclips and other items turned at the sound of his voice. He appeared about five foot ten inches tall and wearing a grubby baseball cap the color of faded blue or maybe that was black, it was hard to tell. The loose hanging mechanic's shirt offered no hint of a shape and upon closer inspection, the clerk was a woman. The look she landed on him was one of boredom or irritation more than anything else.

"Are you now? I think we've got a few of those out back." She pulled a dusty three ring binder from under the counter and slapped it on top, creating a small dust cloud. Opening the cover, her faded blue eyes locked on him. "Gotta VIN?"

"No, I didn't think to bring that."

"Really?" She shifted to a stance of disbelief. "You've been looking at places like this and no one has asked you for a VIN?"

Tucking his fingers into his front pocket, hoping he looked casual, he shrugged. "I guess the places I've checked haven't been that good at keeping records."

She nodded once then crossed her arms on top of the counter. "Why don't you tell me what you're really looking for?"

Taking in a deep breath, he let it out slowly and rubbed his chin with his fingers. "My friend's sister committed suicide in a black Pontiac Grand Prix. I'm hoping to check it out and make sure a necklace that she always wore, but didn't have on, isn't laying on the floor of the car or something. Their family wants it back. They're distraught as you can imagine."

She sniffed once, scratched her forehead with dirty fingers, and he noted that the dirt under her nails seemed as if it had been there a while and likely permanent. "I've got a car like that out back. We're scheduled to demolish it in the morning. We told the guy who dropped it off that we only keep cars for two months. We strip them and then crush what's left. Sorta creepy having it out there."

"I'd be so grateful if you'd let me take a look at it."

She hesitated, staring at him, indecision on her face. He gauged her at around forty years old, nondescript, and not a very happy woman. But working in these conditions could do that to a person. Or maybe it was a source of refuge for her, hiding out here with the junk and few people to bother her throughout the day. He didn't want to insult her by offering money, but the thought crossed his mind that may be what she was waiting for.

Deciding to try bringing it around a different way, he asked, "Are there fees owed on the storage of the car?"

Her brows rose in the air. She grunted, "You think that's what I'm waiting for?"

"Ma'am, this means so much to my friend's family, which makes it important to me. I'd love to be able to find that necklace and bring it back to them."

"No fees. He paid up front."

"What did he look like? Do you remember him?"

"Creepy guy, light hair, almost white, and eyes the color of ice. He tried being coy with me, but when he smiled it never reached his eyes. Didn't trust him then, wouldn't now. He had the car towed here by some local station. Gus's I think."

Killian. It had to be. "Did he give you a name?"

"Nope, and I didn't ask either. Paid me two thousand dollars in cash. We stripped what we wanted from it, the motor's gone. The tranny, too. Other parts that we could sell off are gone, too. But, the seats were shit and we didn't take anything from the inside, so you should be able to go take a look at it. You can't drive your truck back there though; you'll need to walk."

"Okay." Last thing he wanted to do was walk through a junkyard in the growing heat, but he figured as much when he got here.

She walked around the counter, maneuvering around various parts laying on the floor and a couple of vinyl stools with an older tall table between them. Locking the glass door, she then turned to him, "Follow me."

She led him to a side door, which looked much the same as the front door, covered with old fliers and wanted notes from people looking for parts they must have asked for here and she just taped them up on the doors. The sunlight hit him in the face and for an instant he was blinded by its brightness. Turning to look past the fence he could see Sophie watching from inside the truck. He half saluted to let her know all was good, but he wished he was holding her hand now. It would be horrible for her to see the car Kate died in, or at least was found dead in, so he was glad she was where she was.

The ground was dusty, almost sandy, and it swirled around his shoes as he walked. She led him past junked out cars and trucks, stripped bare of anything of value and ready for crushing. Looked to be around ten or so of them. "That one right there. Have your look."

"Thanks." He approached the car and a sense of dread settled over him. He wasn't naturally uneasy but knowing something evil happened in this car set his nerves on edge. Pulling his phone from his back pocket, he looked in through the windshield and snapped a picture of the VIN. Opening the driver's door, he could still smell the faint decomposition that had occurred. Based on the medical examiner's report he'd seen, Kate hadn't been found for more than a few hours after her death, or at least she'd been in the heat and exhaust for around that long. And that was only because the tenant, who rented the garage came home from work and opened the door to put his car inside. He'd gotten home from work early and had taken a late lunch, so they were able to piece together some of the timing. The exhaust billowed out and he called CID and fire brigade on base.

Taking pictures of inside of the car, he glanced at the dashboard and was happy to see an analog odometer. Taking another picture of the mileage, he walked around to the passenger side of the car and opened the door. Leaning in, he knelt with his knee on the seat and looked around. A quick glance told him his escort was watching and he needed this to look good in case anyone came around asking questions. Stepping back out of the car, he knelt on the ground and looked under the passenger seat. Using his phone as a flashlight he scanned under the seat and something glinted in the light. Focusing on the shiny object he couldn't make out what it was, other than round. Reaching his hand under the seat, he retrieved the object only to see it was a waded up gum wrapper.

Tossing it onto the passenger side floor, he opened the glove box and found old dirty papers stuffed inside. Fingering through them he saw the name of David Sams on an old electric bill. Another envelope had the same name on it, a cable bill. Opening up the bills he noted that they were around a year old. A CD case lay inside. It was dusty and somewhat clear, the CD inside had DS - Favs in marker written on the front and nothing else.

Fighting the feeling that nothing here was of assistance to their case, but hopeful the VIN and the name David Sams would lead to something, he closed the glove box door and began to pull himself from the vehicle. Another glint of something dark by the driver's floor mat caught his eye, and since he was already here and this car would be gone tomorrow, he walked around and opened the driver's side door. Shining his phone light on the floor where he'd seen something glimmer, he saw a stone, looked to be dark reddish in color resting in the crack between the floor mat and the carpeting closest to the door. Pulling it out he examined the floor around the same area in case there was something more. Finding nothing he wrapped the stone in his hand and turned to the woman who offered him this privilege.

"Nothing?" She asked.

"No, ma'am. But I appreciate you allowing me to look."

She turned and began walking back to the building leaving him to follow. Time was up here.

32

The waiting was killing her. She couldn't see anything from her vantage point in the car. They'd disappeared around a rusted out, dilapidated pickup truck. Watching the time on her borrowed phone from GHOST, she saw it had only been eleven minutes. How long should she wait before getting worried something bad had happened? Probably longer than eleven minutes. Next time they had to do something like this, she'd get that information up front.

Relief swept through her when she saw the woman walking back to the building. Waiting to see Gaige she held her breath. It seemed forever before he finally walked past the old pickup. He briefly glanced her way, then looked straight ahead and her stomach rolled.

Sitting up straighter she lay her hand across her stomach to quell the roiling. Not sure why she was so nervous, other than the obvious, she was wanted for murder and had no way to prove otherwise. Oh, and there was a rapist and killer out there somewhere maybe preying on his next victim. And, Gaige didn't smile when he looked this way and he sure as hell didn't seem happy.

Finally, he emerged from the building and stalked straight to the truck. Climbing inside, he started the vehicle, pulled his seatbelt across his chest and put the SUV in reverse before saying a word. Twisting in her seat to look at him, she allowed the silence to settle over both of them. Finally, out of the parking lot and down the road a way, he pulled into a grocery store parking lot and put the SUV in park. He turned in his seat and stared into her eyes.

"First of all, I'm glad you didn't have to see that car. My guts are a bit twisted just knowing someone you loved may have died in the car, or, at the least, been placed in it after she was killed. That's all I'll say except, no, there's no blood or anything to prove that someone died in it, except a creepy feeling. Even the clerk said that. But, I found this." Opening his hand to reveal the deep red oval stone, she couldn't stop staring at it.

"What is that? What does it mean?"

"I was hoping you could tell me."

Reaching out to pick it up she halted, looked into his eyes to make sure it was okay to touch it. Gaige nodded and she reached again for the stone. Fingers shaking, she lay her left hand under the stone so if she dropped it, she'd also catch it.

The stone was a deep red in color, cut with many facets, so probably by a credible jeweler, and it seemed of high quality. That wasn't her specialty by any means, but she loved jewelry and paid attention to such things. She also had a friend in the jewelry business who taught her so much about jewelry and stones.

"Tell me what you see, Soph."

Clearing her throat, she pulled her shoulders back

and winced slightly as her sore shoulder pinched a bit then replied, "I see quality. A stone cut by a professional. A fake ruby is too bright and clear, but this one is deep red in color, and while it sparkles it doesn't look like a piece of glass. I'd guess a reputable jeweler in town would be able to tell us what kind of setting it had been in."

He leaned forward and kissed her lips quickly. "You're smart, Soph."

Putting the SUV in gear again he headed into town. "Grab your phone and find a jeweler in town we can visit."

"I don't need to; I know a jeweler who is very good at his job and would be able to tell us what we need to know.

Glancing briefly at her, his brows rose. "Do tell."

She turned to face the windshield once again. "I used to date him for a time."

"So an ex?" He said no more but she turned to see his face just in time to see his jaw clench.

She grinned, could it be he was a bit jealous? "He's an ex for a reason, Gaige. We didn't work out, but we ended it on decent terms. I know he'd help us."

Nodding, he replied, "Yeah." Letting out a long breath, "Just tell me which way."

"Turn right at the intersection and head downtown. The store is located on Main Street."

Turning where she requested, Gaige pulled his phone from his back pocket, tapped a couple of times, then held the phone to his ear.

"Wyatt, see what you can find out about a David Sams. Also find out if he's had a black Pontiac Grand Prix stolen and if there is a police report in California."

He listened to Wyatt on the other end of the line a moment, then said, "I'll send you pictures of the VIN and odometer reading on the car Kate was found in, too. I'd like a full report on the vehicle. When was it titled? Who titled it? How many miles were on it at each titling? The works."

A feeling of relief flooded through her as she felt as though they had leads. Finally.

33

S tretching his shoulders back he tried loosening the knot forming in the middle of his back. His phone rang and he pulled it from the cup holder in the console. Hawk's name read on the screen.

"Hawk. Fill me in. But hang on just a minute and I'll put you on speaker."

Softly Sophie said, "Turn left at the light. We can park around back." She pointed to a large brick building, burgundy awnings over the front windows said "Crowne Jewelers" and that knot grew a bit more.

Stopping at the red light he tapped the speaker icon on his phone and said, "Go ahead, Hawk."

"I found the medical examiner, Candace Phillips, on base out here. She reluctantly agreed to talk to me. She was puzzled as to why she was suddenly transferred and it left a sour taste in her mouth. She's bitter. But that's good for us."

The light turned green and Gaige turned into the parking lot behind the jewelry store, he put the SUV in park. "She spilled?"

"Oh yeah. She said just before she was transferred she knew someone had accessed Kate's autopsy report and she could tell the report had been altered because she wrote it. Other documents which are part of the report also were missing. Candace was outraged. She didn't have the security clearance to see who had changed the report, including deleting some of it, so she went to her superior. He said he would look into it. Then, suddenly she was transferred, but not before looking at her report and taking detailed notes as to what had been changed that she wrote and what was missing."

"Was she willing to share those notes?" He glanced at Sophie, whose eyes were locked on the phone as if it were a lifeline. Biting her bottom lip, her hands were both balled in her lap.

"Yes. I snapped pictures and I'll send them to you. I'm at the airport now and getting ready to board the plane. I'm just waiting for Gavin to finish his pre-flight check."

Sophie swallowed and he watched her closely. "Hawk, give us the low-down before Sophie dies of suspense."

Her eyes flicked to his and he grinned. The smile on her face was so sweet and innocent his heart flipped. Relaxing back into the seat she blushed, and he wondered if she ever looked more adorable.

"Kate didn't die in the car. She must have been placed in the car after she was killed. At least before the hose was shoved into the window and the car left on. According to the toxicology report, there was no carbon monoxide in her lungs or blood. There was a high level of lorazepam in her system and that seized her heart. She did not find any opioids. Of course, the toxicology report was not in the report.

At the scene and during the autopsy, she saw bruises on Kate's arms that looked suspiciously like finger marks, but those observations were removed from her original autopsy report as were the lorazepam test results. Also, Kate had bruising on her hands that appeared to be defensive wounds, most likely to ward off fists. She said the forensic techs' notes written at the scene, which had mentioned the bruises, were missing from the report. The photographs that the techs took at the scene and the ones she took during the autopsy were removed as well. Candace concluded that she struggled with someone prior to her death, she was injected with lorazepam, likely to calm her or make her drowsy, but the dose was too high causing her death. Then, whoever drugged her panicked and put her in the car to make it look like suicide."

Sniffing from the passenger side of the vehicle had him looking at Sophie, who silently sat across from him, tears streaming down her cheeks, but staring straight ahead. Once again, trying to be stoic and only partially succeeding.

"Thanks, Hawk, I'll look at the documents when they get here. Safe travels."

"Out."

"Hey." He reached across the console and lay his hand at Sophie's nape. Pulling her toward him, she rested her head on his shoulder and cried. His gut twisted at the anguish she released. Though her right shoulder was still tender, she slowly reached forward and took his hand in her right hand and squeezed. He sat with her while she cried, not sure what he could say to her or how to console her. Sometimes you just had to get it out of your system. He remembered crying exactly twice in his life. When

Tate died and when his dad died. Kate was Sophie's Tate. He knew exactly how she felt learning that her friend didn't take her own life, but that someone else had. And the guilt of not having been there to help your best friend in the whole world when they needed you most. That was probably the worst feeling. It's what drove him daily to be the best he could be, train his team to be the best, and to kill every mother-fucker who'd earned it by harming another and thinking they could get away with it.

Taking a deep breath, Sophie pulled away and sat up straight. While she was swiping her eyes with the pads of her shaking fingers, he hopped out of the truck, pulled the back driver's door open and pulled a tissue pack from his duffle. Quickly making his way around the truck, he opened the passenger door and handed Sophie the tissues.

She gratefully took them, swiped at her eyes, and gently blew her nose. She turned to him then and exited the truck. But her arms instantly wrapped around his neck and he wrapped his arms around her waist and lifted her so her body was pressed to him and her feet dangled. Holding her as close as he dared without squeezing the breath from her, he reveled in the contact and comfort they brought each other in that moment. It shook him seeing her grief and remembering his own from so long ago.

She softly whispered, "Thank you."

He squeezed her once more, then gently set her on the ground. Before letting her go, he whispered back, "Always."

Taking another tissue, she dabbed at her eyes once more, reached into the truck, pulled the stone from the cup holder in the console, then turned and said, "Let's go see if JJ can help us figure this piece of the puzzle out.

His jaw tightened, but he inhaled a deep breath, then stepped back, took her hand in his, hit the lock button on the fob and walked with Sophie to the backdoor. Time to meet the ex.

34

Entering through the backdoor brought back memories. She'd meet JJ after she finished her shift at work and they'd have dinner somewhere downtown before going back to his place. More often than not, she spent the night and left early in the morning to make it to work on time. Though they only dated for six months or so, they spent much of that six months together. Then she learned his family had a better pairing in mind for him than her. She remembered her own parents forcing her into a marriage she didn't want and tried explaining that to JJ, but he was to inherit his family's jewelry stores, all eighteen of them, and he wasn't willing to fight for her. That probably said it all right there. She'd broken it off with him, and Kate had told her it spoke volumes that she'd only cried once, that first night, then not again. Right after the breakup she'd thought about him though, and wondered if he did finally marry this "right person", but she didn't snoop to find out. It'd be easy enough to do, but she'd unfriended him on all social media platforms soon after and then went on with her life. That was three years ago. Since then, she'd seen him at one charity event for veterans in town, but he was alone. They chatted, busy polite conversation. "How are you? You look good. Still working?" But nothing too personal. It was better that way. But, something told her he'd help her with this. She hoped anyway.

The brick hallway was still so old world and pretty. She'd always loved this part of the old building and admired how his family had restored it and all of the others they owned. It was their signature to refurbish older buildings in a downtown area and settle their business there. And they did it well.

She squeezed Gaige's hand as they neared the doorway that led out to the main store area. They'd passed several closed doors along the hallway, which she knew were cutting rooms and storage areas. One was a break room for the employees. The old, heavy, wooden door squeaked as she pushed it open and JJ, who stood behind a glass jewelry counter, turned to see her. It only took a split second for him to recognize her and the smile that lit his face made her heart beat a bit faster, but not like Gaige did, more like she hoped this would go well.

Then his eyes moved passed her and to Gaige and his smile faded away. "Hi, JJ, how are you?"

He cleared his throat, and stood a bit taller before responding. "Sophie, it's great to see you. I'm well. And you look fantastic."

He walked the few steps to stand before her, his arms outstretched for a hug. She stepped into his hug, briefly wrapped her arms around him and quickly stepped back. Taking Gaige's hand in hers once again, she introduced them. "JJ, I'd like you to meet Gaige Vickers. Gaige, this is JJ Crowne. His family owns this store."

The two men shook hands. She'd always thought JJ was handsome. He had that California male look you saw in the magazines. Tall, though not as tall as Gaige, he stood around six feet tall. He was slim, and his sandy brown hair and blue eyes were classic and attractive. Though looking at the two men side by side, he'd never match up to Gaige. Not in a million years. Gaige was tall at around six foot six, broad shouldered, muscular, thick, and manly. Not a metrosexual in any sense of the imagination and never would be. It was part of the attraction, he was all male. Gruff when he needed to be but gentle with her in all ways that counted.

"Ah, the famous Gaige Vickers. I've always wondered about you. Sophie talked about you often. Too often for my taste. And now here you are together."

Gaige chuckled. "Nice to meet you as well." He left it at that, no need to explain that he'd only just heard about JJ fifteen minutes ago. The fact that JJ was jealous and made his snarky comment was enough.

JJ clapped his hands together. "So what brings you here to Crowne Jewelers, getting engaged and need to see my finest diamonds?"

Sophie opened her mouth to say something, but Gaige beat her to it. "Not yet. We're cleaning up some loose ends first. Then, no offense, but I've always thought a Cartier would look simply spectacular on her finger. Don't you?"

Her mouth instantly dried out. Had he actually thought that? And tying up loose ends was probably just his way of being snarky in return and Cartier? Holy crap. She couldn't let her head think like that, he was just posturing and staking his claim, no matter how temporary it might be.

Clearing her throat, she decided they'd played their

male posturing games long enough. "JJ, I actually had hoped you'd be able to help us figure out what kind of stone this is and what type of setting it would be set in or had been set in."

She held open her hand and the ruby colored stone lay in her palm. Always the jeweler, JJ looked at the stone and slowly picked it from her palm. Stepping to the glass counter, he pulled a felt pad from the back counter with the Crowne logo on it, lay it on the glass and gently set the ruby colored stone on it. Quickly pulling out his jeweler's eye from a drawer on the back counter, he set it up to his right eye and looked at the stone, turning it from side to side.

Her heart fluttered as she waited and her stomach knotted. She clasped her hands together in front of her and watched his face, looking for any expression.

After he'd examined the stone, he pulled his jeweler's eye away from his face, tucked it in its case in the drawer, and turned to look at her. "This is a ruby of fine quality. Few inclusions and the two I could find were minute and almost nonexistent though the stone is of a darker hue, keeping the value down some. Of course, a trained eye can see them, you probably couldn't. No offense."

Gaige responded. "None taken. Can you tell it's worth and the setting it would have been in?"

JJ pulled a catalogue from a drawer at the far end of the counter and brought it back to the end where they stood. He opened it to a section, color coded on the edges of the catalogue, and thumbed through the pages until he found what he was looking for. Turning the large book to them he pointed to a man's ring, that looked similar to a class ring, with imprinting in the sides of different military symbols.

"I'd say it had been set in a ring such as this." Picking up the stone he turned on a light mounted on the glass jewelry case and held the stone under it. "If you look along this very edge, you can see marks in the stone where the setting had dug into its surface and some of the stone has been worn away on this end, allowing it to slip from the setting. Though probably because it caught on something and then pulled free of the setting. And I'd say it was somewhere in the twelve-thousand-dollar figure."

Pointing to the end of the stone where now she could see it was a different height than the other end, she had to admit, he was very good at this.

"Wait here a moment. I have a setting such as this in the back that came in for repairs about a month ago."

He walked to one of the back rooms they'd passed as they entered the building and she looked into Gaige's eyes. He smiled at her, seemingly more relaxed now that the initial meeting and sizing up was over. His right hand reached up and he ran the backs of his fingers along her jaw, then slid his fingers behind her nape and brought her face to his. "So beautiful." His lips touched hers, softly but still possessively and her nipples puckered as the wetness gathered between her legs. He simply did it for her.

JJ came out of the hallway and snorted lightly. She pulled away from Gaige, though not far, stared into his eyes, then whispered back to him, "So handsome." Before turning to JJ.

He cleared his throat and showed them the setting he had. "As you can see, when I set the stone into this setting..." He pushed it into the setting from the back, using a fair amount of pressure to set the stone as it should be. "You can see that the stone on this end is worn away allowing something small to catch the gold at the edge and pull the stone from its setting."

JJ stopped talking and looked closer at the ring. Taking his jeweler's eye from the drawer once again, he looked at the ring through the glass. His brows furrowed and his jaw slackened, as if not believing what he was seeing. She glanced at Gaige and saw that he was at attention, watching every move.

Gaige asked, "What are you seeing, JJ?"

Pulling the jeweler's glass from his eye, he looked at them both, then said, "It's almost as if this was the ring this stone came from. When this ring came into the store, it had a tear in the gold right here." He pointed to an area at the end of the stone where the stone was worn away and you could see the lip created leaving room for the gold to catch on something.

Gaige looked JJ in the eye. "Do you take photos of broken jewelry when they come in to show the before and after to the owners?"

"Yes. We do." He turned to the computer station behind him, and typed his password into their program, then scrolled and typed until he found the file he was looking for. Turning his monitor to them he waved them behind the counter for a closer look. "This is the before. You can see the gold had caught on something and pulled open which would have allowed a stone to fall from it."

Gaige stared at the screen and so did she. The oval stone fit in the middle of a gold setting, with United States Army around the stone. Unbelievable, but then again, not. There weren't many jewelry stores in Riverton and this was the finest. Whoever wore this ring, paid money for it, so they'd come here for repairs.

"JJ, I know this is a breach of confidentiality, but the

man who owns this ring may have killed Kate. Please, will you tell us who that is?"

She placed a hand on his forearm and squeezed. Not openly flirting, but if she had too, she sure would for this information.

"Sophie, you know my father would kill me if I pissed off a client."

"He might be a rapist and a murderer. Do you want rapists and murderers as clients?"

He looked into her eyes and she tried appealing to him with just a look. Please God, let him give her the information.

35

E xiting the jewelry store from the backdoor once again, Gaige opened the passenger door for Sophie, and helped her inside. Closing the door, he walked around the front of the SUV to get into the driver's side. The backdoor opened and JJ said, "Gaige."

Halting and staring at JJ, he waited a beat, but only that long before walking toward him. It didn't escape his eyes that JJ glanced into the truck at Sophie and swallowed. It also didn't go unnoticed that JJ didn't have on a wedding ring, but had a slight demarcation where one used to be.

Before he could say anything, JJ handed him a piece of paper, ripped from a small spiral notebook with a name written on it. Chet Forest. In smaller print below Chet's name, was a notation – not the owner.

"He's the one who brought the ring in. Said it wasn't his but he was bringing it in for a friend and that the friend would be around to select a new stone for the ring in a couple of weeks. That's why we still have it, Chet hasn't returned our calls and no one has come in to claim the ring."

Fisting the piece of paper in his left hand, he reached out his right hand to shake JJ's hand. "If the owner of that ring does come in, we'd appreciate it if you'd give me a call." He pulled his phone from his pocket. "What's your phone number, JJ? I'll text you and you'll have my number."

"I'm not even supposed to give you this much information."

"Let me tell you a bit about what we're up against, JJ. Chet Forest is dead and the killer just may be the owner of this ring. He's also likely the person who killed Kate. And, now he's after Sophie. Her life may very well depend on us finding this guy before he finds her. Not only that, Sophie is being framed for Chet's murder."

JJ swiped his hand through his brown hair and mumbled, "Holy Fuck."

Quickly giving Gaige his phone number, Gaige held out his right hand once again and firmly shook JJ's. "Thanks, JJ, I'll let Soph know what you've done." Then he had another thought. "Was that ring purchased here in the first place?"

"I'm afraid not. It's Army issue. It's called the Freedom Ring. They sell them on base and are purchased directly through Balfreed."

JJ turned and slipped into the back of the jewelry store and Gaige walked the few steps to the SUV, feeling better about the progress they'd made today.

Climbing into the driver's seat, he swiftly pulled his seatbelt across his body, clicked it into place, started the truck, and turned to Sophie. "Glad he had a change of heart."

Handing her the piece of paper he watched her face as she unfolded the paper. Her right hand flew to cover her mouth as soon as she read the name on the paper.

"Oh my God, I told Chet that I was looking for the autopsy report and that I could prove Kate was murdered. He knew all along who killed her. Probably helped him for all we know."

Leaning on the console, he softly replied, "But you didn't know that then."

Putting the vehicle in reverse, he eased out of their parking spot and turned out onto the street. Sophie composed herself then cleared her throat. "At least we have a bit of a lead. Sort of." Her shoulders slumped. "We really don't have anything more than we did before."

"I told JJ that Chet was dead and that you've been framed for the murder. He didn't look like that made him happy. I sent him my number and asked him to call if someone comes by looking for it."

"That could be never."

"Right, but JJ said that Chet told him the owner of the ring would pick it up because he wanted to select a new stone. JJ also told me those rings are purchased directly through Balfreed and we have a computer whiz at our disposal." He tapped his phone and said, "Call The Whiz." He smiled as he told his phone to call Jared – The Whiz was his code name in Gaige's phone. Genius.

"Yep." Short and sweet. Jared wasn't a chatter. The fewer words said to him, the better in Jared's world.

"Gaige Vickers."

"Yeah. I got the numbers, most of them and most of the pictures from that phone you wanted me to hack into. You have a new phone you want me to download them on?"

"I will in an hour. I'll call you with the number. In the meantime, I need you to hack into Balfreed's purchase records and focus on names you've been previously given in this investigation. Reed Killian. Chet Forest. Tommy Taylor, Jeff Taylor. For starters. If you don't find those names, we'll try another avenue."

"On it. Anything more?"

"Nope. I'll call you with a phone number soon."

"Out."

A click was heard and the line went dead. At least he never had to worry about Jared taking up too much time.

"We need to get you a new phone, Soph. The Whiz has some of your numbers and pictures. Tell me where there is a cell phone store. Nowhere near base."

"Why don't we head back to Canyon Creek and find a store there."

He chuckled. "Sounds good. Glad you're thinking, 'cause right now, I'd like to get back to Gigi's, take a shower, and touch you. Everywhere."

And he did. After spending the day with her, watching her compose herself time and again, continue to be tough and smart and gorgeous as she did it all, he did just want to lay in bed with her in his arms. Smell her hair and skin and feel her soft curves pushed up against him. His cock thickened just thinking about it.

"Gawd, that sounds like a little piece of heaven."

Glancing at her, he was met with the shiny, deep brown eyes he'd fallen for twenty-ish years ago. Gut punch. That's what it was like. In the best possible way.

36

Before exiting the shared bathroom with Gaige and Hawk, Sophie unlocked the door leading to Gaige and Hawk's, actually it seemed, Hawk's room so he could get in if he needed to, then slid the door open to her bedroom. There was Gaige, laying on her bed, leaning against the headboard, no shirt on, only boxer briefs covering his man parts, and his laptop on his lap. He looked delicious.

"Hey." He picked up her new phone, which was plugged into his laptop, looked at the screen then lay it back on the bed, "only about fifty-three percent finished downloading. It'll likely be after dinner before it's finished."

Laying her dirty clothes in the basket for that purpose, she smiled when she saw Gaige's dirty clothes already in there from today. Crawling across his legs to lay next to him, her long hair still wet, the tank top she wore dampening from where it absorbed the water from her hair and the denim shorts Gigi had given her on, she sidled up to see what he was working on.

"What are you working on?"

He kissed her lips, stared at her for a few moments then inhaled. "Reading the autopsy report and Candace's notes, Hawk sent over. He'll be here in about a half hour, he just called. It's all as he said earlier."

She nodded 'cause it choked her up a bit talking about Kate's autopsy report. But, rather than becoming morose again, she kissed Gaige, then whispered. "I'm going to go help Gigi with dinner. She shouldn't have to wait on us like this."

His left hand reached behind her head, and pulled her in for a deep kiss. She felt the moan come from deep in her chest, her head felt light and swirly, as if the world faded away and no one was left in it but her and Gaige.

A phone ringing broke the beautiful spell and she ended their kiss with a light peck. "Get your phone, I'll go help with dinner."

Scooting off the end of the bed, she looked back at him once, to see he was still looking at her. Tapping his phone his voice was a bit gruff when he said, "Vickers."

Walking through the living room she marveled at the light colors of greens and faded orange on the walls which gave the home a comfortable feeling while still feeling larger than it was.

"Shower feel good?" Gigi stood at the stove, stirring something that smelled amazing.

"It sure did. That smells fantastic."

She stopped at the counter across from Gigi and watched her for a moment. "I hope you like it. It's my grandmother's Boeuf Bourguignon. It'll stick to those men's ribs and keep them full all night. How was your day?"

Giggling at Gigi's quick change of the subject. "It was

as good as it could be under the circumstances. We got a couple of leads, but we're still waiting on results. I did, however, replace my phone. For some strange reason, it makes me feel like a complete person again. I've felt so out of touch and lost since my phone's been gone. I guess because I have to rely on everyone else to tell me what's going on."

"I get that. We've come to rely on them so much, haven't we?"

"Yes. Tell me what I can do to help, please. And don't say nothing, I need to do something."

Gigi pulled a cutting board from under the counter, lay a knife across it, and pushed a bag of potatoes toward her. "Leave the peelings on but cut these up in large chunks, I've already washed them."

She looked at her new friend for a longtime before saying anything, not really sure how to broach the subject. "Gigi?"

Her friend turned to her but said nothing.

"Thank you for not saying anything to those soldiers in the bakery today asking about me."

"Ah, you did hear. I wondered." She tapped her wooden spoon on the side of the pan and picked up a bowl of cut up carrots. "I'd never turn you in. I don't know the severity of what you're up against. And, I've been trying my best to keep my nose out of it, 'cause I can tell you've got enough going on right now, but I'll help you in any way I can, Sophie."

"You're truly a special person and I'm so glad you found me huddled outside of your bakery."

She cut potatoes and told Gigi all that was going on in her life and to her credit, Gigi listened and asked minimal questions. And it felt good getting it all off her chest.

"So, it seems you're wanted for murder. You're looking for a rapist and murderer of your friend Kate. The murderer is after you because he thinks you know who he is. Gaige's cousin is mixed up somehow and framed for the rape. The medical examiner was transferred. And Gaige and your ex-boyfriend met today. And the Army is looking for you for murder and being AWOL. Sweetheart, that's more than most people do in a lifetime. I think you're handling it all with amazing poise."

Tears sprang to her eyes and she had to set the knife down so she didn't cut herself. The backdoor opened and Hawk filled the opening leaving little room to spare.

"Damn, smells fucking amazing in here."

Both women laughed and that felt wonderful. It had been a long time.

37

S etting his laptop on the bed, he dug through his duffle for a clean pair of pants, typical tactical black pants and a t-shirt. Hawk just got back and he had news to share.

Snagging his phone off the bed, he tucked it into his back pocket as he walked out to the kitchen. Hawk stood next to Sophie at the counter, leaning his hip on the edge, a beer in his hand, and a smile on his face. Gigi laughed at something he'd said and Sophie's cheeks were bright pink. She had a pile of cut up potatoes in front of her along with a glass of wine.

"The mood has definitely lightened in this house today. It feels good."

Sophie turned to him, picking up the second glass of wine on the counter. She handed it to him, her cheeks flushed, her hair beginning to dry and curl in the most luscious way, swirling around her breasts, perfectly framing her fabulous nipples through the tank she wore. Turning to pick up her glass she turned back to him and tapped her glass to his. Hawk leaned forward and tapped his beer bottle to his wine glass, a smirk on his face.

"What's so funny out here?"

Hawk replied first, "We were just teasing Sophie about sharing her bedroom."

Gaige chuckled. "Jealous. You're all jealous that I have the best roommate ever." He kissed her flaming red cheek, then turned to Gigi. "My God, you have the best smelling kitchen in the world." Looking at Hawk, then Sophie, he said, "If either of you ever tell Mrs. James or Kylie I said that, I'll deny it till my dying breath."

"Who's Mrs. James and Kylie?" Sophie asked, a look of worry on her face.

"They take care of us at the GHOST compound. Mrs. James does the majority of the cooking, does all of the laundry, housekeeping, packs our go bags, etc. Her daughter, Kylie does the cooking some days."

"So, she spoils you." She and Gigi giggled and all he could do is shrug.

"What's wrong with being spoiled? Plus, they get paid well."

Hawk chimed in. "And, they get to hang with us every day."

Sophie groaned. "Oh my Gawd. Gigi, grab a shovel, the shit's getting deep in here."

Gigi giggled, "I'm on it."

He laughed and it felt good to feel carefree for just a few moments. He loved that this side of Sophie was coming back. She'd always been so fun loving and happy. Her smile lit up the room.

His phone rang and he grabbed it from his pocket, saw Tommy's name, and frowned. Tapping the answer icon, he responded, "Tommy, what's up?"

He walked into the living room and sat on the sofa for a small amount of privacy, but also so the others could continue to joke around if they wanted.

"Gaige, I just remembered something. It just flashed into my head while I was taking a shower. Kate and I went back to her apartment. I remember that now. We weren't drugged at the restaurant we were drugged at her apartment."

"How do you know that?"

"We got to her apartment and entered. Kate went to the kitchen to make us a drink and I was putting a movie into the DVD player. I heard Kate gasp and walked into the kitchen. There was a man in the kitchen, just staring at her. She looked scared and puzzled. She asked him what he wanted and how he got in and all he said was, "Sit down."

We both sat at the table, he took his time picking up two drinks and bringing them to us, then leaned against the counter with his arms crossed."

"You just sat down and didn't say anything?"

"I didn't know who he was. For all I knew Kate knew him, so I guess I was stunned and went along. She seemed a bit nervous, but she wasn't screaming or anything."

"Who was he? What was his name? What did he look like?"

Tommy went silent for a moment; he could hear him moving around but not saying anything. "Tommy?"

He whispered, "Dad just got home and I have to be quiet. Listen, it's still so foggy. He didn't say who he was. After we sat down, I watched Kate's face and realized she knew him, but she wasn't happy about him being there. I thought he might be an ex or something. Someone with a key. He had light hair, super light and the creepiest ice blue eyes I've ever seen. Like they would glow in the dark or something. Sort of like that picture your friend showed me yesterday."

"There aren't many people who look like that, Tommy. Was it him?"

Sophie came back into the room and sat at the edge of the sofa. Her eyes were locked on his, clearly in tune to what was going on.

"It's still fuzzy, Gaige, I hate these moments in time that are gone. I can't seem to fit it all together. I hate to accuse him if it wasn't him.

"But if it was, Tommy, we've got to get him in custody."

"That's all I remember right now. I've gotta go, Gaige. I'll call you if I remember more."

"One more thing, why did you drink the drinks?"

"He seemed evil. Cold, calculated and not someone who would just let us say no. Kate picked up her drink and took a small sip when he told us to drink up, so I did as well. It didn't taste like anything was in it."

He heard a click. "Tommy?" No response. Gaige took in a deep breath and let it out slowly. What were they on, day three now? Or was it four?

Hawk entered the living room and sat in one of the arm chairs. He quietly waited as Hawk does, but Sophie reached forward and lay her hand on his arm. "Gaige?"

"Tommy remembered that they weren't drugged at the restaurant and that someone was in Kate's apartment when they got back there. Said he had ice blue eyes and white hair and told them to drink the drinks he had made, so he probably put the Versed in their drinks. I asked if it was the same guy in the picture Hawk showed him yesterday and he's reluctant to say for sure."

Sophie sat straighter. "You mean Reed Killian?"

Sophie sat back against the arm of the sofa, her right knee bent and her leg on the sofa between them. Laying her right elbow on the back of the sofa and resting her head in her right hand, she said, "He'd been after her."

Looking into her troubled brown eyes, he asked, "How long has Killian been on base here?"

She shrugged, "I'd have to look at the roster, but maybe a year or so."

"Do you know where he was before that?"

Sadly shaking her head sideways, she stared at him.

"Hawk, call GHOST and ask Wyatt or Josh to look further into Killian's record. Where has he been and for how long."

The gentle giant walked to his bedroom and he watched Sophie's face. Concentration, certainly, but maybe a bit of lost hope, too. "Don't worry, Soph, we'll get him."

His phone rang again. Seeing Jared Timm's name on the read out, he hoped this would be some good news on the Balfreed records. "Jared, tell me something good."

38

She listened as Gaige talked to Jared, whoever that was. It seemed he was with GHOST or affiliated somehow. Hawk was in the other room getting records run on Killian and she felt unable to help herself. Kate was murdered, 'cause that's what it was, no way she killed herself. She'd never believe it. She and Kate had been trying to figure out how to prove that Tommy had raped Kate to get around all the stonewalling they were getting from CID. Now, she doubted Tommy did it, because honestly would a rapist stay the night with a woman he'd raped? Why hadn't they seen this before? It really made no sense.

Oh. My. God. She sat up straight, and Gaige's eyes snapped to her. She just remembered. He sat up straighter and stared at her, his brows furrowing.

She whispered. "Does GHOST have someone who can get into Kate's old phone records?"

Gaige nodded, "Can you get into Kate's phone records?"

Pulling his phone away from his ear, he asked, "What's he looking for, Soph?"

"Kate received an anonymous text from someone, who told her to look at Killian. That was it. Nothing else and she thought it was Killian trying to get her to go out with him. *Look at Killian.* She'd always tried ignoring him because he creeped her out. But maybe that person meant to look at him for her rape."

"Did you hear that?"

Gaige gave her a thumbs up and listened to Jared's end of the conversation.

Too edgy to sit, she got up and went to the bedroom. Picking up her new phone. Actually, GHOST's new phone. Gaige had insisted for the time being it be in GHOST's name so no one could track her with it, but it was hers to use for now. Whatever happened when this was all over would determine if she needed to once again get another phone. But, she picked it up to see the download was still only at 73%. It seemed to be taking forever. Needing something to do until some of their information came through she picked up their laundry, cut through the bathroom to Hawk's room and found him sitting up on his bed much as Gaige had been doing not long ago in their room. He looked up at her when she entered and her cheeks flamed bright red.

"Sorry. I just need to burn off some steam so I thought I'd do laundry. Do you have clothes I can wash with ours?"

"You don't have to do my laundry, Sophie."

"I didn't say I had to, I said I had to burn off some steam. I'm offering."

He seemed undecided if he should let her do his laundry or not and it became uncomfortable. "Are you afraid I'll mix up your underwear or turn them pink?"

He laughed then and she'd be dead not to notice how attractive he was. He usually hid his feelings, he was always so stalwart and quiet, so his laugh was truly nice. Plus, shit, he was scorching hot. Badass. You name it, he had it. Just not her heart that had always belonged to Gaige. Even JJ felt that.

"Knock yourself out, Soph. I've got my dirty clothes in that basket over by the dresser."

She smiled back at him, walked to the basket and pulled his worn clothing from the basket and mingled it with theirs. She left the room without another word as he was already back to typing on his laptop. Weirdly quiet, that one was.

Gigi was still puttering in the kitchen humming again, but now she was frosting a cake. You'd think she'd be sick of baking after spending the day in a bakery, but here she was, cooking and baking for them all. She'd find a way to repay Gigi no matter how long it took her. She was one in a million.

Walking to the laundry room, she sorted their clothing, tossing the light clothes in the washer, the dark clothes on the floor, to go back into the basket until it was their turn to be washed. Adding a soap pod and closing the door, she pushed the button, turned the knob and pushed the start button. Hearing the washer lock she tossed the dark clothing into the basket and tucked it alongside the washer so no one tripped on it. Turning she stopped in her tracks as Gaige filled the doorway, his right shoulder leaning against the frame. His gaze was intense and goosebumps raced along her arms.

"Hi." She squeaked out.

His full sensual lips curved into a beautiful smile, his eyes never left hers. "I love watching you, Sophie. I feel like I've waited a lifetime to just be in your presence. Watching you do mundane chores like our laundry does weird things to me."

Taking the few steps to stand in front of him, she brushed her fingers along his forehead. It was a stretch for her, the man was tall, but his face always held such intensity, it seldom relaxed as it did now. Running a dangerous operation where the team put their lives on the line every day and keeping all the balls in the air must be a monumental task. Doing it well, was an even bigger one.

Her fingers trailed along his temple to his cheek, where she then cupped her hand and held him there. Her thumb brushed along his bottom lip softly, and he held perfectly still, his eyes locked on hers. Standing on her toes, she lightly touched her lips to his, a feather soft kiss. Just one. Then her arms wrapped around his waist, and she stood there laying her head on his chest. His arms wrapped around her shoulders and squeezed her to him, his head rested on top of hers and she closed her eyes. No feeling in the world would ever beat this feeling. Her heart told her this was love. Her head told her not to go too fast. Her body said, rip your clothes off and ride'em cowgirl.

"Gaige, I've got records."

39

H is voice was gruff when he responded to Hawk. "We'll be right there."

Kissing the top of her head, he softly said, "Duty calls, Soph."

His heart pounded when she squeezed him tightly to her before stepping back. His fingers began shaking as he placed them under her chin, bringing her eyes up to his. "When this is over, Sophie, you and I, we'll go away for a week of R&R with nothing to do but enjoy ourselves and make love. Deal?"

"Deal." Her eyes glistened and he felt as though he hit a nerve or something, but no time to talk about it now. They'd have time. This time he wasn't just walking away and he wasn't letting her walk away either.

Holding his hand out for hers, he allowed himself a minute to enjoy the feel of her hand in his. The size difference was both amazing and exciting, and he wanted that feeling for the rest of his life. Entering the living room, Hawk had pulled down the desk, set up their portable printer, and was printing out reports. The hum of the printer and Gigi's humming were the only sounds in the house right now. The aromas of dinner and a freshly baked cake swirled around his head and he admitted he was beginning to get hungry.

"What do you have, Hawk?"

"So, here's a list of all of the bases Killian has been at during his career. He moves 'round a bit, not totally uncommon, but I'd say more than the average soldier."

He turned the list for them to see and the list filled a page and a half. Twenty-four years in the service and the man had been stationed at eighteen different bases.

"So, here's what we need to do now. I don't know if you heard Sophie before when she mentioned the anonymous text Kate received but, thinking as Sophie, perhaps Killian is the rapist, and piecing in the rest, I'd say he's raped someone else. Maybe someone else at another base was raped and was either afraid to say anything or did and was stonewalled just like Kate and Sophie were. So, we need to find out how many other rapes were reported during the times Killian was at these different bases."

"Oh my God. Do you think that's why he's moved around so much?" Sophie's face drained of color and he held her close and pulled the desk chair out for her to sit on.

"We need to find out." He looked at the list and drew lines after every five bases. "You take the top five. I'll take the next five. Soph, your phone should be ready in a few minutes, using that to access the internet and our clearance with the military, you take the third five. That leaves three and I'll text them to Dodge and Jax. Let's research the fuck out of this." He went into the bedroom and grabbed his laptop and Sophie's phone. The update was complete, so he unplugged it and handed it to her.

"You're good to go."

She smiled, so brightly, he thought the sun would be jealous if it saw her. He leaned down and kissed her soft lips, then stood and walked to the sofa with his laptop. "Let's crack this bitch. If we can nail down evidence to prove Killian is our rapist, we can put him behind bars where he'll never destroy another soul and clear Tommy. Then, we should also be able to link him to the Fentanyl that killed Chet. And the lorazepam that killed Kate."

Sophie's voice was quiet when she called him. "Gaige?"

He turned to look at her. Her shapely legs looked fantastic. The little denim shorts she wore fit almost as if they'd been made for her. Her cute little toes wiggled around as her right leg swung to and fro perched on top of her left leg. When women crossed their legs it was sexy, when Sophie did it, it was unbelievably sexy. No lie.

His eyes rolled from her toes to her face and the smile she wore told him she'd seen the whole thing.

"Did Jared find out anything about Balfreed?"

"No, he'd run into a problem and wanted to know what GHOST's budget was. I told him we didn't have one right now."

"Gaige, please don't run into huge expenses for me." The look of dread on her face was heartbreaking.

Hawk chuckled. "He can afford it."

"But, I don't know how or when I'll be able to pay you back. I'm so screwed right now it'll take..."

He held up his hand to stave off any further complaint from her. "I told you not to worry about it." He looked at his laptop again and continued to search rape complaints at bases. "Research." He told her when he could see her still watching him.

"Dinner's ready, come on in."

Closing the lid on his laptop, he stood, set it on the desk and held his hand out for Sophie. Hawk stood, chuckled, and moved past them to the kitchen. Following closely behind, he was surprised to see the table set and laden with food. Drinks were set at each place setting. Wine for he and Sophie, beer for Hawk and a mixed drink for Gigi.

"I hope you don't mind that I guessed at the drinks, and you can certainly have something else if you like, but I wanted to fuss a bit."

"Gigi, you're spoiling us."

"Yes, I hope you feel that way. Having you all here has made me realize that I love being around people again. Sure I have the occasional battered woman show up at the bakery due to the spread of word through those who I've helped in the past, but I don't often have them come out here to stay with me. I miss having people to take care of and just the noise of people in the house again makes me so darned happy. So, I've made a decision and you're the first people I'm telling."

She took a deep breath and let it out slowly. "There's a bed and breakfast in town that I've looked at over the years. I've always wanted to own one then life got away from me. But, the bakery is successful and I enjoy having people around and baking, eating with them, then doing my own thing during the day. So, I'm going to buy it and run it and the bakery."

"Oh, wow, Gigi, that's just fantastic. You're going to be so darned busy, but I'm so happy for you." Sophie jumped up and ran around the table to hug Gigi.

"It's because of you, Sophie. You made me realize that life can get out of your control even when you don't do anything wrong. I have the opportunity and I'm going to take it. There may not be another."

Gaige swallowed the giant lump that just formed in his throat. Gigi was right, when opportunity comes along you have to take it, there may not be another chance. He wasn't going to risk letting this opportunity go with Sophie either. He couldn't. Silence fell around them and he noticed everyone looking at him. "Congratulations, Gigi. I didn't mean to withhold congrats. Your comments about opportunity made me think of something else."

"Well, thank you all. Now, let's eat before dinner gets cold."

"Wait!" Sophie held her wine glass up. "To Gigi's new adventure."

They toasted Gigi, ate an enjoyable meal, and chatted about the bed and breakfast and all she wanted to do with it. He barely heard a word as his thoughts were on clearing Sophie and repairing her Army record so he could bring her home to GHOST.

40

"Okay, I've found one rape complaint at Fort Stewart at the time Killian was stationed there. It was three years ago but after the charges were made, nothing happened, then Killian was stationed at..." She looked down at the piece of paper she'd written her notes on. "Fort Lewis in Washington state. The complaint was made by Carlee Brown."

"Okay, let's find out where Carlee Brown is now." Gaige instructed.

Hawk responded then, "I've got one too at Fort Riley around five years ago by Gayle Stout. Then he was transferred to Fort Stewart about six months later. Nothing came of the report."

"Okay, find her." Finally, they were on to something. He continued searching his bases until his phone rang.

"Jared, tell me you've got something."

"I do. I hacked into Balfreed records and found out each ring has an ID number imprinted on the inside of the band, up in the setting so it doesn't get worn away. So, I hacked into Crowne Jewelers records, which by the way, was child's play, and found the ID number associated with the ring they have. I was able to match it to a purchase five years ago at Fort Riley to a Rand Gillman."

"That's a new one."

"Purchased on June 13. I'll send you the purchase record. He paid a hefty sum for it. Close to thirteen thousand dollars. The notes on the purchase were that he wanted a real ruby not a simulated stone."

"Thanks, Jared." Ending the call, he turned to Sophie and Hawk. "The ring was purchased by Rand Gillman."

Hawk began typing and both he and Sophie waited. "Found him. He's here. In California."

Gaige set his laptop aside and went to look over Hawk's shoulder. Scrolling the page of Rand Gillman, a picture populated on the screen and Gaige's stomach twisted. "What the fuck?"

Sophie jumped up and ran around the desk. She gasped as her hand flew to cover her mouth. They stared in disbelief for a long time, no one saying anything.

Finally, Sophie mumbled. "He looks just like Reed Killian. But younger."

Disbelief. "What the fuck is going on here?" His head spun a bit, his mind tried catching up with this crazy bullshit.

"Log into the Military records database and see if there is a Rand Gillman listed as military personnel." He leaned over and kissed the top of Sophie's head. She stood stone still disbelief clearly in her eyes. "Hey, search for Carlee Brown, 'kay?"

"Yeah." She whispered.

He watched her walk around the desk and sit opposite Hawk. She picked up her phone and began searching. Earlier, when he got out of the shower, he called Josh at the compound and had him overnight a new laptop, set up with their search capabilities for Sophie to use while they were here. Maybe it would be hers to keep. That was a discussion he hinted that the team would have, but part of him pulled back thinking it was too soon and her life was in too much disarray at the moment. He wanted her to want to be with him, not feel as if she had to. That was more important than anything for a long future. He was at a loss to figure out how to know without doubt that she wanted him for him. How did anyone ever really know?

"Oh no!" Sophie cried out. Hawk stopped searching and looked over to her. He walked around the desk to see what she was looking at on her phone.

Reading her phone screen some puzzle pieces were coming together, but not in a good way. Looking over at Hawk, he said, "Carlee Brown is dead. It appears to be suicide."

Hawk sat back in the chair dismay in his eyes. "This pattern is not only smarmy, its deadly. I've got to find Gayle Stout."

Hawk went back to searching.

Sophie swallowed but squared her shoulders and mumbled. "We're going to get this fucker."

"That's my girl." He was proud of how strong she was. The total package right here, brains, beauty, and brawn.

He continued his search of bases for rape reports and found two that had been reported at two different bases. One in Texas and one in Florida. It seemed Killian was a serial rapist and the Army continued to move him around to keep him instead of locking him up. He remembered a similar mission they'd been on when he first came on board with GHOST. There was a bad egg in uniform, not raping women, but stealing from them. Mementos, undergarments, necklaces and personal items. The behavior was thought to be the beginning of sexual deviant behavior by taking mementos to see if he would get caught. But he also was watching these women, border-line stalking. Instead of locking him up, the Army moved him around because they didn't want the bad press. He ended up killed in action in Afghanistan during deployment. This smacked of the same thing, move him around to keep the bad press down.

Then he remembered, "Serial rapists generally take trophies from the bodies of their victims. Later, they can hold a trophy when they relive a rape. They usually have a signature. Serial killers do all of the same things. We need to find out if things were taken from these women."

Sophie looked up at him. "That's true. How do we find this out?"

"Gayle Stout committed suicide a month after reporting her rape to command," Hawk reported.

"How."

Hawk rubbed his forehead with his fingers, then ran his fingers around his tired eyes before looking over to him. "Found in a garage with her car running."

Sophie's anger bubbled to the surface. "This is ludicrous! This bastard is raping then killing the women who report it and getting away with it. We've just got to stop him. Even if it means he needs to die instead of trusting the system."

She stood and paced around the living room, clearly too agitated to sit.

"I have to agree with you, Soph, he must be stopped. But we have a new player in the game and that is Rand Gillman. Who is he and why was it the stone from his ring that was in the car Kate was found in?"

Hawk chimed in. "There are no military records for a Rand Gillman, but I found him on social media. Says he was born twenty-four years ago in South Carolina." Leaning back in his chair Hawk locked eyes with him. "Remind me, Gaige, isn't that where you were stationed for AIT and that's where you met Killian?"

"Yes, it is. So you're thinking Rand Gillman is Killian's son?"

"According to his pictures and his friends, his mom is Irene Gillman. She's married and Rand has a brother and sister who look nothing like him. And mom is dark hair, dark eyes. Rand looks nothing like his mother. I'd bet, after Rand was born, Killian may or may not have made support payments for the kid, but he's certainly never claimed him as far as I can tell so far."

Standing to get his blood flowing again, he looked over Hawk's shoulder at the social media pictures Rand Gillman had posted.

"Does it say why he's here on his social media?"

"Working at a hospital in Riverton."

Sophie stopped pacing and faced them. "So he'd have access to drugs."

41

She was going to make sure he didn't rape anyone again. No matter what she had to do, but what did his son have to do with it all? Was he the rapist? Or the murderer? Just when it seemed they'd found the answer, more questions popped up. Her head swam with the facts.

Undressing for bed, she slipped her arms through a loose fitting t-shirt Gigi had given her in the stack of clothing. She was grateful for the clothing and for Gaige giving her a phone, but she missed her things. Her apartment sat empty now, all her clothes hanging in her closet waiting for her to claim them. Hopefully anyway. The first of the month, when rent was due, would be coming shortly. But the fact that they'd reported her as AWOL may give authorities permission to go in and confiscate her belongings. That would be another shit show she'd have to deal with. It never ended it seemed.

Reaching behind and braiding her hair she watched fireflies buzz around outside, playing as they created twinkle effects in the darkness. It was pretty here. Gigi had found herself a nice little place to heal. She'd have to do that when this was all over, find a place to heal. The first thing she wanted to do is plant a tree for Kate. Actually for Kate and Tate. They never found their way to each other in life, she sure hoped they did in death. And that brought her thinking around to Gaige. She didn't want their story to be one of Kate and Tate. Never finding their way together in life. They had a chance now, how deep did they delve while her life was in such turmoil? Again the questions piled up.

"What are you thinking about?" Gaige entered the room from the bathroom, freshly showered, and smelling fantastic. He still wore the Cattleman's cologne, she loved it. He smelled like a spa but manly.

Taking him in, the whole of him, standing across the room from her. No shirt on, his muscles prominent, his abs clearly defined. He'd always worn his hair cropped short, she'd assumed at first because of the military, but he'd been out for close to twenty years, so it must just be his style. He wore it well, it fit him in some way. Short, clean and precise. But oh so handsome.

"I was thinking I hope Kate and Tate have found each other in heaven because they never found their way to each other here on earth."

She saw him swallow. He stared at her, indecision in his expression. Finishing her braid, she secured the band and let her hands drop to her sides as she watched him wrestle with his thoughts.

"We should talk. I was undecided about it earlier, but we have some time alone now, we should take it to sort a few things out."

Suddenly it felt as though her legs wouldn't support her. Walking to the end of the bed, she slowly sat and waited to hear his words. He was undecided if they should talk which meant he didn't want to be with her for the long haul. Her stomach rolled at the thought of him saying the words, but it would be better to know and not think there could be anything more than just the now. Right?

She couldn't respond with words, her throat felt so tight and the blood thrumming in her ears seemed to amplify. This was it. All these years she'd thought, some-day. That was likely to end now. She'd survive, wouldn't she?

He came to sit beside her on the end of the bed. She felt it dip under his weight but couldn't look at him. He turned his body, his right leg folded and laid on top of the bed to face her. His fingers tucked under her chin and gently pulled her face to look at him.

"I want you to look at me when we have this conversation."

Ohmigod, he wanted to watch her destruct.

So slowly she felt slothful, she turned, folded her left leg so it laid on the bed, her bare leg parallel to his, the contrast between the two was stark. Raising her eyes to his, the intensity of his look nearly brought tears to hers.

"I've been stupid. All these years, Soph. All these fucking years I dreamed of you. Thought of you and wondered what it could be like with you. But something held me back from picking up the phone. I told myself at first it was because of Tate. There's this bro-code where you don't go and he was my best friend. The only brother I've ever had. Ever will have. I ignored even you for him. Then you married, I got engaged, and I made my mind up that it wasn't meant to be."

Could he hear her heart breaking? Couldn't he hear it?

"When Tate died, you were still married and we were both hurting. And then, the years passed and we lost touch. And I thought of you so much, but I couldn't bring myself to call you."

He reached forward and took her hands in his. His large strong hands had touched and held her so sweetly last night and this morning again, her heartbeat increased. She could feel the heat climbing up her torso as the dreaded words came closer to being said.

"Then you called me. You were in trouble and needed me. On the flight here I wondered about it. After all this time, you called me. I told myself not to get revved up and excited because you were in trouble and of course you knew I would help you. GHOST has developed into an organization with so much to offer and, yes, you'd know that.

He stopped talking, swallowed and cleared his throat. Here it comes. Blinking furiously to stop the tears, she struggled to breathe.

"But I dreamed of Tate last night. He just kept popping into my subconscious laughing. He looked happy and alive. He didn't say anything, he just kept showing me random pictures of him and us and the two of you in happy moments. Of both of us laughing at your mom's 45th birthday party and Christmas that same year. I worried all day about what that meant. That he was reminding me that you are his sister. Was it a warning to not destroy the bro-code? Then Gigi said she couldn't let an opportunity pass her by. I now honestly believe Tate was trying to tell me he approves. He's happy that we're together."

She felt the lone tear slide down her face, but she couldn't let his hands go.

"I think that's what it was, Sophie. I believe Tate was telling me he approves. I don't want to let this opportunity pass us by. But I don't want you to be with me because you need my help, you have it, always, no matter what. I want you to want me for me because Sophie, I love you. I always have. I always will of that I'm convinced."

A sob tore through her body, it came out louder than she'd intended, but the relief ripped through her so fiercely and so fast she had no control.

Her hands covered her mouth to keep the cries from coming again and again. She closed her eyes and the flood of tears continued to pour out.

He gently pulled her to him and wrapped his arms around her shoulders. Wrapping hers around him she reveled in the warmth and strength of him. She could feel his heart beating rapidly as if he'd just run a marathon, but she took a moment to compose herself. Finally, when she thought the words would come without sobs, she whispered. "I thought you were going to tell me you didn't want to be with me. I was trying to be so brave."

He pulled her away from him to look into her eyes. His thumbs brushed under her eyes, feeling tears and swiping them away. "Say again."

"No, I don't want to say that. I love you, too, Gaige. And not to sound like a parrot, but I always have and I always will."

42

R elief. Euphoria. Overwhelmed with...what? Love? Probably.

Staring into her sparkly brown eyes, her lashes spiky and wet with her tears, her smile grew, changing the stern hardened look she'd worn a few minutes ago to one of unparalleled beauty and light. She'd just blossomed in front of him and it was like witnessing a caterpillar turn into a butterfly. Stunning.

Her hands framed his face and pulled him closer. Watching her eyes close before her soft full lips touched his was a joy. The shock that ran through him as her lips molded to his was like the first time and in a way it was. They'd declared their love, she felt the same way he did and it was powerful. Snaking his arms around her waist, he pulled her down, rolling so she landed on top of him, his lips never leaving hers. Her legs framed his, the weight of her body on his like the best blanket on earth. Her elbows rested next to his shoulders, her hands circling in his hair. Their bodies touching from head to toe. Perfect.

He dove his hands into her braid, felt down to the

bottom, pulled the band free and began freeing her hair. The warmth from her body brought the aroma of her hair into full bloom and he inhaled taking that smell into his lungs. Once all of her hair was loosened, he slid his hands into it and brought it around so it's silk veil framed their faces. Sliding his hands down her back and to her ass, he squeezed her firm globes and pulled her tightly into his body. A thrill ran through him when she moaned into his mouth and her hips arched and fell in a rhythm as old as time. His cock had hardened in a nanosecond the instant their lips met, but having her move against him, seeking more from his body, well, that just made him crazy.

He felt something lacy covering her ass, digging his hands under the fragile fabric, he fisted the little strip from the thong and ripped it apart, she pulled her lips from his.

"I just bought these."

"When?"

"When you bought the condoms."

"I'll buy you more."

Wrapping his arms around her once more, he rolled so he'd be on top of her, his body not interested in playing it slow tonight. He lifted his head to look into her eyes, but first he saw her silky hair fanned across the bed in a messy array of curls, catching the light. He had always enjoyed her hair, it was always beautiful, thick and shiny. The richness of the dark color complimented her skin and eyes. Looking down into her face she wore a sultry smile that caused fine lines to crease at the corners of her eyes and he got the feeling she was assessing him. Then the little vixen bit her bottom lip and he wanted to do that, so he bent his head down and nipped her lip, sucking it in slightly then nipping once more.

Her legs lifted around his ass and he felt her lock her feet together, she was going to hang on for the ride. That was fantastic 'cause it was going to be a fast and furious one.

He croaked, "Fast or slow?"

"Fast." She whispered. "Very fast."

"Good answer."

Arching his hips, he felt the instant his throbbing cock fell against the slit he wanted. Tightening his hips slightly, he felt himself seat into place. Raising himself up on his hands to perfect the position, he slowly entered her warmth.

She moaned as he slid as far in as he could. He ground against her clit, slid out and repeated, this time sliding in further, his cock coated perfectly with her cream. They were ready. He increased his speed, pumping in and out, enjoying the way her lips rippled along his cock, it was the perfect massage and friction for their mating. Yeah, he wouldn't be wearing those condoms. Not ever.

He continued his pace, grinding against her clit as he pushed all the way inside, pulling out and doing it again. Sophie moaned, her hands on his back squeezed and she whispered, "Gaige."

She whimpered and he gruffly said, "Let it go."

Her hips kept time with his, both of them trying to reach the pinnacle. She cried out his name. His name. Never would he have thought it could sound so good. He pushed all the way inside of her and applied pressure to her clit while she rode her high. He could feel her spasms and it was all he could do not to let go, the sweat formed on his back and arms, he could feel it trickle down his head.

He began pumping again, it wouldn't be long now. His

balls tightened up to the point of pain, his cock felt as though it would rip apart, the heat and pain from being so hard nearly unbearable and then he came. The throbbing caused him to groan into her hair, still fanned out on the bed. Her legs tightened and pulled him in fully, her arms squeezed him tightly. His hands found her head and cupped her as he breathed in the scent of her skin and hair and allowed the feeling of floating to overcome him. If this was heaven, he didn't want to leave.

He jerked a few times as his seed flowed into her and two thoughts reached his brain. They'd have to talk about birth control and it wouldn't involve condoms.

---

liding the door closed quietly she walked out to the kitchen to find Gigi sitting at the kitchen table with a cup of coffee and the newspaper. Her mug had a cute saying on it, *People say I'm condescending (that means I talk down to people)*. Sophie giggled, "I love your coffee cups, Gigi, how fun."

"Thanks. I collect them. I can't seem to stop it actually. I've got some pretty sassy ones on the top shelf. Those are my favorites."

Making her way to the coffee pot and the cupboard with the cute cups, she picked out one with a bright sunflower on it and no saying. Adding a spoon of creamer and pouring coffee in it, she glanced at Gigi who shook her head no.

Taking the seat across from Gigi she sat and sighed. "It's peaceful here."

Gigi looked out the patio door and stared for a minute. "It is. It's what I love most about this place. That and the fact that I feel safe here."

"Are you going to sell this place and move into your bed and breakfast?"

Gigi tightened her lips for a moment then looked into her eyes. "I may, someday, but certainly not now. The thought actually makes me nervous. So, I'll have locks inserted on the kitchen and laundry doors. When I'm not there or one of my staff, then those doors will be locked. I'll have snacks out that can sit and guests will be treated well. I may even find a caretaker to live there and help out for free room and board, we'll see."

"You've certainly given it all a lot of thought."

Gigi giggled. "I have. It's time for me to branch out and do some of the things I've always wanted to do. I'm not getting any younger. Having you all here has helped me realize that I enjoy people and I'm ready to move forward. How about you, Sophie, what are your plans when all of this is over?"

She let out a long breath. "Well, first I have to get my record cleared up. Then I have two months left on this contract with the ARMY, so I'll have to finish them. But, this has certainly spoiled the military for me, so I think I'll need to do something else. I'm not sure what that is just yet."

"What have you trained to do?"

Giggling she responded. "Oh, gosh, I've trained for all sort of things. Communications is my major specialty, but I also finished college in Business Administration and Kate and I used to dream of opening a craft shop. Selling our crafts but also teaching other people how to do them. I may give that some thought. Or not. I honestly haven't given it any thought since Kate's been gone. I've dealt with one thing or another since her rape, then her death and to be honest until Gaige had arrived, my only thoughts were how to stay alive."

Gigi's hand reached across the table to hers. "Oh, honey, I'm so sorry."

That simple gesture made tears form in her eyes. The simple act of someone caring made such a difference. "Thanks, Gigi." She cleared her throat and swiped at her eyes with the pads of her fingers. "I guess if something good could come of this, Gaige and I found each other again. Though, I'd give anything to have Kate here to see it."

"She can see it." Gigi's warm smile and simple confidence made her feel so grateful.

Her bedroom door slid open and Gaige stepped out into the living room. His eyes still looked sleepy, but when they landed on her, they lit up. Butterflies formed in her tummy at the sight of his face brightening just by looking at her.

Gigi whispered, "Now what woman wouldn't want to be looked at like that?"

Gaige walked directly to her, leaned down and kissed her upturned lips. "Morning."

"Morning."

Gigi sighed but mumbled, "Morning."

Gaige walked to the coffee pot, took out a mug, chuckled at the saying, then poured his coffee. Walking to the table with the pot in one hand and his cup in the other he refreshed both of their cups, then took the pot back to the coffee maker and set it on the hot plate.

Sitting to Sophie's left and Gigi's right he sipped his coffee quietly, looking out onto the backyard at the flowers in bloom and the birds swooping here and there.

"Well, I'll get breakfast cooking, I suppose you all have a busy day ahead."

Sophie stood but Gigi motioned for her to sit. A couple of minutes later she brought apples, strawberries, peaches, and blueberries in a big bowl to the table with a knife and cutting board and a big platter. "Cut these up while you and Gaige chat. I've got the rest."

"Thanks, Gigi." She pulled an apple from the bowl and set it on the cutting board. "What are we doing today, Gaige?"

He grinned at her. "First, I have reports coming in soon, I hope, on the rape victims that have died. Autopsy reports, rape allegations, police reports, all of it. My military contact, Casper, was quite eager to help out on this one. He's pissed they have a piece of shit like Killian on staff. GHOST is pulling up records on Rand Gillman. Birth Certificate, employment records, family members' records, etc. We'll pour over all of that and see if anything leads us to be able to pin down Killian or Gillman. Then, I'm going to go out and talk to my Uncle Jeff."

"Oh no, Gaige. I thought he didn't want this to go any further."

"He didn't. He used Killian to clean up what he thought was Tommy's mess only it was Killian's own mess. No wonder Killian was eager to help out. But, it's time to let Tommy off the hook. It's time for Uncle Jeff to face the fact that not only did he treat his son horribly by not trying to clear his name and by making him quietly live with this shit, but he may have let the rapist and killer into a lot of places that helped him cover up all of the evidence. Then, he's going to clear your record, Soph, and Kate's. Then, we're going home." She sat staring at him for the longest time, knife midair over the apple she was cutting. He told her he loved her last night and always would, but they didn't talk about what would happen from here. He sipped his coffee and his eyes landed on hers. Setting his cup down he tilted his head and furrowed his brow.

"I guess we didn't talk about this last night. I have to be at GHOST. I would love it if you'd come back with me. Live with me. Be part of my life. The biggest part of it. But, we have to do it in Indiana. Do you think you can live there?"

Her smile felt impossibly huge. Setting the knife on the cutting board, she looked into his eyes. "I can probably make that work." Then her eyes opened wide. "But, speaking of work, I'd be unemployed. I'd have to find a job and do you have room for me there or where would we live? I don't know any place around there to even begin looking. And, I'm rambling."

Gaige laughed and it was glorious. "It'll all fall into place, Soph. One thing at a time. We have to clean this all up first."

"Did I hear that Sophie's coming home with us?" Hawk walked into the room, freshly showered and smelling divine!

"Once we get her record cleared."

"Well, along those lines, I got the employment records for Rand Gillman at the hospital. You have them in your email, too. He's only worked there for six months. But, get this, I have his employment history from the social security records. He'd moved to each town a few months before the death of each rape victim."

44

They each sat huddled around the kitchen table, their laptops and phones burning up the internet downloading files and reports that had been pouring in. The doorbell rang and Gaige jumped up to get it. Gigi had left for the bakery hours before and this was likely the package he was expecting today. Glancing out the window, he instinctively reached behind him for his gun, right hand on the stock, just in case.

Seeing the delivery driver uniform, he cracked the door open. The driver, a younger man not more than twenty-eight years old, looked him in the eye and smiled. "Afternoon, sir, package delivery for Mr. Gaige Vickers."

Releasing his weapon and leaving it holstered, he took the box from the driver. "Thank you."

"You're welcome." And off the porch he went, already making time to get back to his truck.

Seeing the bright pink bra and panties on the mailing label, he felt secure bringing the box into the house.

Turning around, Hawk stood behind him, gun in his

hand, pointed at the floor. Nodding to his comrade he locked the door once more, carried the box to the kitchen table, and using a pocket knife he slit the tape open. Lifting the lid and unwrapping the box, he glanced over at Sophie who was watching his every move.

He smiled at her and Hawk resumed his seat at the table.

Lifting the new laptop from the box, he lay it in front of Sophie, "Welcome to GHOST."

Her head tilted, her dark hair hanging freely over her shoulders and he thought again she was without a doubt an unparalleled beauty. He'd thought that from the first moment he'd seen her. All those years did nothing to change that about her or change his feelings.

"That's for me?"

"Yep. We can't ruin your eyes by having you stare at that phone all day."

She ran her hands over the top of the computer, lovingly petting it, whispering, "Oh, wow."

Then her brows furrowed and she reached over and lifted the lid on the box where the pink bra and panties sticker was affixed.

"Laptops come from a lingerie store?"

Hawk laughed which made him laugh. "No, it's our front."

"Your front? As in a dummy company?"

"Yes. There are times, such as these, that we have to ship things. I didn't want to bring an unknown box into the house, so they labeled it so I'd know it was legit."

"What do you call this front company?"

"GHOST Lingerie." He and Hawk chuckled again.

"So you guys all think this is funny, I see. What about Jax, does she think it's funny, too?"

Hawk stopped typing for a minute. "She thinks it's a riot."

She lifted the lid and turned it on. It startled her when it almost instantly popped on. He continued to pull the cords, a cordless mouse, mouse pad that had the GHOST shield on it and the instruction manual.

"It's all set up with all of our programs. I'll help you learn the software we use, but you'll have full search capabilities just as Hawk and I and the entire team at GHOST have.

"You're serious? Really?"

Hawk chuckled and continued reading through his reports, but his eyes slid to Sophie periodically, his amusement evident on his face.

"Don't abuse it, Soph."

Her head shook vigorously, "I won't, I swear."

He pulled his phone up, forwarded a text he'd gotten from Josh with Sophie's user name and password and sent it to her.

Her phone pinged and she looked down at it. "Your sign in credentials."

She logged in using the information he'd texted her and as her screen appeared her mouth dropped open. Her eyes scanned the screen then she looked up at him. "So, what does this mean? Do I work for you now?"

Hawk laughed. "Sophie, in a matter of a few minutes you became a member of the team and you're sleeping with the leader of GHOST. Record time right there." Her hands flew to her cheeks to hide the red that tinted them. He laughed and she jumped from her chair and wrapped her arms around his neck. "Thank you."

Taking the opportunity to give her a squeeze he responded, "You're very welcome. But, once we get back to

GHOST, all the team members will meet with you, then they'll vote on whether or not you're a permanent member of the team."

Fear passed across her face, then she said, "You'll vote yes, right?"

He couldn't help it, he laughed. "Probably, but no guarantees."

Her head swung to Hawk. "Hawk, will you vote yes?"

Hawk looked up from his computer, a smile on his face. He waited a few beats then said, "Jury's still out for me, Soph."

She leaned across the table and swatted at his shoulder.

Looking at the laptop Sophie said, "We'll need to have ground rules though. You can't grab my ass or anything while we're working."

"Darlin', you're the one who just jumped up and hugged me. Those rules go both ways."

She laughed and he and Hawk joined in.

"But, really Gaige, what does this mean? We didn't talk about me working for GHOST. And, my specialty is communications but I can learn, but I'm not sure I want to work for GHOST. I mean, I don't know anyone other than you two and what do you all do, just sit around and look at reports all day? Not sure I can do that. But, I guess I'd like to know..."

He laughed then held his hand up to halt her. "Honey, let's work at this slowly. Right now, we need to wrap this shit up. Then, we need to get you and Tommy cleared. Then, we need to get home. You can talk to Jax, who by the way will be thrilled to not be the only woman on the team, if it works out that way. Then, we'll talk again. Some of our missions are extremely dangerous. We've lost members on the job. Jax and Josh are twins, their brother and father were both killed while on duty. Hawk was recently shot as was another team member, Dodge, on our last mission. It's not for everyone and, as I say that out loud, I don't like the idea of you being in situations like that. But then again, Dodge probably hates it when Jax, his fiancée, is too."

Hawk chuckled. "He hates it. They make it work. I'll bet it all changes after they're married and she gets knocked up."

Gaige simply nodded, that would be a bridge they'd cross if and when that happened. If Sophie were pregnant with his child, no way he'd want her anywhere near some of the shit they dealt with. He wasn't going to borrow trouble on this though, he'd take it one day at a time.

Hawk's computer chimed, then his phone pinged. "I've got reports on Rand Gillman."

Waiting to see what those said, he and Sophie both watched as Hawk read through them. "Killian's kid. Killian is on his birth certificate and it looks like he paid child support until Rand was 18. But, he didn't raise him or spend any time with him. He signed over legal rights to Rand three years later when Irene married Donald Gillman. Donald adopted Rand and gave him his last name. But, Reed continued to pay child support, even though he didn't have to." Hawk looked up at him. "Isn't he swell?" The sarcasm was thick.

Chuckling he responded, "Okay, so we have that connection in place. Now we have to confirm that Rand was in the area after each of the rapes. And, why was Rand on base to buy the ring from Balfreed at Fort Riley?"

"On it." Hawk typed away, as he lost himself in his mission. Glancing at Sophie, he said, "Soph, I need you to dig into Chet Forest. How did he know Rand Gillman? I'm going to work on digging up information on David Sams, the former owner of the car Kate was found in and see if he can give us some answers."

45

Her head was swirling with all that had gone on over the past few hours. Gaige loved her and she loved him. That was the biggest and best thing. She felt hopeful she'd be cleared of Chet's murder and her AWOL status. A few days ago, she thought she was going to die at the hands of someone she didn't know. Now, she assumed and would prove that anonymous someone was Killian.

"Oh, wait a minute!" The thoughts and memories were running through her mind at breakneck speed. "The men that tried grabbing me at my apartment complex...I think I know who one of them was." Flipping her hair over her shoulder, she stared out the patio door for a moment. "We had some guy hanging around, said he was hired on for maintenance. There are tons of civilians who work on base and this guy was fairly new. Now that I think of it, he had a tattoo on his hand of a spider. It was about the size of a silver dollar on his left hand between the thumb and forefinger, but faded. I saw that. He tried grabbing me and said not to talk to another person about what I knew.

Then he said to the other man, "The Captain will be..." and the other man told him to shut up. Anyway, while this was happening, I twisted and ran around the building. He tried grabbing me again and I remember seeing that spider. At the time it didn't come together who he was and how I'd recognized him."

Gaige sat next to her at the square table, and leaned across. "That's great. What's his name?"

"I never knew his name. But there must be a database of civie employees on base. Profiles?"

"Yes, you can access it by clicking on this icon." He pointed to the icon on her computer and she clicked on it. A screen opened up asking her for a name. Biting her bottom lip, Gaige scooted his chair around the table.

"There's a work around. Click on "More Info" just below that field. Now type in Maintenance or Grounds and see if his picture comes up."

She did as he instructed and she waited as picture after picture of the civilian employees populated the screen. She'd be here for days scrolling through all of these pictures. She remembered he had his head shaved, but that didn't mean at the time his picture was taken it was shaved. The top of the screen said "838 profiles found."

She groaned, yep, days she'd be sifting through these pictures. Gaige chuckled. "Now click here and sort by sex. You can rule out all females. That will cut your search down."

Following instructions, she was pleased to see that removed more than 398 civilians from the search. She began scrolling through the photos of the civilians employed by the Army and Gaige whispered, "You've got this."

He scooted his chair away and she scanned her screen to locate Spiderman. She chuckled at her nickname and sent up a silent prayer that he didn't have Spiderman's skills, or he'd be a bugger to find and capture.

After two hours, she found a picture of someone who looked very similar to one of the men, the man who tried grabbing her. Reading through his profile, she found his high school was in South Carolina. She'd bet her first born he had been in high school with Rand Gillman.

"Hawk, that information you got on Rand Gillman? Did it say where he graduated?"

Hawk began typing. "Yep. Clemson."

"Spiderman went to high school with Gillman."

"What's Spiderman's real name?" Gaige asked.

"Tony Guilianetti."

"Okay, you have an address on Spiderman? I think I'll go pay him a visit." Gaige declared.

"I'll go, too."

"Soph, people are looking for you all over, I don't think it's a great idea to have you running around out there."

"We were out yesterday."

"We went to a junkyard and your former boyfriend's jewelry store. Not out looking for a person, who, by the way, has tried to kill you."

Turning to Hawk, Sophie said, "Hawk, tell him I can take care of myself."

"Oh, fuck no, you're not getting me in the middle of this shit show."

She stared him down, but he wasn't squirming in his seat, he simply chuckled. "That won't work either. Sorry, Soph."

Turning back to Gaige she saw his grin and that irritated her further. "I'll stay in the car."

"Why go at all then?"

"'Cause I get stir crazy sitting here. I've never been so sedentary in my life. I'm used to moving around, working, PT."

Gaige scraped his hand through his hair and heaved out a deep breath. "Alright, you stay in the car."

"Scouts honor." She held up her hand as if taking a pledge.

"You're not a scout and neither am I."

Closing the lid on his laptop, Gaige stood and carried his computer to the bedroom. She followed suit. Hawk tucked his in a computer bag and pulled the strap over his right shoulder. Apparently they were going on a road trip. Finally.

When taking her new laptop to the bedroom, Gaige was sitting on the foot of the bed tying his boots. He looked up at her when she entered. "What caliber weapon are you most comfortable with?"

"9 millimeter."

"Okay." He stood, walked to the closet, knelt down, and began pulling weapons from his duffle. Laying a 9 mm handgun on the bed, he dropped a box of bullets next to it and a holster. Tossing a badge on the bed next, he said, "Load your weapon and carry it on you at all times. That's an ankle holster which will fit under your jeans. The badge is for you to only show if a cop stops and wants to see credentials. You're not officially GHOST until you're voted in, we do the paperwork and get you permission to carry on our behalf, but hopefully you won't need to use that this time."

"Okay."

Setting her laptop on the table next to the bed, she shimmied down her shorts and grabbed her jeans from a hangar in the closet. Gaige was busy loading his weapons and holstering them.

She strapped her ankle holster on, and adjusted it to fit her. As she reached for the 9 mm, he lay on the bed and put his arms around her from behind. "I love you, Sophie. Do not do anything to get yourself killed or hurt. I don't have body armor for you here and I don't like that you're coming along, but I do understand. If we were at home, we'd be in the Beast, which is a vehicle outfitted for us and our needs, including bulletproof windows. Here we have a rental, so this is not the way we like to go in, but we have to."

Laying her head back on his shoulder, her heartbeat increased. Part excitement and part Gaige. "I love you, too, and I won't do anything to get myself in trouble. Promise."

He kissed her neck, squeezed her waist, then pulled away. "And, tell me you're current with weapons training and self-defense."

"Yes, current on both."

"Let's roll."

46

The ride to Spiderman's home was quiet. Usually before a mission they got quiet, contemplative, and putting their heads right. A few prayers usually went up. Not that this was a usual mission, but clearly, they were now beginning to dig into where all of this bullshit started and it wasn't unreasonable to think that Spiderman or anyone else they might encounter would defend themselves from possible prison time. And, since they weren't cops, people usually didn't fear them as they did cops, so usually a fight developed. Frequently involving weapons. Certainly fists.

"Turn right up here and it's the second driveway on your right." Hawk instructed from the passenger seat.

After turning right, they found themselves in a trailer park. And, a less than nice one at that. They found Spiderman's number quickly. The first place on the right was a white trailer with faded aqua detailing. The three wooden steps that led to the door had been painted white at one time, but mostly the bare gray wood showed now. The curtains were faded and tattered from what they could see from their viewpoint in front of the trailer. An older pickup truck sat next to the steps, probably twenty years old or more and used to be black. Rust showed through in many spots along the bottom of the truck, and the paint had long ago faded and spider-cracked.

Putting the SUV in park, he turned to look at Sophie. "Keep your head down and only use your weapon if you're seen and fired upon."

"Okay." She smiled but it was weak. Likely her stomach was rolling as it had been some time since she'd seen any action like this. Her last deployment had been more than six years ago.

"Soph, do you have PTSD?"

She swallowed. "Not really. But I do stay inside under the covers during the 4th of July celebrations."

"Most of us do." He winked, "You good?"

"Yeah. Go get'em."

Glancing at Hawk he nodded and received a nod in return. Opening their respective doors they got out, he hit the lock button on the doors and proceeded toward the steps.

They walked up the decrepit steps to the trailer door and knocked. Footsteps could be heard walking from the back of the trailer to the front. The door opened and a young man around twenty-five-years old stood before them. Dark eyes, dark shaved head and reedy in build. He had two black eyes and his nose was swollen and misshaped. "Yeah?"

"I'm Gaige Vickers and this is my colleague Hawk. Reed Killian asked us to come and ask you some questions."

"That so? Why would Reed want you to ask me questions? Why don't he ask his kid if he wants answers?"

"That's what he asked us to find out. He'd like to have a conversation with Rand but can't get Rand to return a phone call." It was a guess and he hoped it'd pay off.

Instead of moving aside to let them in, he crossed his arms over his chest. "If Rand don't want to talk to him, then Reed should just go and fuck himself."

"I'd say I agree with you, but this is important. It's regarding his will."

"Yeah? He leaving Rand some jack?"

"Yes, actually, a substantial amount."

Rubbing his chin with his hand, Gaige was able to see the spider tattoo. "What's he want to know?"

"Can we come in and have this conversation?"

Spiderman looked over his right shoulder toward the back of the trailer, then stepped back and pointed them in the opposite direction to the kitchen. "Make it quick, I gotta be at work."

Hawk stood in the doorway between the kitchen and the living room and Gaige sat at the old scared wooden table. The trailer was surprisingly not filthy, but it could use a good tidying up. Dirty dishes were stacked in the sink and no dishwasher was visible.

"Where can we find Rand?"

"First of all, why do you need to find him? If Killian wants to put him in his will, why does he have to have an address or know where he is?"

"For the legal documents the address and phone number need to be added. That way, if something happens, he can be reached to make arrangements to receive his inheritance." He sure hoped he was sounding convincing.

Spiderman looked between him and Hawk indecision on his face. The sound of a backdoor closing caused Hawk to turn his head just in time to see a white head pass by one of the windows. Following the direction the head was taking, Hawk glanced out the front window and saw Rand Gillman try to get into the rented SUV. Gaige saw it at the same time and both men turned to the front door. Gaige heard the click of a pistol and turned in time to see Spiderman pointing a gun at him.

Pulling his gun from its holster, the first shot rang out from Spiderman's gun and then a second shot sounded from behind him. Hawk had shot Spiderman in the chest causing him to fall back against the counter, but he was still holding his gun, raising it to shoot Hawk. Gaige had time to raise his pistol and shoot three more rounds into Spiderman to stop him from shooting any more.

Hawk ran out of the trailer just as Rand Gillman shot out the windows of the SUV. Sophie shot back and hit Rand in the upper right torso. His attention was diverted enough that Hawk managed to run behind him and knock him to the ground before he shot again.

Sophie jumped from the driver's side backseat, small spots of blood spattered here and there on her face, from the broken glass. Running around the vehicle, she stopped when she saw Hawk on the ground pulling Rand Gillman's gun from his hand.

Gaige ran to Hawk's aid, taking Rand's gun and laying it a few yards away on the ground. Sophie grabbed her phone from her back pocket and tapped a couple of times before putting her phone to her ear.

He half listened as she directed a 911 operator where to send the ambulances. This would be local PD involved, which might get things rolling faster on their investigation. Looking around to see if there were other threats coming their way, the odd thought struck him that not one other person in this trailer park bothered to come out and see what was going on. Sirens could be heard in the distance as he glanced at Sophie's face. She stood calmly alongside him and they both watched Gillman lay on the ground on his stomach, Hawk's knee on his back. That white hair and his icy blue eyes sizing them both up, clear hatred in them. So much like his father it was scary.

47

S he was bone ass tired. They'd spent the past five or so hours at the police station, getting their situation sorted. It took a while but Gaige got Casper to talk to the Chief of Police with respect to Sophie shooting Gillman in self-defense, she was released on personal recognizance. They'd offered her a private cell in the jail to keep her safe, but she'd blanched profusely at that notion, and Gaige nearly lost his shit at the thought. He worked tirelessly to explain the situation and not divulge GHOST. She watched him argue his point, explain who he was, that he was here to help, and in the end it was Casper who had gotten the local police to let Gaige and Hawk go. Then Casper convinced the Chief of Police that her military charges are the sole jurisdiction of the Army. He sent in some of his own people to get her out. It was tenuous, but she was grateful just the same. It was past ten o'clock when they entered Gigi's house, and quietly slipped off to their bedrooms.

"Do you have to deal with local PD's often when you go on missions, Gaige?"

"Once in a while, but never to the level of today. We usually have what we call "friendlies" in local PD who are willing to help us. Today was brutal. And, our top contact who even Casper reports to is in the State Department if we would have needed more assistance tonight or anytime."

"What will happen to Rand now? Will they let him go or will he get put in jail under suspicion?"

"Casper is sending someone in to question him as soon as he's stable from surgery. Probably not until early tomorrow morning."

"Okay." She unstrapped her ankle holster, pulled her weapon from the holster, released the magazine and checked the chamber for a bullet. It was empty; the police department had emptied the chamber as they examined the gun. They'd run ballistics tests on it, which of course would come back positive, because she'd shot Rand. But they also checked to make sure it wasn't stolen. GHOST had sent them the paperwork on the gun showing Gaige owned it and it was legal.

Laying them on the bed she then grabbed a t-shirt and entered the bathroom, sliding both doors closed and locked them. Should she feel bad that she didn't feel bad? She didn't. At all. As she stood there looking at him on the ground, his hateful creepy ice blue eyes staring at her all she felt was disgust. She didn't question him about Kate or his involvement because she didn't want to put him on guard that they suspected him of anything, even though it was clear that he thought they were on to him about something.

Dressing in her t-shirt she splashed water on her face. One of the ambulance crews had looked her over and pulled a few small pieces of glass from her face and arms. She was fine, just a few little cuts, she'd had worse.

Brushing her hair, and then her teeth, she unlocked the door to Hawk's room and then opened the door to her room with Gaige. He lay across the bed, which was now void of weapons, and patted the top for her to come and lay down with him. Laying alongside him, he kissed her forehead then lay his head next to hers, his right arm solidly around her waist, pulling her into his body. "You did good today."

"Hmm. Really?"

"Really." He kissed her temple. "How do you feel?"

"I'm good. The only thing I feel bad about is not feeling bad."

He chuckled. "There are worse things to feel bad about. Rand isn't alright. He's got evil in his soul; I could see it in his eyes. His face. His father isn't much better, but he's even worse. He's a sociopath. He has no remorse for anything and this is all a game to him."

"What do you think his involvement is?"

"I don't want to speculate. We'll know tomorrow. Casper is sending his best investigator and has invited me to watch the interrogation." Half sitting up she turned to face him, resting on her elbow. "Seriously? Why?"

"Because GHOST has a lot of information about what's been going on and some of the key players. So, I can be there, I can't say anything, but I can write things down for the investigator to ask. There will be a court reporter there to take down the interrogation and so will the CID and the local police. Since Killian is Army, but Rand isn't, it can only work with cooperation on both sides. But it seems they are willing to work with each other, so that's a bonus. That doesn't mean there isn't a power struggle. But, let's not worry about that just yet, our priorities are to find the killer of Kate, who may or may not be the rapist. Then, clear you and Tommy. Then go home."

"And your Uncle Jeff?"

He took a deep breath. "Uncle Jeff will be forced to retire. That's at a minimum. For trying to cover up a crime. For using military personnel to do it. There could be a court martial involved, too. But, to be honest, I can't worry about that, he made his own bed. It makes me so damned sad that he behaved the way he did. But he'll have to pay the piper, however that is to be done."

Laying her left hand against his cheek she looked into those beautiful green eyes, the lines at the corners added character and were likely well deserved. "I'm sorry, Gaige. I know how much you respected him."

"Yeah. But, the most important person right now is Tommy. He's going to need help once he's cleared of Kate's rape. Therapy for sure. Then he's going to have to deal with his father and whatever happens to him. Aunt Bev is going to be distraught. I'll help them however I can, but Uncle Jeff has to come to terms with his actions in all of this, no matter that he thought he was helping Tommy."

She kissed his lips, softly. Then she turned with her back to him and closed her eyes as he spooned her tightly to his body. His breathing was deep and even before she fell asleep and her mind was able to turn off the events of the day. But, one thing she did know, they were several steps closer to clearing this all up now than they were this morning and that was something.

48

C asper had clout, that was for sure. Gaige walked down the hallway of the hospital, just outside the wing where Rand Gillman was recovering from his gunshot wound. Military personnel guarded the entrance to the wing, no one entered without special permission.

"Sir, I need to see ID." One of the guards said.

Pulling his driver's license and his GHOST badge out for him to inspect, he nodded. "Room 413."

Walking to 413 he noticed each hospital room door was opened along the hall and all rooms were empty. Throughout the night staff must have been moving patients to another wing while Rand was here and under protection or guard, whichever it was.

At the entrance to 413 he was halted. A guard turned and opened the door. "Sir, Mr. Vickers is here."

Apparently the first guard had radioed ahead. Casper's chosen investigator walked out and shook his hand.

"Mr. Vickers, my name is Colonel William Ashton."

"Thank you for including me, Colonel Ashton."

"Come this way." He turned and Gaige followed. Entering a room which at one time was the waiting area for families, the large room had been divided into two sections. One section hidden from the other by a panel, which had been brought in and held a one-way mirror.

"You'll sit behind the mirror so Mr. Gillman can't see you. You'll ask questions on this iPad." He handed him an iPad with a text box opened for his use. "You can only see him through the one-way mirror, but you can't speak to Mr. Gillman. The court reporter, my assistant who will be monitoring the iPad, a police officer, an investigator of CID, and myself will be the only people in the room with Mr. Gillman. I did receive your information last night. I've briefed myself on it and I'd like to say good work. You've been busy."

"Thank you." Colonel Ashton held his hand out toward a grouping of chairs behind the panel. He walked into his side of the room and sat in a chair in front of the window. Colonel Ashton turned and left the room, more important things to attend to.

Two more people sat in the room with him, not introducing themselves and not speaking to each other either. One in uniform, one not. A door was closed, sealing them off from the other room and not long after, Rand Gillman was wheeled into the room on a hospital bed. He was slightly reclined and had two IVs inserted into his left arm, which were arranged by a nurse. The blanket covering him was straightened and then Colonel Ashton, his assistant, the court reporter, the CID investigator, and the police officer entered the room. Gaige bit his cheek as the thought ran through his head. A criminal, a court reporter, a cop, an Army investigator, and a Colonel walk into a room...

The police officer started. "Mr. Gillman, you were read your rights last night. Do you remember?" The cold icy blue stare landed on the officer but he didn't budge from his standing position alongside the bed. "Yes."

The officer nodded. "And you've declined an attorney."

"Yes."

"And do you object to giving your statement under oath?"

"No."

"And you're aware of the reason we are all here this morning?"

Gillman chuckled. "Yeah."

"Do you think this is funny, Mr. Gillman?"

"Yes. It's funny. You're all funny. All your procedure and protocol bullshit."

His creepy eyes swung to Colonel Ashton and froze. Colonel Ashton was what women called a handsome man in his late fifties. Physically fit, sharp, he had deep brown eyes framed by thick lashes and a nice smile. But he didn't scare easily. You didn't make it this far in the military by being a pussy and he wasn't. He stared Rand down, not a twitch in his stance or demeanor. It was impressive to watch. Rand first began fidgeting with the blanket covering him, his fingers moving the material around subtly, then the toes on his right foot began moving back and forth and then his eyes finally looked down at his lap.

Colonel Ashton began asking Rand questions.

"The court reporter having sworn you in, I'll proceed. What was your involvement with the death of Kate Ryan?"

"I don't know a Kate Ryan."

"Then why was the ruby from your ring found in the car her dead body was found in?"

Rand's eyes rounded, but he said nothing.

"What was your involvement with the death of Gayle Stout?"

His lips curled up slightly at the mention of her name. But still he said nothing.

"What was your involvement with Carlee Brown?"

When Rand refused to speak at all, Colonel Ashton finally said, "We have you in the towns of all three of these women at the times of their deaths despite the fact that the towns all are in different states. We have evidence you left behind at each of the murder scenes and the local police have found evidence in your home that you stole from each of these women." Turning he opened a case and pulled out clear plastic bags with necklaces in two of the bags and a ring in the third. "This necklace belonged to Gayle Stout and was reported missing by her family. Her parents have identified a text photograph of the necklace as Gayle's missing necklace."

Holding up the second necklace, he said, "This necklace was reported missing by Carlee Brown's family. Likewise, her parents have identified a text photograph of the necklace as Carlee's missing necklace."

Holding up the ring, he said, "This ring belonged to and has been identified as Kate Ryan's class ring by her parents in the same manner. All of these things were found in your dresser, all have been identified by the families of these young women."

Rand smiled as he looked at the personal items. It was eerie and disturbing. Gaige's stomach twisted as he watched this person derive pleasure from so much pain. But it was his words that brought it all together.

"Do you think I look like him?"

"Excuse me?" Colonel Ashton asked.

"My father, do you think I look like him? They all did.

They all thought I was him. They even called me by his name. I can't tell you how happy that made me."

"When did they call you by his name?"

"Gayle called me Reed as I was raping her. She threatened to tell the authorities who I was. I loved that and it made my orgasm spectacular. But, I knew I had to give them more drugs. As much as I liked that they thought I was him, I couldn't let them say anything. But, she did that little bitch. Even though I threatened her. I told her I'd kill her if she said anything and she did anyway."

It was hard to listen to his glee. He was proud of himself.

"How about Carlee Brown?"

Rand played with the blanket a bit more and his smile disappeared for a minute. "She wasn't as much fun. I gave her too much of the drug and she laid there like a corpse. So, I had to adjust my dosages. I almost had it perfect for Kate. She was lively enough to try to fight me but couldn't."

He was so happy Sophie couldn't hear this. It would make her vomit to see how proud he was of himself.

"Why did you kill them?"

Anger rose to the surface and he balled his hands into fists. "Didn't you hear me? I told them to shut their mouths. So many women don't report a rape, they're ashamed. But these stupid bitches had to go and report my dad."

"Was that your plan, to get your father in trouble?"

He lay his head back against the bed and laughed. Then his hand flew to his chest, his face contorted as if he was in pain. "Yes. I wanted him hunted and on the run from his precious military. That's all he ever gave a shit about. Not me. Just his fucking promotions and military career. So, I thought I'd taint it for him."

"How does Tony Guilianetti fit into all of this?"

"Tony is a great hacker. He was able to hack into places to get me information."

"What information did Mr. Guilianetti obtain for you?"

Rand chuckled. "Ah, so you don't have all the pieces to the puzzle pulled together yet."

"Why don't you fill them in for us?"

"What's in it for me?"

Colonel Ashton moved a step closer to the bed, his face unreadable. "How about the difference between prison and a death sentence."

Rand chuckled again, held his chest and said, "California doesn't have the death sentence."

"That's correct, but Kansas does and you murdered Gayle Stout in Kansas. Extradition to Kansas would put you on death row."

The sickly smile faded from Rand's face, and he visibly swallowed.

"Now, let's try again. What records did Mr. Guilianetti access for you?"

Taking a breath, Rand's face changed again to one of resignation. "He was able to hack into the DMV records for me and change the name on the title of the car I put Kate in to make it look like it was hers."

"Okay. Anything else?"

"Yeah. He could tell me when my father was being restationed and where."

Colonel Ashton flinched at that. Some military records were not secure. He'd bet heads would roll on this one, but that was to be expected.

Gaige typed into his iPad. *How did he know Chet Forest?*

Colonel Ashton's assistant handed him the iPad. The Colonel read it and handed it back to her.

"How did you meet Chet Forest?"

"He came by the hospital where I work to pick up a corpse. One of your finest was killed in a car accident and at our hospital and the Army wanted him back. Chet came to pick him up and we chatted. Tony dug up some information for me on Chet. Turns out he liked to gamble a bit and owed some money to some folks. I offered to pay his debt for a favor. I needed Kate's autopsy report changed to show that she had carbon monoxide in her lungs and blood so it looked like a suicide. I also needed other conclusions altered and documents removed. It's just amazing what someone will do for money."

Colonel Ashton stared him down again. Maybe to get his own thoughts in order. "And, why did you kill Mr. Forest if he was willing to help you?"

Rand shrugged. "He didn't have the stomach for it. His medical examiner was transferred to another base suddenly, thanks to my father, and he had a change of heart after that. Threatened to tell someone that I paid him to fix the report."

"Let's talk about your father for a moment. How much of your activities does he know about?"

"That you'd have to ask him. I saw him following me these past few months. I saw him drive past my place a couple of times. I saw him a few times sitting in his car outside of Kate's place. I saw him at the hospital once, too."

Gaige quickly typed in, *Why was his father watching Kate?*

Colonel Ashton's assistant handed him the iPad. His eyes scanned the text then asked Gillman the question.

"The sad sack liked Kate. He'd asked her out a couple of times. She wanted nothing to do with him. I overheard her talking to that friend of hers as they were walking to her friend's car one day."

"Is that why you targeted Kate?"

Gillman chuckled, picked at some invisible lint on his blanket then closed his eyes. "Yes. I wanted him to suffer."

Why was he on base at Fort Riley to buy the ring?

Colonel Ashton pulled the ring from the same case he had the women's jewelry in. It also was in a clear plastic bag. "Why were you on base to buy this ring and why did you buy it with the Army insignia on it?"

He laughed again, held his chest, and then responded. "That was my gift to me to remind me of my father and his precious military. My mom saved every dollar that prick paid her for me. When I turned 18 she gave me half and when I turned 22 and graduated from college, she gave me the other half. I splurged. And since they let civilians on base, I went to the commissary and bought the ring as a gift to me. I paid a pretty penny for it, too."

Un-fucking-believable.

49

Her phone rang and she grabbed it before it rang again. "Gaige? What happened? I'm dying here. My stomach is in knots."

"Soph, he confessed. To everything. He raped and killed Kate and the other two women. It sounds as if more were raped but those women haven't come forward. Not yet anyway. Some of them likely will never be able to come forward."

"Oh my God." She plopped down in a chair, her heart hammering, her stomach in knots. It took a moment and she felt like she'd throw up.

"Soph, put me on speaker so Hawk can hear and I don't have to repeat."

Her fingers shook and another wave of nausea caused her hands to sweat. Hawk gently took her phone, nodding once to her, and hit speaker. "I'm here."

She listened and her stomach twisted and turned as he told them what had happened. It was disgusting how this pig Gillman derived so much pleasure. Her heart hurt for Kate and Gayle and Carlee and every other woman out there who'd been violated and abused and murdered. "I'm on my way out to Uncle Jeff's right now. I'll be home later."

Good thing Hawk was thinking clearly 'cause she sure wasn't. "What's going on with Killian?"

"Colonel Ashton is meeting with him now to find out what he knew and how complicit he was in all of this."

"Okay, good luck with your uncle. I'll be wrapping up my reports then. Is the plan to leave in the morning?"

"Yes. Please make arrangements with Gavin."

"Will do. Out."

"Sophie, are you still there?"

Her voice shook when she answered him. "Yes."

"Baby, I know that was hard to hear. I'm sorry. For all of it. But, Casper is working on your status right now. I'll hear from him later tonight. We'll talk when I get back, okay?"

"Yeah."

The phone clicked and he was gone.

"Hey, you okay?" Hawk's concern made tears spring to her eyes.

Swallowing, she nodded, cleared her throat and said, "Do you think it's okay for me to call Kate's parents?"

"I don't see why not. It sounds like they know something's going on 'cause Kate's ring had been identified by them."

She nodded. "Thank you. I'm going to go and call them. Unless there's something I'm supposed to do now." She nodded to her computer.

"Nah, it can wait. After each mission we write up reports that we keep on file. Each person on the mission writes up their own, but Gaige can show you how to do that, where to access them, and where to save them when he gets back. Go on, girl, call your friend's parents."

"Thank you." And without thinking she leaned over

and hugged him, sniveling in his ear. He patted her on the back, clearly uncomfortable with her closeness, but she pulled back and nodded then took her phone to her room and closed the door. Calling Kate's mom would be difficult, but she wanted to talk to her and commiserate with her. Then she'd call her own mom and chat. She'd purposely avoided contact with her during this time because she didn't want her to worry. And, her mom didn't have her current phone number, so there was no chance of her calling while all this turmoil was going on.

But first, she was going to take a long hot shower, and cry, and get it out of her system so she didn't blubber on the phone like a baby.

Grabbing her clean clothes from the top drawer, her mind raced back to her apartment, hopefully this meant she'd be able to go and grab her own things. That thought gave her goosebumps. Normal. Oh, to have life get back to normal again. Though even that was going to be different.

Taking a deep breath to keep the panic at bay, she gathered her clothes and walked to the bathroom.

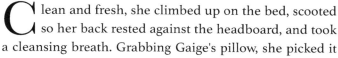

Clean and fresh, she climbed up on the bed, scooted so her back rested against the headboard, and took a cleansing breath. Grabbing Gaige's pillow, she picked it up and smelled it, then pressed it tightly to her body. "Okay. I can do this." She whispered.

Picking up her phone, she dialed the number of Kate's mom and closed her eyes as the phone rang on the other end.

"Hello?"

"Sandra?" Her voice cracked. She cleared her voice and tried again. "Sandra, this is Sophie Turner."

"Oh, Sophie. It's so good to hear from you. We just got a call from someone in Colonel Ashton's office. He told us who..." Her voice cracked. "About Kate's rapist and kil..." There was a pause.

"Yes. How are you, Sandra? I know it was hard to hear all of that, but at least we know. It's small consolation, but we had to know."

"Yes. It won't bring her back, but we all knew she didn't kill herself. We knew."

Her soft crying on the phone cracked Sophie's barely there composure, and she softly cried with Sandra.

"Thank you, Sophie. Thank you for Kate. You are such a good friend. To our whole family."

"Actually, Gaige did most of the work. He's amazing. He did so much to help Kate. And, Tommy."

"Tommy. Oh, I have to go to church and pray for forgiveness for all the bad thoughts I heaped on that young man."

Sophie actually smiled. "Gaige is there now talking with them. Tommy is his cousin. Can you believe how small a world it is?"

"Oh, my heavens. So, he flew out there to help his cousin and met up with you again?"

"Actually, I called him. I was in a bit of trouble trying to dig into Kate's death and he came out here to help me."

She heard Sandra sigh. "How is that going?"

Sandra knew about her love for Gaige. Kate had told her mom a long while ago much to Sophie's mortification at the time, but over the years Sandra asked now and then about Gaige and if she'd seen him.

"He loves me, Sandra. And, as you know, I love him."

"I know it well. I'm so happy for you. Richard and I were just talking this week about Kate and Tate and we wondered if they finally found each other."

"Oh, I just told Gaige that this morning. I think they have Sandra, I really do."

Their conversation lasted for a while longer and she was about to call her mom when she heard a car pull into the driveway. Hoping it was Gaige, she left the bedroom and walked out to the living room then into the kitchen. Leaning against the counter her heart rate increased as she waited. Gigi walked in the door and her face must have fallen because Gigi said, "I'm happy to see you, too."

"Sorry." Her face scrunched.

Hawk walked out of his bedroom, then he stopped and turned to go back to his room.

"What in the hell is going on here? No one wants to see me?"

"It's not that, Gigi. We love you. But, we're waiting for Gaige to get back and tell us what happened with his uncle."

"Oh, he's doing that now?"

"Yes. I'll fill you in while I help you make dinner."

50

"What the hell were you thinking, Uncle Jeff?" His once proud and strong uncle sat behind his desk in his home and rubbed his forehead with shaking fingers.

"I just didn't want Tommy to be labeled a rapist and I didn't want him to go to prison."

"But you assumed he was and that may haunt him forever."

"Dammit, Gaige, I'm aware." he yelled. "I've let my son down in so many ways. I'm so ashamed."

"I don't know what's going to happen to you, Uncle Jeff, but I'm afraid your military career is likely over."

His sad and tired uncle turned his head and gazed out the window that looked over the bluff and out onto the ocean below. All he had here was due to his military career and how well he served the United States Armed Forces. Now, he was faced with losing it all.

"I suspect on some level I've known that for a while. Trusting Killian with something like this was the biggest mistake of my life. He came to me and told me that

Tommy was a rape suspect, but he'd help me if I could see to his next promotion. I had no idea he was framing my son for something his son had done. Or at least he was willing to use the situation to make it look as though he was helping me."

"But, what made you even think this was the best way to handle it?"

"I don't know."

"Uncle Jeff, why did you trust Killian more than you trusted Tommy?"

"I didn't. Not really. I just saw a way to help Tommy keep his record clean."

His uncle scraped his hands through his hair, his face filled with defeat, worry and embarrassment.

"Why didn't you try to clear Tommy? Why didn't you hire a lawyer or an investigator? "

"He said he couldn't remember. Neither of us knew if he'd done it or not. And no, the facts didn't add up, but he couldn't remember anything."

"Even when he couldn't remember anything, he wanted to tell Kate that he never could have raped her, but you wouldn't let him. Then when he started to remember and knew he didn't do it, you wouldn't listen to him."

"But, you don't understand, he just folded up into a ball and wouldn't come out of his room. He hasn't worked since it happened. Not much anyway. If he weren't self-employed, he'd have surely lost his job by now. I just thought the best thing was to sweep it under the rug and it would go away. It was poor judgment. I know. I'll pay the price for that for the rest of my life, but it wasn't about me or my career, I swear, you have to believe that."

His Aunt Bev came home from wherever she'd been

for the day and interrupted their conversation. "Hi, Gaige, will you be staying for dinner?"

He stood and hugged his aunt. "I'm sorry, Aunt Bev, but I have to go and Uncle Jeff has something to tell you that doesn't need an audience."

He turned and shook his uncle's hand. "I do believe you. Good luck, Uncle Jeff. Please stay in touch and let me know how things are going for you. I'll help you all out however I can, but only legally."

"I'm proud of you, Gaige. And, I'm sorry."

"I'm going out to the shop to visit with Tommy before I leave."

He left his Aunt and Uncle's house and his heart was heavy. The look on his uncle's face when he told him the facts of what had happened, Killian's son's involvement, and that Killian was being interviewed now was devastating. His uncle's eyes teared up, and his look of defeat was gut wrenching. Watching a man crumble was never easy. Especially when you loved him like a father.

Walking behind the house and down to the shop, he smiled when he heard a power tool running. When Tommy first started building boats, he began out here. After his business had grown, he was able to move to a larger shop and he bought a nice little house not far from his shop.

Opening the door, the smell of fresh cut wood wafted to his nostrils and fond memories of helping Tommy sand boats and oars flooded his mind. "Good to see you out here working, Tommy."

A sad smile lifted the corners of his mouth, but it didn't reach his eyes. "Thanks, Gaige. I've been off long enough and after speaking with you earlier, I realized I need to get back to life."

"Did Colonel Ashton's office call you and tell you what happened today?"

Gaige walked around a pile of wood pieces and skirted sawdust that had been swept to a section of the floor. The boat Tommy was working on was small but was his signature boat. It was the style of boat he'd started with as a young man learning his craft.

"Yeah. Colonel Ashton told me they were interviewing Killian soon and that they'd spoken to his son and he'd confessed."

"Yeah."

Gaige leaned against the work bench, his back supported by the wooden surface, his eyes locked on Tommy. "Did they say anything else?"

"Only that their investigation was on-going and they'd recommend that I don't leave the area until they wrap this all up."

Nodding, Gaige watched his cousin closely as he said his next words. "Your dad is in trouble for his role in halting the investigation. He's the one who kept CID from doing their full job. It's likely going to end his career."

Tommy slowly shook his head, his eyes now lovingly locked on his boat. "I figured he'd be in trouble, I wish he'd listened to me. But, he made his decisions on his own."

"You're right there including his decision not to listen to you." Gaige straightened, then approached Tommy and hugged him. "If you need help, or your mom does, call me. I'll do what I can for you both. Your dad, too, but only if it's legal. Love you, Tom."

His cousin's arms held him tight. The longest hug he'd ever gotten from Tommy. "Love you, too. Thanks, Gaige. I don't know how I'll ever repay you."

Pulling back and looking into Tommy's eyes, he said, "I love you all, you're my blood. No repayment necessary. We'll stay in touch as we always have. Just move on, and live your best life."

Tommy choked up, but managed to keep his composure. "I will."

The drive home was long even though it was in actuality only about a half hour drive. Right now he just wanted to get back to Sophie, pack up, and go home. With her. And start a new life that included he and Sophie together. But first, he hoped Casper was true to his word and would be able to clear up Sophie's record.

He finally pulled into the driveway at Gigi's and let out a long breath. He couldn't remember such a long day filled with so much emotion. His gut had twisted watching Rand take pleasure in his horrendous crimes. Clearly he'd developed ongoing mental illnesses somewhere along the way. Some people weren't as strong as others. It was apparent that his mother was able to provide for him financially; she'd never spent any of the money Killian had sent her. But, he'd harbored a fascination with his father that developed into something dark and sinister.

Entering the kitchen, three faces turned to stare at him, but he only really saw one. Sophie jumped up from her chair and ran to him and the instant she was in his arms, part of him felt better. She fit him perfectly, in so many ways. Physically, sure. Emotionally, for God's sake, yes. She filled his heart.

"Are you hungry? I saved a plate for you." She whispered into his neck.

"I'm not starving, but I should eat."

She pulled back and looked up at him. Resting her hand on his cheek she softly asked, "Are you alright?"

His lips turned up slightly. "I am now. Mostly."

Taking his hand in hers she led him to the table and nudged him to sit down. She walked to the refrigerator and pulled a plate out, uncovered the plastic wrap and set it in the microwave. Then she pulled a beer from the refrigerator and held it up to him. He nodded, her eyes traveled to Hawk who also nodded, then Gigi, who said, "I'll have a glass of wine with you."

Sophie passed the beers to the guys while Gigi got up and poured their wine. Sophie pulled his dinner from the microwave and grabbed utensils before setting it in front of him. It smelled fantastic, as usual. Waiting till everyone was seated again, he held up his beer.

"Here's to success and the best hostess in the world."

Everyone said, "Cheers." And took a drink.

He began telling them about his meeting with his uncle, filling in when questions were asked and answering more questions about Gillman. He was certainly happy this mission was almost over. But, he was also so happy Sophie had called him in the first place.

51

Hugging Gigi good-bye, Sophie let the tears fall. "I don't know how I'll ever be able to repay you, Gigi. Your kindness when I had no one was a life saver. Literally."

"Oh honey, I'm so happy I was able to help. You can repay me by living a great life in Indiana."

She giggled and stepped back so Gaige could hug Gigi; and then she watched as Hawk lifted her off her feet and squeezed her hard. Setting her gently down on the ground, he chucked her under the chin, and Sophie looked at Gaige and mouthed, "Did they...?"

He shrugged and walked out of the house to the car. The plan was to go to her apartment and gather some things she wanted for the time being. A company would be hired to pack the rest of her belongings and ship them to her at GHOST.

Casper had not only expunged the charges from her record, he'd ended her contract with the Army and called it deployment gratuity for all the time served in saving her own ass. He also expunged the four Article 15s from Kate's record and restored her to the soldier she was with a stellar record. She was both excited and nervous at the same time. But, she'd find a way to send Gigi some money as soon as she was earning a paycheck again. And, she had pay coming from the Army for the two months she had left on her contract, so that would keep her until she figured out what she wanted to do.

Arriving at her apartment complex, she had a hard time keeping her stomach from twisting. The last time she'd been here was pure hell. She couldn't help looking around for any signs of danger. "Don't worry, Soph, we're with you." Gaige said from the front passenger seat.

She smiled at his concern. "I know and thank you both for being here."

Hawk looked at her from the mirror and she smiled. He said nothing, which was his usual.

"This building here. I'm on the second floor."

They walked up the steps to her place and her knees shook so bad she was afraid she'd stumble. Pulling the key from the plant pot next to her door, she unlocked it and looked around. The place had been ransacked, someone had gone through her things and tossed them around. They were likely looking for clues as to where she was. Hawk walked passed her, gun in hand, and moved down the hallway as Gaige did the same thing in the opposite direction toward the kitchen.

Hawk yelled, "Clear."

A few seconds later so did Gaige. Closing her door, she turned and began picking items up off the floor and laying them on the sofa. Trying to straighten things up, Gaige softly said, "Soph. Honey, don't clean. Just pack. We've got to get on a plane and I promise you, we'll have all of this packed up nicely for you and brought to GHOST. Okay?"

"Yeah. Sorry. It's just habit. I don't let things lay around like this."

"It's okay, babe. What can I help you with?"

She looked around. "If you can grab my computer, and electronics over in the desk, if they're still there, I'll pack some clothes."

"On it." And true to his word he began at her desk, pulling electronics from drawers. Feeling a little violated, she walked down the hallway and pulled her duffle from her closet floor and began packing as many of her clothing items as she could fit in it and the suitcase she had on hand. Less than an hour later she had all of her toiletries, her undergarments, and clothing packed and she was ready to start all over.

They climbed in their rental and drove to the airport. Gaige called Gavin, GHOST's pilot, "We're on our way. ETA twenty minutes."

Then he called GHOST. Wyatt answered. "We're on the plane in twenty. What's happening there?"

"I just took a call from Casper. A couple and a foreign dignitary were killed outside a State dinner in Washington and investigators are having problems putting all the of the pieces together. The press is bitching that the investigation isn't going well and saying the President is hiding things from the public. Casper wants this wrapped up and he wants us involved discreetly working with Washington PD doing things they can't."

Gaige looked at Hawk, tapped the speaker icon. "Repeat that for Hawk."

Wyatt repeated what he'd said for Hawk's benefit.

"I want in." Hawk glanced at Gaige.

Gaige nodded. "Wyatt, have everyone at the compound when we get back so we can round table and decide who's going to Washington. And, to meet Sophie. We have to interview her and then vote on her joining GHOST."

"Ten-four. Anything else?"

Gaige glanced at Hawk, then back at Sophie. She shrugged and he responded. "That's it for now. See you in a few hours. Out."

As he finished handling GHOST's business, she allowed her mind to say goodbye to Riverton and all the good times and the bad times she'd had here. She silently said good-bye to her military career and readied her mind to move on. There'd be hard days for sure, but she'd get through. Gaige promised her a visit out here one of these days so she could say good-bye to friends. But, she'd be able to touch base with them when she wanted to and her best friend was no longer here. She was in heaven. She silently told Kate and Tate she hoped they were happy, that she loved them both, and to watch over Gaige and her as they started this next chapter of their lives. Something told her it was going to be amazing. Scary. Adventurous and un-fricking-real. That's what she'd also told her mom when she'd finally spoken to her last night.

"Okay, I'll let her know." Gaige twisted in his seat. "Jax said it's about fucking time. Her words, not mine. That there's another woman in the organization."

She laughed then. "I think I'm going to like Jax."

"You will, definitely. She's tough. Strong. And, if it's on her mind, it'll be out of her mouth in no time."

"Sounds like Kate."

He looked into her eyes and held them for a moment.

Nodding, he said, "Only you can determine that, but a word to the wise. Don't tell Jax she's like anyone. She works hard to be unique."

He and Hawk both burst out laughing and Sophie made that note to herself. So had Kate.

52

A xel met them at the airport, the Beast was running and ready to get them back to the compound. Stowing their gear in back, they climbed in, Hawk taking the passenger seat, while Gaige climbed in the back with Sophie.

"Axel, meet Sophie. Sophie, Axel." Gaige turned to Sophie and by way of background said, "Axel is one of the best at what he does, which is largely surveillance networking. He's also fun to have around, but don't let him bust your chops, 'cause he'll certainly try."

"I'll do my best to keep my chops unbusted. Nice to meet you, Axel."

Axel laughed and shook his head. "Nice to meet you too, Sophie. We've all been dying to get a look at the woman who kept Gaige off the market all of his life. Well, there was that one close call, but other than that, you know."

Sophie laughed. "We've all had close calls or worse. I'll bet you have, too."

Axel laughed but said no more. Feeling the pull to get

back at running his Hidden Ops organization or GHOST, Gaige pulled out his phone and began texting team members to meet them at the conference room in an hour.

H awk and Axel talked crap in the front seat and though he was texting and catching up with his email, he often glanced at Sophie to see her looking out the window and watching the scenery as they drove. Taking her hand in his, he began pointing out landmarks and notable places.

His phone rang and he glanced down to see "Casper" on the readout. "I've gotta take this, Soph." She nodded.

"Vickers."

"Gaige, I wanted to follow-up with you on Killian so you can give your team an update."

"Hold on, I'll put you on speaker." Tapping the speaker icon, he said, "Everyone, I have Casper on the line. Casper, I have Sophie Turner, Hawk Delaney and Axel Dunbar with me."

Without a large preamble, Casper dove in. "Hello, everyone. I wanted to update you all on Captain Killian so you have the full story. My investigator was able to glean the final pieces of the puzzle of this mess. First of all, Killian has confessed to manipulating information regarding Thomas Taylor and doing so to keep the heat off his own bad acts and those of his son. He suspected his son had raped the women who accused him. He said he first suspected Rand when Gayle Stout filed rape charges against him. He knew he hadn't raped her, but she was so adamant it was him. Admittedly, he has a distinctive look, as does his son, and Ms. Stout kept talking about, 'His icy dead eyes'. He tried making contact with his son, but was rebuffed. He began searching for him, going so far as to contact Mrs. Gillman and was told to leave them alone.

After being transferred to avoid issues on base, which was also a deal made with Ms. Stout by the Army to keep her quiet about the rape, he spotted Gillman at Fort Stewart the base to which he'd been transferred. Thinking he'd catch up to him eventually, he kept an eye out but didn't get concerned until he heard that Gayle Stout had committed suicide. Unlike Killian, he said he wasn't sure what to do at that point. Clearly, what he should have done was go to his superiors and ask for assistance, but that escaped his thought processes."

The sarcasm was strong in that last statement.

"Thanks to your intel, we did retrieve the video footage from the Medical Examiner's Office and Morgue complex. Gillman did enter the office where Mr. Forest was working. Looking at the time on Ms. Turner's phone, it was planted in the Medical Examiner's desk where Mr. Forest was sitting at that same time. Mr. Forest died less than 30 minutes later. Gillman has confirmed this in subsequent interrogations."

Taking a deep breath, he caught Axel's eyes in the rearview mirror and Hawk turned to him and nodded.

"Thank you, sir, we appreciate the wrap-up."

"You're welcome. I've already spoken to one of your men regarding another mission I have for you. This one is of major importance. Send your best." The line went silent.

*

The landscape changed as they left town and headed out to the outlying area where GHOST was located. Slowing to turn into the driveway, he watched her face as the gates came into view. Her eyes rounded and her mouth formed an "o". Axel pulled into the driveway, rolled his window down, waived his security card, and the gates silently slid open. Sophie looked at him, then out the window once again as Axel drove them up the drive and turned the corner bringing the Southern Mansion style home into full view.

"Holy moly, is this GHOST?"

Laughing, Gaige responded, "It is."

Axel then waived his security card before the garage panel and the door lifted. Entering the garage, the drive sent them down to below the compound house.

"This is our garage which as you can see is below ground. Since we have so many of us, and each of us is allotted two vehicles, and for safety reasons, we decided below ground was more logical. We have two vehicles for the group, this is Beast One and the other one is Beast Two, I'll show you that one later."

Her amazement was evident, and he'd be lying if he said it didn't give him pride to see her expression.

Axel parked the Beast and they began exiting the vehicle. Grabbing their bags from the back, Sophie reached in and took out her duffle and suitcase. Walking to an elevator, Hawk scanned his security card and the doors slid open.

"So, we have two levels below ground, Soph. The garage and the next level up is for operations. We're bulletproof in case we're found out, so our lower levels are a bunker should the worst happen and we have to be in lock down for any length of time. Operations is where we'll meet the rest of the team in a few minutes, but first let's drop Axel off on that level, which is also where we have a shooting range, our computer systems, workout facility and more. Then, I'll take you upstairs to drop your bags off before giving you a tour and coming down to meet everyone."

"Okay."

He saw her swallow and his heart went out to her. She must be nervous as hell to be the new girl. Actually, new home, new person in an established group, new job, new everything. Taking her hand in his, he squeezed, and she looked up at him. She smiled but it was stiff.

The doors slid open and Axel exited. "See you guys in a bit."

The doors slid closed and they continued upward. Hawk turned to Sophie and smiled. "You'll be fine. Everyone here is family. That doesn't mean we don't disagree at times, it means that on some level, we love each other. When we go on missions, we protect each other. We kill for each other. We respect each other. Gaige has assembled the best of the best."

She smiled, "Thanks, Hawk. I'm sure it will be fine. There's just been so much change for me in the past weeks, and especially this past week. But, I appreciate all you've done to help me and Kate. I want you to know that."

"My pleasure."

The doors opened and Hawk stepped out first and walked down the hall to the left without another word.

"We'll follow Hawk until the top of the stairs, Soph." He led her down the hall and to the grand staircase. She was silent as they ascended the stairs, and a quick glance told him she was looking around and impressed.

"This is simply amazing, Gaige. I'm absolutely speechless as I look around."

Chuckling he replied, "You'll get used to it, but yes, the

designer did a fantastic job with this place. You can see that it started out as an old mansion, but we had many needs to address. Safety first. I wanted to conceal that it is GHOST headquarters. But then, I wanted a place for all of us to be able to live should team members want to. Everyone lives here now, except Ford and Megan, Lincoln and Skye, and Dodge and Jax. Though Jax still has her room and they do stay periodically when missions get long and they are too tired to drive out of town."

"Wow. I feel like a child with no vocabulary, but all I can say is wow."

He stopped before double doors at the end of the hall-way. Opening the doors he stepped aside, allowing Sophie to enter the rooms first. She slowly walked in and stopped after a few feet. This first room was a large sitting room, a brown leather sofa and a coffee table sitting in front of it with only a metal bowl on top with decorative balls in various tans and browns inside for decoration. A large, rich brown plush rug lay in front of the table, and across from the sofa on the wall was a television. Below that a fireplace, though it was not burning at this time.

"So, this is our sitting area. Through that doorway to the left is our bedroom and inside the bedroom to the right is our bathroom." She set her bags on the floor alongside the sofa and walked into the bedroom, her sigh said it all.

"Oh, my! Gaige, this is beautiful."

He looked at it through her eyes and his pride expanded ten-fold. He'd always been proud of the mansion, but, watching Sophie view it for the first time renewed his love of it. And, honestly, right now, his heart felt close to bursting that she liked what she saw. It was as if all that he had was great, but it didn't mean as much as it did right now because she loved it. He was speechless thinking about it.

He watched her walk around the room, running her fingers along the smooth surface of the large dresser and the chair in the corner. Turning on the bathroom light, she giggled and he set his bags down on the chair and went to see what she was giggling at.

"Gaige, I've never lived in anything this spectacular before. I feel like I've been transported in time and I'm a princess or something. This is simply stunning."

He watched her walk to the double sinks and run her hand along the cool granite, then step over to the claw foot tub and run her fingers along the smooth edge. The glass shower stood next to the tub and her eyes took it all in before landing on his.

"Unbelievable."

"Glad you approve. I'll admit I've been a little nervous about your reaction."

She laughed. "I don't know why. My gawd, this is fantastic."

She walked into his arms and hugged him tight. He eagerly reciprocated. Pulling her tightly to his body, he inhaled the smell of her hair, and whispered, "I needed this. We've been together all day, but we've barely touched. Thank you."

"Thank you. For everything. For so much, my mind is still reeling from all that you've done."

Pulling away he turned her toward the door and walked her out to the bedroom. Gently sitting her on the foot of the bed, he knelt down in front of her and looked into her eyes.

"Sophie, look at me. You don't have to thank me. I would have moved heaven and earth to make sure you were okay. I'm sorry I haven't picked up the phone all the times I wanted to. I'm sorry for all the lost time between us. I'm sorry you've had to lose Kate and all that happened to you these past weeks. But, part of me believes that was our journey to each other. And now that we're finally together from our separate paths, we'll be stronger as we begin our journey on one path together."

He took her hand in his. "I'm sorry I don't have a ring to put on your finger, but I will soon. In the meantime, Sophie Turner, love of my life, will you marry me?"

Her gorgeous mouth opened, closed, opened again, but nothing came out. Tears began rolling down her cheeks before she finally responded. "Oh my God, yes. Oh yes, Gaige."

He stood and pulled her up with him, wrapping her in his arms and lifting her off the floor. Her arms wrapped around his shoulders and her lips close to his ear whispered, "I love you so much, Gaige Vickers. I always have."

His heart would have beaten out of his chest if it could have. His mind tried to grasp everything about this moment. The way she felt in his arms. The way her hair fell around them. Her scent. Her warmth. Her voice. Her.

***

Her parents were murdered and she's determined to find out who did it. No one will stop her, even Hawk.

Read Defending Roxanne - https://books2read. com/u/bwKnge

Keep in touch and learn about new releases, sales, recipes, and other fun things by signing up for my newsletter - https://www. subscribepage.com/PJsReadersClub_copy

ENJOY THIS BOOK? YOU CAN MAKE A BIG DIFFERENCE

Reviews are the most powerful tools in my arsenal when it comes to getting attention for my books. As much as I'd like to, I don't have the financial muscle of a New York publisher. I can't take out full page ads in the newspaper or put posters on the subway.

(Not yet, anyway.)

But I do have something much more powerful and effective than that, and it's something that those big publishers would die to get their hands on.

A committed and loyal bunch of readers.

Honest reviews of my books help bring them to the attention of other readers.

If you've enjoyed this book I would be so grateful to you if you could spend just five minutes leaving a review (it can be as short as you like) on the book's vendor page. You can jump right to the page of your choice by clicking below.

Thank you so very much.

ALSO BY PJ FIALA - PAPERBACK

To see a list of all of my books with the blurbs go to:
https://www.pjfiala.com/bibliography-pj-fiala/

You can find all of my books at https://pjfiala.com/books

Romantic Suspense

Rolling Thunder Series

Moving to Love, Book 1

Moving to Hope, Book 2

Moving to Forever, Book 3

Moving to Desire, Book 4

Moving to You, Book 5

Moving Home, Book 6

Moving On, Book 7

Rolling Thunder Boxset, Books 1-3

Military Romantic Suspense

Second Chances Series

Designing Samantha's Love, Book 1

Securing Kiera's Love, Book 2

Second Chances Boxset - Duet

Bluegrass Security Series

Heart Thief, Book One

Finish Line, Book Two

Lethal Love, Book Three

Wrenched Fate, Book Four

Bluegrass Security Boxset, Books 1-3

Big 3 Security

Ford: Finding His Fire Book One

Lincoln: Finding His Mark Book Two

Dodge: Finding His Jewel Book Three

Rory: Finding His Match Book Four

Big 3 Security Boxset, Books 1-3

GHOST

Defending Keirnan, GHOST Book One

Defending Sophie, GHOST Book Two

Defending Roxanne, GHOST Book Three

Defending Yvette, GHOST Book Four

Defending Bridget, GHOST Book Five

Defending Isabella, GHOST Book Six

RAPTOR

RAPTOR Rising - Prequel

Saving Shelby, RAPTOR Book One

Holding Hadleigh, RAPTOR Book Two

Craving Charlesia, RAPTOR Book Three

Promising Piper, RAPTOR Book Four

Missing Mia, RAPTOR Book Five

Believing Becca, RAPTOR Book Six

Keeping Kori, RAPTOR Book Seven

Healing Hope, RAPTOR Book Eight

Engaging Emersyn, RAPTOR Book Nine

MEET PJ

Writing has been a desire my whole life. Once I found the courage to write, life changed for me in the most profound way. Bringing stories to readers that I'd enjoy reading and creating characters that are flawed, but lovable is such a joy.

When not writing, I'm with my family doing something fun. My husband, Gene, and I are bikers and enjoy riding to new locations, meeting new people and generally enjoying this fabulous country we live in.

I come from a family of veterans. My grandfather, father, brother, two sons, and one daughter-in-law are all veterans. Needless to say, I am proud to be an American and proud of the service my amazing family has given.

My online home is https://www.pjfiala.com.
You can connect with me on Facebook at https://www.facebook.com/PJFiala1,
and
Instagram at https://www.Instagram.com/PJFiala.
If you prefer to email, go ahead, I'll respond - pjfiala@pjfiala.com.

Made in United States
Orlando, FL
30 August 2022

21775826R00174